Seat Mates

Anna Harbom

ISBN: 979-8-9907332-1-3

Any references to historical events, real people, or real places are used fictitiously. Names, characters, and places are products of the author's imagination.

Front cover art and book design by Bailey McGinn.

Printed by Anna Harbom in the United States of America.

First printing edition 2024.

www.AnnaHarbomAuthor.com

For Christian

Contents

Chapter 1.. 1
Chapter 2.. 15
Chapter 3.. 23
Chapter 4.. 29
Chapter 5.. 36
Chapter 6.. 45
Chapter 7.. 59
Chapter 8.. 63
Chapter 9.. 77
Chapter 10.. 84
Chapter 11.. 94
Chapter 12.. 100
Chapter 13.. 108
Chapter 14.. 118
Chapter 15.. 160
Chapter 16.. 174
Chapter 17.. 186
Chapter 18.. 194
Chapter 19.. 211
Chapter 20.. 222

Chapter 21 237
Chapter 22 239
Chapter 23 244
Chapter 24 250

Acknowledgements..263
About the Author 265

Chapter 1

"What the hell, asshole!" I smash my foot onto the brake of my Mini Cooper as the BMW that just cut me off swerves and then rights itself. The traffic is heavy as all get-out, and I'm already late for my flight.

"Not today, Satan," I grumble with a glance at the large red-eyed statue of a stallion that greets me as I approach the Denver airport. That thing has always given me the creeps. I don't know who thought it was a good idea to greet travelers with a demonic horse on their way in and out of our city, but whoever it was is in desperate need of PR training.

The douchebag in the black BMW holds up their hand for the universal courtesy wave of apology. I'm not having it. I'm already late for my flight. A flight I really don't want to be on in the first place.

"Oh no, I don't think so," I growl and flip the bird at the car in front of me. It's not like they see me anyways. Traffic is hectic, and they aren't looking. But the BMW taps its brakes twice and pulls back into the lane next to mine and slows down, hard.

"Oh, shit."

I look to my right and see a man's profile. He turns his head as his window comes down, and he hangs his hand out, middle finger aloft. In the span of a moment I register dark hair, a straight nose, the shadow of a beard, and a cocky grin.

I shrink in my seat as a spike of fear shoots through me. He really wasn't supposed to see that.

"BMW douchebag," I mumble as I hit my turn signal and pull my tiny car off the road and into a parking lot designated for compact cars only.

I look around me before I get out. This day has been bad enough already. The last thing I need is a road-rage idiot suffering from affluenza coming after me in the airport parking lot.

Alright, no time to lose. I jump out of my car and haul my suitcase out of the trunk. It barely fit in there. It's way too big. I'm only going to be gone for a week, but I'm equipped for at least a month. Some people overpack. I pack like there might be some sort of a natural disaster and I'll have to stay forever.

After hauling my monstrosity behind me and catching the bus to the airport terminal, I go through the ridiculously complicated check-in process. All those automated machines are supposed to make things faster, but I can never get them to do what I want them to, and it ends up taking me twice as long. The terminal is packed today. It's Thursday, the very beginning of Labor Day weekend, and everyone, I mean everyone, has someplace to be.

The line stretches, zigzagging across the white linoleum floor. Harried travelers stare at their phones, leaning on one foot, then the other, sighing with impatience. Dammit. I might really miss my flight. Which might not be a bad thing. If I miss it, I won't have to go. I *shouldn't* be going, as Cara has told me repeatedly over the last several months.

As if she's reading my thoughts, my phone pings, and I see a text from my best friend:

Are you at the airport? I'm so so soooooo sorry I couldn't make it! I'm there with you in spirit! You can do this!

I smile at the screen. Cara was supposed to be here with me as moral support, but her grandmother got sick and is in the hospital with pneumonia. So, when Cara showed up at my apartment apologizing profusely, I gave her a hug and told her that she should go be with her family and not to give it a moment's thought.

The line inches along. I crane my head, up on the toes of my sensible airport ballet flats. Easy to get on, easy to take off. I double-check that my computer is ready to place in a bin, and my phone is already in my hand, slippery with sweat from my nervous fingers. I tap out a quick message:

I'm here. Security is a nightmare. If I miss my flight, I'm not going.

The phone immediately pings in response:

In that case, I hope you miss your flight!

Ahead of me, I watch as some lady works on the tiny buckles of her stilettos. I suppress a groan. Who wears stilettos to the airport? What the hell is she trying to prove? Although they do make her legs look killer, and her outfit is perfect. But never mind. There's no excuse for this. Airports are a place for efficiency, and I've got this down to a science. I traveled nonstop as a kid, and I still travel all the time for work.

The line shuffles forward again. I look with envy next to me, where the swift pass, or the pre-check or whatever that line is called, moves right along while the rest of us undress for the TSA. I should have gotten the pre-check. I meant to. I keep meaning to. Every time I'm at the airport I go through this inner monologue, but then I never do it, because I'm the sort of person who procrastinates, and overpacks, and has a to-do list as long as a CVS receipt. But at least I'm ready for the TSA.

Ahead of me, in the fast lane, I see the guy in the Beamer. I grit my teeth as I inspect him. He's frowning down at his phone, typing in hyper speed. He's wearing sleek charcoal slacks, cleanly pressed with a crease down the front so sharp it could give you a paper cut. His black knit top looks soft. Not the slouchy comfy sort of soft, the expensive sort. He's wearing the right kind of shoes. Loafers. Easy to slip off, easy to put back on. Not that he'll need to. Nor will he have to take off his belt or remove all his worldly possessions to place in separate bins.

With a huff, I turn my focus back to my own lackluster reality. When it's my turn I lay my computer into one bin, my shoes in another. My leggings don't require a belt, and I have no pockets to empty. My backpack contains only a book, a sandwich, a spare pair of underwear (just in case), and my crochet tools. I'm making a baby blanket for Cara, who just announced that she's expecting her first with her unbelievably sweet husband, Billy. I'm thrilled for them. I really am. I can't wait to be Aunty Daisy. I'm going to be a kick-ass aunt. I even bought a book on babies, just in case Cara needs me to know something about her newborn, as if she doesn't have three actual, biological sisters ready to dote on her.

I walk to the machine that takes nude pictures of you and stand with my arms up in the air, and proceed to hustle my shoes back on my feet and sling my belongings into my backpack, and then I'm off, storming towards the terminal like a woman possessed. The image of the man from the Beamer taunts me. He's probably already relaxing in business class, sipping a glass of champagne, and purchasing an overpriced watch from *SkyMall*. Ugh. I should have just accepted the apology wave, so I wouldn't be ruminating on him like he's the source of all my problems.

I get to the gate just in time. The last of the passengers are lining up with their tickets and phones ready to scan, and the flight attendant directs them down the ramp towards the plane. Some small part of me, the part I have been resolutely ignoring since I got that invitation six months ago, groans regret. Once I get on that plane, there's no going back. I sigh. At least I have a stay in a plush hotel room to look forward to. And room service, and access to a pillow menu that I absolutely plan on abusing. All paid for by Michael, my mother's soon-to-be husband.

I make my way down the aisle of the crowded plane. First past the smug faces of the business class passengers, comfortably lounging with drinks already in hand, then to the back, with the normal people with normal problems—like being seated next to a screaming toddler, or trying to film the person flipping out because they had one too many at the airport bar and forgot we live in a society. They're all in various states of disarray. Shoving slightly too large carry-on bags into overhead bins and making awkward introductions to their seat mates.

I head down towards the back of the plane. I have a middle seat because of course I waited until the last possible moment to book my ticket.

I find my row, and look to the right and then to the left. My stomach plummets through the floor, right down to the cargo hold.

The man who wagged the middle finger at me like he enjoyed it, and smugly strolled through security without a care in the world. He's on my flight, and because I must have done something terrible in a previous life, he is seated next to me.

The word pops out of my mouth before I can stop it.

"Beamer." It comes out like an accusation.

He looks up from his laptop abruptly, where he's typing like he *must* get this email out or calamity is imminent. He looks startled for a moment, and an awkward pause ensues as recognition lights his eyes. Then his mouth curves up in a slow smile. Not a smile. A smirk. It's a rather appealing mouth. He doesn't say anything, only stands, to let me get past and take my seat in the middle. To my left a middle-aged woman is already lightly snoring, her head slouched against the window. I look around frantically, just to make sure the plane really is full, which it is. No empty seats anywhere. I quietly damn Cara for having the foresight to book herself a refundable ticket.

I slide my backpack under the seat in front of me and sit. My heart is jumping in my chest at what just came out of my mouth. I cannot believe I said that. He takes his seat next to me, and I am excruciatingly aware of the fact that I just called attention to myself, and now he has clearly recognized me as the unhinged woman who gave him the finger instead of just accepting the courtesy wave. This is the universe punishing me.

A few minutes pass while the flight attendants begin closing the overhead compartments. Maybe he will ignore the ridiculous nickname I just gave him, and we will sit in silence for the entire three and a half hours it will take to get from Denver to DC. But fate is not on my side today, and from my right, where Beamer is still making a show of doing very important things on his laptop, I hear his voice for the first time.

"Mini Cooper." The words are smooth, like a Bond villain who's been expecting his nemesis to arrive at any moment, informing me that, yes, he is aware of precisely who I am, and no, he's not going to let it go.

I huff at him and rummage through my backpack at my feet until I find my crochet hook and ball of yarn. The baby blanket will be green and yellow—gender neutral, since Cara has decided she wants the sex of the baby to be a surprise.

The flight attendants are now instructing all passengers to put their devices into airplane mode. Beamer closes his laptop and slides it into the seat pocket at his knees. The watch on his wrist flashes at me, like it needs the world to know it was expensive. This is when he notices the canary yellow yarn in my lap.

"Go ahead, Mini, and be more cliché. The world didn't think you were cute enough with that ridiculous car you drive."

I look at him, my jaw hanging open. "Excuse me?"

He nods at my baby blanket. "You knit? What are you, a sixty-year-old woman?"

"It's crochet," I correct him, hooking my needle aggressively through the yarn.

"Tomato, tomahto," he says with an indifferent shrug.

My lips press into a flat line, and I exhale hard through my nose like a dragon. I can ignore him. I can just ignore him for this entire flight. I don't have to even reply to him. But of course I do, because he basically just called me a nerd, and now my temper is officially up.

"What, are you in high school?" I spit back at him.

"You started it, Mini." The smirk returns as he pulls out his in-flight magazine and begins leafing through it. A full-page ad alerts us to the existence of Montana. I examine him for a moment before I reply and realize that the smirk has subtly transformed into a quiet sort of smile. This is entertaining to him. He's trying not to laugh.

"At least I *have* a hobby, and I'm not glued to my work computer." He might find this funny, but I'm not laughing.

"How do you know it's work?" he asks lightly. He turns a page, eyes still on his magazine. "I could be a poet. I could be writing the Great American Novel."

The plane begins taxiing the runway.

"Oh, I highly I doubt that."

"Why does that seem so unbelievable?" He looks at me as though affronted.

"Because poets don't cut people off at the airport," I explain.

"I apologized for that. Didn't you see me wave? It was an accident."

I ignore him. "And poets don't drive BMWs."

"Successful poets might," he points out. "And let's not forget, Mini, you gave me the finger first."

I set my crochet down and turn to look at him squarely. "I was late for my flight, and you"—I jab a finger towards him, nearly touching his arm—"almost killed me."

"Well, I was late for my flight too. I *apologized*. I gave the wave."

I should just say sorry for the middle finger, but as is easily displayed by my packing tendencies, I lack self-control.

"Yes, well, we don't all have the TSA fast pass."

He looks momentarily startled before he laughs. "So, you've been stalking me through the airport? You should learn to control those anger issues."

"You aren't going to let this go, are you, Beamer?"

He looks at me and gives me an evil grin with his very nice mouth, and a single dark eyebrow raises. "I'm afraid not, Mini."

"Well, I'm not sorry for flipping you off, because now I can tell you deserved it. I'm a good judge of character."

"Are you? And what is my character like?" I swear he's really enjoying this. His eyes are literally bright with mirth. Something about that fact—the fact that my harried stress and borderline mental break on the roadway is funny to him—makes me dislike him even more.

"You wear expensive clothes." I nod at his slacks. "You have a fancy watch. Why don't you make your way up to the front of the plane where you belong? Doesn't your poet's salary pay for that?"

The plane swoops up into the air with a roar of the engines and my stomach dips a little.

"All booked up," he says easily as he reaches for his computer.

He pulls down his tray table, and the screen lights up, revealing a wall of text in what must be nine-point font. Good God, whatever this man does for a living seems horrible.

He begins typing again, this time in red, making track changes. Tearing up someone else's work. How very predictable.

I return to my crochet, taking a deep breath, focusing on the thought of Cara's baby nestled in the blanket. It's just three hours next to this man. To my right the woman lets out a snort, and then another snore.

"She took a pill," Beamer says absently.

"What?" I snap.

"The lady next to you. She took a pill as soon as she sat down. I was relieved that I wouldn't have too much chatter to distract me."

"You're the one still talking," I say, sliding the yarn over the crochet hook and pulling it through the loop.

He doesn't reply but continues typing away. The flight turns, tipping my body to the right. Through the window the checkered quilt of the Great Plains expands into the distance. Behind us, the flight attendants rummage about with bottles and cups, glass clinking and cabinet doors opening and shutting as they prepare the drink cart. Beamer's elbow is firmly planted on the armrest between us. My jaw tightens, and I press my elbow against his, still working my crochet hook. He doesn't budge.

It's a universal understanding amongst all air travelers that the person in the middle seat gets the armrest. All of us on this journey are trapped in an aluminum tube together, thousands of feet in the air, and only a few unspoken rules separate us from becoming a reenactment of *The Lord of the Flies*. This is one of them. Beamer and I are locked in an air travel cold war, each of us hell-bent on claiming these few square inches of precious real estate for ourselves. I press my elbow harder against his, but I might as well be working against a brick wall.

Finally, I huff, "Beamer, the armrest is mine."

"Says who, Mini?" he asks without looking over at me, his fingers working across the keys as smoothly as a pianist.

"Says the laws of nature and every person who's ever flown. Are you new to air travel? First flight? You must be *excited*."

"Those laws only apply to people who are tall enough to ride a rollercoaster, Mini. And who don't have a woman on a dose of horse tranquilizer sitting on their other side."

My small stature has been the source of many a joke in my lifetime. It's not original.

"Way to grasp at the low-hanging fruit, Beamer."

"I bet you know all about low-hanging fruit," he says and then grins at his own joke.

I roll my eyes. "Got any other knee-slappers for me? Your work looks boring as hell, by the way."

"I can go all day."

"I bet your girlfriend regrets that."

His lips purse into something like a frown. "Is that jealousy I hear, Mini?"

"Not in a million years."

The keys clack under his fingers. My crochet hook works with increasing force. Our elbows are still smashed together.

A moment later a flight attendant charges up the aisle with the drinks cart, headed with determination towards the elites in the front.

There's a grunt of pain, and Beamer rubs his elbow as the cart hits him with a rattling thump, and the attendant moves past as though she didn't just risk fracturing his arm.

I stifle the urge to cackle at him in vindication. Instead, I sigh. He has broad shoulders. I think about myself waving my finger at him through the windshield of my car, and his apology wave in return, and I relent. Damn conscience. I silently slide my elbow off the armrest. A small show of humanity in an increasingly inhumane world.

A few moments of silence pass between us, and all the bluster has gone out of me.

"Thank you," he says in a low voice, almost like he regrets having manners.

"Is your elbow hurt?" I ask.

"My professional tennis career is likely over, but beyond that I expect to survive."

"I thought you were a poet."

"I'm a man of many talents," he answers smoothly.

I smile in spite of myself as I hook and loop the yarn.

He sighs then, as though in resignation.

"My name is Charles." He reaches his right hand across his body in an offer to shake mine. I regard it with suspicion for a moment and look up to meet his eyes. They're a lovely shade of hazel, gold and green and soft brown. It annoys me that every time I notice a detail about this man's appearance, it turns out to be something attractive.

I reach up and meet his grip. It's firm. "Daisy."

He tilts his head back with a laugh, although it's good-humored now, rather than sarcastic. "Oh, come on, not Daisy!"

"Why not Daisy?" I say, affronted.

"Because you drive a Mini Cooper, and you knit, and the name

Daisy is practically the same as being called Dot." There's a twinkle in his hazel eyes.

"Please tell me we're not back to that." I want to continue being angry, but I'm finding it difficult. "I get it, I'm short and I *crochet,*" I correct him. "And besides, it's not like you aren't a walking cliché yourself, with your very important laptop and your fancy car and country club name."

He's twisted towards me now, his broad shoulders turned in my direction, "Hey, I go by Charlie, and I *could* be sitting up front, and I'm not. So that blows a hole in your whole cliché theory."

"Because they were all booked up," I say pointedly.

He turns back to his computer. "The point still stands. A lesser man would have taken the later flight."

I huff a laugh and shake my head.

"I didn't mean to cut you off, Daisy," he says softly.

Finally, I give in to the urge to offer an apology, "I'm sorry I flipped you off. This just hasn't been my day. Or my year, actually."

I grimace inside at this little slip of vulnerability, and all at once I remember exactly why I'm on this flight and what I'm flying towards, and the desire to talk leaves me. I move to put my crochet away and take out my book, but Charlie interrupts me, his eyes back to me, his computer seemingly forgotten, his expression sincere.

"I take it this isn't a trip for pleasure, then?" he says.

The way the word *pleasure* comes out of his mouth makes me nervous. "It's not, exactly. It's more of a chore, to be perfectly honest."

"I'm sorry it's not a happy trip."

It's a platitude, but I'm struck by a brief moment of insanity during which I think I could tell him everything. I could tell this stranger the whole ugly backstory and then waltz off the plane unburdened, never to see him again. Instead, I reach for my book and open it, signaling the end of the conversation.

We sit in silence for a while as I attempt to read through the distraction of Beamer's presence beside me. He works diligently, making progress in whatever it is that he does with his life. Periodically, he murmurs under his breath. Sometimes he snorts derisively. Finally, he mutters, "Jackass."

I look at him with concern. "Are you okay?"

I shouldn't have issued commentary of any sort. Why I decided to reopen the door to conversation isn't something I fully understand, beyond the fact that when I'm talking to him, I'm not thinking about anything else, and my novel isn't putting any effort into holding my attention.

"Sorry." He looks sheepish. "Just this guy I work with. Everything he does just sounds so… pretentious. And overblown. He uses a paragraph to express something that could be said in just a line."

"Like he likes the look of his own writing? Likes the thought of someone hearing the sound of his voice?"

"Yes." He points at the screen. "Exactly like that. And I happen to be one of those people who hears what they read in their head, so unfortunately, I've had his voice in my ear this whole flight."

"Except when you've had my voice in your ear," I say.

"Yeah." He tilts his head slightly, as though weighing his words. "But you have a nice voice, Daisy. I don't mind it at all, it turns out."

All at once, my cheeks feel warm, and I turn my head back to my book.

When the plane lands, Charlie does not stand up right away. In my mind, that receives brownie points. I've never understood the people who stand up the second the wheels touch the ground, as if they will suddenly be free to sprint towards the front of the plane and jump out of the hatch.

"Do you have anything in the overhead?" he asks when we finally stand and it's our turn to head down the aisle. The show of consideration surprises me.

"Nope," I answer, "but thanks."

He nods and slings his laptop case over one shoulder. He, also, is carrying nothing else.

He holds an arm out. "After you." The gesture is oddly sweet, coming from a man who spent the first half an hour of our acquaintance blithely enjoying making fun of me.

I walk ahead of him, and at baggage claim we do the thing where we stand in proximity to one another, but not exactly *next* to one another. As though we are unsure what the etiquette is for people who have become sort-of pals on a flight after being sort-of enemies.

My obscenely large suitcase, in an undignified shade of purple, is dumped onto the carousel and as I haul it off, I catch him out of the corner of my eye, chuckling with one hand over his mouth, shaking his head.

And that's that. Beamer is now filed away in my mind, as a funny story about the time I gave a hot guy the finger on my way to the airport.

Chapter 2

It turns out the hotel my mom's wedding is to be held at is in Georgetown—a charming, wealthy section of Washington, DC without access to the metro. But it's not until I get off at the nearest stop that I realize I've made a grave error. Too late now. I already made the decision to save myself the cab fare, and what have all those spin classes been for if not to prepare me for this moment?

It's an old city—well, old by American standards—and the uneven sidewalks aren't doing me or my gigantic suitcase any favors. The air feels about a thousand degrees, and the humidity exceeds sauna levels of saturation. By the time I arrive in Georgetown, my suitcase bumping and rattling the whole way, I have a blister on my foot and pit stains beneath my arms, and my previously tasteful ballet bun has devolved into a frizzy pouf on top of my head.

The neighborhood is bubbling over with charm. Colorful townhouses line the streets with window boxes full of tumbling, flowering vines. Lush trees do their best to provide shelter from the baking sun. Tourists snap photos as they walk, and students from the university dart in and out of salad shops and bookstores. Cars pack the street running down the center of it all, competing for impossibly small parallel parking spots.

As I approach the glass doors of the elegant hotel, I make determined eye contact with a bellman who's looking at me apprehensively. As though he's unsure about the protocol of allowing a deranged bag lady into the lobby. All around me, black sedans sit with calm serenity, with tinted windows and interiors undoubtedly clean, and fresh with air conditioning. A woman saunters past in white flowing slacks and a beige silk camisole. Her blond hair is twisted into an elegant chignon, and she talks on her phone in crisp syllables. I march past her, determined to claim my place here, among these beautiful, wealthy people. It doesn't matter that I'm limping on what I am fairly sure is a bloody foot.

When it becomes obvious that I'm not slowing down, the doorman seems to accept the fact that he's going to have to acknowledge me, and he swings the door open with a white-toothed smile and a nod. The cold air hits me like a divine blessing from God himself. On a large glass table, adorned with a stunning display of orange and pink flowers that I'm too hot and exhausted to fully appreciate, there are tall glass vessels containing ice water with sliced cucumbers. I stagger towards it like a woman wandering out of the desert, dragging my purple suitcase and simultaneously trying to wriggle the heel of my foot out of my shoe to give myself some relief.

It's not until I'm on my second glass of cucumber water that I take the time to really absorb my surroundings. The air is scented with lavender, and discreet sconces glow softly so that no one here will ever have to face the prospect of being seen under bad lighting. Here, everyone gets to be beautiful. A modernist chandelier soars proudly from the ceiling overhead. To the left are the doors to a restaurant and bar, and on my right a bank of elevators. A man seated at a large, black grand piano plays a soft tinkling tune, and ahead of me, behind a long desk of blond wood, a stunning woman in a dark suit is squinting in my direction. She must have deduced by my luggage that I am, in fact, in the right place, despite everything else about me screaming intruder.

When I've checked in and collected my key card, I ride the elevator up to the fourth floor. I've never been so grateful to reach a hotel room before. When the door swings shut behind me, the silence comes as a benediction. It's tastefully appointed, all varying shades of unobjectionable taupe and white. The bed's headboard goes all the way up to the ceiling, and a large panoramic image of the city hangs on the opposite wall.

I desperately need the fluffy duvet on the oversize bed, access to the mini bar, and a soaking tub. These things are luxuries, but throughout the day they quickly came to feel like necessities. The talismans I was holding on to, to keep me moving towards my destination. It's not just that I'm exhausted from the journey to the hotel, or the oppressive heat of this city, or the awkwardness of walking into the ritzy hotel while looking like I just went for a swim in the Potomac River. It's everything. The fact that I'm going to this wedding feels like an insult. Plus, Cara isn't with me, and I'm going to have to face my ex-fiancé and meet his new girlfriend who is (I know from my not-at-all creepy or obsessive internet sleuthing) gorgeous, and it means the weekend looming ahead of me feels as appealing as walking into a graveyard in the dead of night.

The last time I saw Rob he was sitting on the opposite end of my sofa looking mournfully at me with his golden retriever eyes and shaking his head.

"It's just way too complicated, Daisy. I can't do this. I can't stop… thinking about it. Every time I look at you it's right there, like a damn splinter."

"When you look at me?" I'd asked, as though I didn't understand.

Although I understood perfectly well. My face, I learned, had become a constant, terrible reminder for him.

Things had become unwieldy. Horribly complicated and painful for us both. Actually, to be perfectly frank, they were fucked up. It was the sort of thing people tune into daytime TV to watch to make themselves feel better about their own small messes. Other people whose lives have devolved into utter chaos. Other people who can't keep their shit together. We were never supposed to be those people, and yet there we were, attempting to untangle a shamble that was so out of control it seemed to have formed a life of its own.

"How the hell are we supposed to move past this?" he'd asked me. "Infidelity is supposed to be a deal breaker."

I'd been unable to look at his face when he said that. I knew what he saw when he looked at me. I knew he saw dishonesty and disloyalty, and that he had come to believe I wasn't the person he thought I was. The injustice of that punched me in the stomach so hard it was almost nauseating, but I tried to win him back to my side—the side that wanted to fight for our relationship.

"We move past it by choosing to move past it," I'd argued. "We can deal with this, just like we've dealt with everything else."

"Everything else? What would you compare this to, Daisy?" His voice had risen as his temper increased, and I shrank back. "This isn't exactly a disagreement about bills, or who does the dishes or something, you know?" He'd run his hands through his blond hair in frustration, gripping his scalp like he could tug an answer from his head. "It's embarrassing! I mean, can you even imagine going out with friends at this point? Family holidays? With what everyone knows?"

I couldn't, but as far as I was concerned, that was beside the point. The point was that relationships should be resilient, and ours was proving not to be. I knew what was happening—our engagement was ending. I should have been crushed. But the overriding feeling was disappointment. Just as Rob had begun to see me as a different person, I realized he had been a different person all along. I wanted to fight for our relationship; he wanted to walk away when things were at their most difficult.

My eyes had welled with tears, but I'd finally accepted defeat and nodded, and Rob had left with a box of his things. When I tried to give him back the ring, he had refused it with a rueful shake of his head. He'd kissed me on the forehead, a chaste kiss, like a child. And that was it—the end of our present, the end of our future.

I'd called my mom immediately and wailed over the phone and she tutted at me, and I heard her talking to Michael in the background while she cooked dinner. Cara had, of course, been there immediately, spending hours watching all of our favorite girl movies while drinking wine and gorging on chocolate. She was irate.

"We should burn his apartment down," she'd suggested while I cried.

"You can't just burn down *one* apartment, Cara," I said through the tears.

"Fine, we sneak in and hold up a lighter to his sprinklers, and we drown his apartment instead." And then I'd begun laughing through all the crying, and she'd held me to her breast like a mother hen and let me fall asleep with my head resting in her lap.

I'd woken the next morning on the sofa, with my own pillow, and the blankets from my bed wrapped around me. Cara was asleep in the Poang chair from Ikea, her head tilted to the side, with a small string of drool leading to a puddle in the groove of her collarbone.

We've since implemented what she calls the Cara Test, which means I am only to date men who live up to her standards of masculine appeal mixed with soft-hearted tenderness. Dates, however, have been few and far between, because I just can't seem to spark with anyone. Apparently, there's something off-putting about a woman wallowing in a universe of self-pity.

As far as anyone else knows, Rob and I had just grown apart. Cara was the only one I'd ever told the full story to, but our modern era doesn't make secrets easy to keep, and just like Rob had predicted, the truth of what had happened was soon clear to anyone who cared to look.

For the next six months I'd gone to work and to the gym and then home, keeping a healthy distance from everyone except Cara, and stayed as far away from social media as I possibly could. But when I had to get on Instagram to work on a social media push for my department, I'd been unable to resist the temptation to check out Rob's social media, and I saw *her*. Tall and slender and sporty with hiking boots (duh, we live in Colorado) and a ponytail that probably swings back and forth like a cute jump rope when she's out on the trail. And that was when the last little glimmer of hope that the life I had imagined for myself—for myself and Rob—was really gone. I didn't begin to come back to life until my boss let me take the lead on my first big campaign—to get a piece of land put into conservation. But then, of course, I lost that fight too, because I haven't been able to do anything right this entire year.

I lie sprawled across the fluffy hotel bed for a while, staring at the ceiling, reliving the last year of my life like a reel of film, and then decide it's time to stop moping and enjoy what's in front of me. The soaking tub and the variety of complimentary soaps on offer are irresistible, and I draw myself a luscious bubble bath. I shave my legs (long neglected) and wash my hair, then read my book while the bubbles slowly evaporate. Finally, when my fingers and toes have turned to prunes, I climb out and wrap myself in a robe and climb under the covers of the plush bed, exhausted and still, embarrassingly, feeling sorry for myself. This won't do. I'm in a new city, in a luxury hotel, and most of the guests won't be flying in until tomorrow, which means that if I want to hit the restaurant downstairs without fear of being recognized, now is the time.

When I open my suitcase to get dressed, I realize right away that it's been riffled with. It's not the first time this has happened. The TSA will occasionally get extra handsy with my things, and I'm not worried about stolen items since I don't have anything valuable to begin with, but I unpack my copious amounts of stuff anyways. I have shoes for any eventuality, including an impromptu trip to Appalachia or a night at the opera, dresses upon dresses, jeans, workout gear, slacks and tank tops, a blazer, a windbreaker, nail polish, earrings, balls of yarn. I don't put it away, exactly, but I do sort of organize things into sections, and hang up the dresses so they don't get wrinkled. And that's when I see *the* dress. The dress for the wedding.

The very important, very expensive dress that I purchased specifically because it's short enough to make my legs look long and the straps thin enough to make my shoulders look delicate. The dress that is supposed to make Rob realize what a mistake he made, and make my mom realize that her daughter is something special after all, and prevent all of our collective friends and family from pitying me. This very important dress has a snag in the silk right across the bust that pulls and bunches in a way that absolutely cannot be repaired. I'm going to have to find a new, perfect evening dress in a city that I don't know, in one day. And I'm a *petite* size. As in, sizes for short people. I can't just walk into a store and expect everything to fit just right. There's a whole special section for the vertically challenged ladies of the world, and most stores have relegated them to the internet. *Shit.*

But, after ruminating over this dilemma, and talking myself off a ledge, I decide that this is a problem not worth worrying about until tomorrow, and I go to dinner.

Chapter 3

With my freshly shaved legs I feel as fabulous as Beyoncé. I want to tell every person I pass, *feel them! Feel how soft!* But I manage to contain myself, and instead I carry myself with dignity, my tiny bag clutched in one hand and my strappy sandals clicking elegantly on the marble. I'm wearing a swishy cotton sundress that is much better in the heat, so that when I walk out onto the patio bar behind the hotel, I don't immediately melt into a puddle of swamp sludge.

The air is warm, but far less intensely so than a few hours ago, and the sun has cast a golden pink glow across the sky. The patio is filled with tropical plants that give it a vacation vibe, even though we're submerged in the pressure cooker heart of American politics. Around the patio, men and women in work attire are frowning at each other over their cocktails, or tapping efficiently on their phones as they nurse a drink. The woman I recognize from when I entered the hotel—the one in the elegant white slacks—is sitting across from a handsome man, spinning a martini glass seductively by its stem on the wooden table. Whatever he's saying rivets her, and she leans in, a slender eyebrow rising.

She looks up from her drink and catches my eye, and I quickly look away, pretending to be fascinated by the plants in the pot next to me.

"Are you snooping again?" a man's voice comes from behind me. Not any voice. *His* voice.

I turn in my seat so fast I nearly fall off, and find him standing there behind me, still in his clothes from the airplane, remarkably, miraculously un-creased. The sleeves of his knit top are pushed up his forearms in response to the weather. They are, unfortunately, very good forearms.

"Beamer? I mean, Charlie?" I correct myself with a frazzled shake of my head.

He shoots me a lopsided smile. "What's a girl like you doing in a place like this?" he drawls as he takes the seat next to mine.

"Is that your usual pickup line?" My heart kicks up in my chest at the sight of him. Why it's excited to see him, I swear I do not know. But it starts drumming away.

"Not a pickup line, Mini. An earnest question." He places his hand over his heart with grave concern. "Are you following me?"

I can't help it. I laugh. I feel like I'm right back on the airplane, but before my mind catches up with what I ought to say next, the bartender emerges and slides a cocktail napkin over with a glass of water and asks for Charlie's order.

"Martini, straight up, two olives, please."

The bartender vanishes to shake up his martini, and I stare at Charlie, last name unknown.

"What are you doing here?" I ask. I'm suddenly nervous, and I pick at the edge of the coaster on the bar top in front of me.

"I thought we were just about to establish why *you* are here, Mini." He takes his drink when it appears and brings it to his lips. His lips continue to be very good. Not so full as to be pouty, but just enough that he's probably an excellent kisser. He's probably kissed his way into dozens of women's beds, with all the trappings of wealth that surround him and clothes that don't wrinkle.

"Wedding." Keeping the details out of it is the best approach to the impending event, I have found.

He nods. "Beautiful place for a wedding." Behind him, the woman from the lobby has noticed the striking man in the perfect attire sitting across from me. Her eyes stray from her tablemate and run the lines of his body. I want to make a face at her, or hiss, or maybe stick my tongue out. But I shove my inner child back into its closet and cross and uncross my legs. Charlie's eyes dart down and linger for a moment longer than necessary before he looks back up at me, and it gives me a little rush of energy.

"What about you, Beamer? I can't imagine you enjoying a celebration. Actually, I can't imagine you… enjoying. Full stop."

His lips twitch. Nearly a smile. "Meetings," he says.

We're both being dodgy.

"Meetings for your boring-as-hell work?"

"You're insightful, you know that?"

"Stop trying to charm me, Beamer."

"Only when you stop looking so in need of being charmed."

That line gives me pause. Is it a barb or a genuine compliment? I can't tell.

"So, who's getting married?" he asks, stirring his drink around by the spear holding the olives.

Are we really doing this? Are we going to sit at a bar next to each other after having an interaction that was only barely tolerable on a flight this morning? His hazel eyes are fixed on me intently, waiting for an answer, so I guess we are.

"My mom." I lean forward so that my elbows rest on the bar ledge and my eyes fall onto the coaster I've been picking at.

"You don't sound happy about that."

"I'm very happy," I say defensively. "She's my mom, and she's in love. Of course I'm happy."

"Of course you are," he agrees.

"What are your meetings for?"

He spins his bar seat from side to side, like a little boy sitting with the grownups. It's an endearing movement. "Oh, you know, corporate takeovers, robbing the little guy of millions, mass layoffs. What you'd expect from a country club master of the universe like me."

Again, it's possible he's not joking, but he clarifies, "I'm a contract attorney, and I have a client in DC that needs some hand-holding."

"Contract attorney? Is it as awful as it sounds? I mean, I barely made it through listening to that sentence, and you have to live that life."

His lips twitch again. "It is *exactly* as awful as it sounds, Mini. But it pays for the Beamer, so you should be grateful. Who would you have around to hate if it weren't for that douchey car?"

Plenty of people, I want to say. Instead, I grin at him, because he's funny and he's actually turning out to be quite charming, and I really need it right now. The Daisy of this morning would give me a whack if she could hear my inner monologue now, but I'm glad he's here and that I'm not sitting alone.

He changes the subject back to me. "So, what does little Daisy Mini do when she's not trotting off to fancy hotels with her oversized purple suitcase?"

"Daisy Mini?" I raise a brow at him. "That the best you got?"

"I don't know your last name, so it's got to be Daisy Mini, I'm afraid."

I roll my eyes over the smile I'm holding back. "It's Daisy Thomas."

"Ah." He eyes me over another sip of his martini. "What does Daisy Thomas do, then?"

I suck my teeth for a minute because I know he's going to find a way to tease me for this. "I'm an environmental advocate."

But he doesn't tease me. Instead, he pauses over his drink, the rim just touching his bottom lip.

"What?" I ask. "What is it?"

He clears his throat and sets his drink down. "Nothing. That's an interesting job."

I eye him suspiciously. "That's it? It's an interesting job? No jabs about how a little old lady like me is trying to save the bees?"

"Well, I mean, if you want me to, I could—"

I stop him with a raised hand, laughing. "No, please don't. I should have just accepted the compliment."

He nods. "So what, precisely, are you saving, Daisy Thomas?"

"Black bears. I advocate, work on policy proposals, do some social media. That sort of thing."

"Your heart bleeds?" he says as he smiles.

I place a hand over my chest, mirroring his earlier pose. "It does."

He twirls his glass in place, and then plucks an olive off the toothpick and chews it, thinking. I'd like to ask him what he's thinking about, but something tells me not to.

"What's your last name?" I ask instead. "Or would you prefer to be known as Beamer?"

He grins and raises his martini. "It's Bond."

I chuckle, "No, really, what's your name?"

"I'm being perfectly serious."

I blink. "That sounds made up."

He laughs. "I'm aware."

"Have you ever asked your mom why she didn't name you James?"

"I've only ever taken the time to feel grateful that she didn't."

This makes me giggle. A fully girlish giggle that mortifies me inside. "Why don't you ask her?"

"She passed away."

My smile falls. "Oh my God, I'm so sorry."

"It's okay." He shrugs. "I was young."

There's an uncomfortable pause—the kind that occurs when you ask someone something too personal. After a moment he turns back to me. "Are you hungry?"

I am, actually. I haven't eaten since the flight, and my stomach rumbles at the thought of food.

"What tipped you off?"

He gestures at the patio around us. "Let's sit down and eat something. You can tell me more about saving the wildlife, and if you're lucky, I'll tell you all about torts."

"Tortoises?" I say innocently, as though I've never heard of a tort, and he tilts his head back as he laughs. The first free laugh I've seen from him. His eyes relax and dimples appear around his mouth, and I hope to God he's not a serial killer because he seems so… nice.

Chapter 4

We're seated inside, where the tables are draped in white, crisp linen, and soft music soothes the weary traveler while candles on each table flicker and gutter with the breeze coming in from outside. Charlie orders a bottle of wine and pours our glasses, and when he asks me questions his gaze penetrates mine with the sort of attention he applied to his work on the plane.

"So, your mom's wedding," he says, and I swallow. "Tell me the story."

I fidget with the handle of my knife, pushing it back and forth so that it pivots from side to side. "It's not much of a story," I lie smoothly. "Mom met a guy she liked, and he asked her to marry him, and now they're getting married."

"Uh-oh." He leans back in his chair. "You don't like him."

I take a drink. "I like him just fine. He's actually great. Super friendly, warm, generous. I get what my mom saw in him."

That's it. That's all he's getting out of me. Charlie is charming, but he's not that charming, and I've been a steel trap about this for a year.

He nods as though he hears my thoughts, and we order dinner. Steak for him, pasta for me.

The food arrives, and I allow myself to sink into my plate of pasta like it's a warm bed. Reveling in it, twirling noodles on my fork and slurping up the sauce. Charlie watches me over his wineglass as he takes a bite of steak.

"Barbarian," I say. I can't help it. The animosity between us has vanished, but I *need* to tease him, or I'll start thinking about how his hazel eyes are greener in this light. The way he's looking at me is making me nervous and warm in places that I can't think about in public, and my thighs squeeze together of their own volition.

"Vegetarian," he replies lightly, like he's not refuting me, just exchanging facts.

"Technically, pescatarian," I answer. "I do eat fish."

"Hmmm, so not all creatures are off the menu," he says. "Fish don't deserve your mercy?"

I laugh. "I don't have the self-discipline." I take another drink. I'm pleasantly tipsy now, warm and relaxed.

"So, Denver," I say.

"Denver." He nods.

"Have you always lived there?" I ask.

"Yep, born and bred. A mountain kid."

"So, you must, like, hike and ski and everything. All the Colorado activities."

"Doesn't everyone?" he asks over a bite of potato.

I shake my head. "Not me."

His eyes widen and he sets down his fork. "You don't hike?"

"I mean, it's not like I've never done it," I say, somewhat defensively. "It's just never been my thing."

"But you love bears," he says in disbelief.

I laugh. "The one thing is not a prerequisite for the other, Beamer. I do love bears, but I don't necessarily want to *meet* a bear."

"How do you even have friends in Colorado if you don't hike?"

"I manage. But *you* like to hike." I circle my fork in the air for him to continue.

"My dad and I used to go camping all the time," he says by way of answer. "He's got a place up near Vail, and we still go every chance we get, although it's not as easy now. My work keeps me busy, and he's slowed down recently."

There's a story there that I don't ask about. It's like we're skating across a frozen lake, moving in careful, slow circles over the fragile surface, avoiding anything that might risk a crack. But I'm curious. I haven't truly felt curious about another person in a long time. I can hear Cara's voice in my head right now, telling me to dig for his whole past.

But rather than push, I take the easy route. "Vail is unsurprising."

"Because it's the town where the stars go?"

"That, and wealthy lawyers."

He grins again. "What can I say? It's important to keep up appearances, Mini. What about you? Are you from Denver originally?"

"Nope."

"Where then?"

Asking me where I'm from is like asking a sea turtle where it's from. I lift my shoulders. "I'm from everywhere, I guess. My dad's been out of the picture since I was an infant, and my mom took us from city to city."

I was born in New York, but we moved to Los Angeles when I was a baby, and then we returned. We spent time in a bright and spacious apartment in Manhattan, and then later moved to Seattle where I wore wellies and raincoats to the playground. For a while we lived in Miami and went to the beach each weekend, and my mother got so suntanned that my own skin looked like porcelain next to hers.

But while every city opened new adventures for my mother, it always meant that I had to start over. I had to make new friends, adjust to new schools, get to know a new nanny, and discover a new neighborhood. It didn't feel like an adventure to me, and with each move I wondered how long I had in this new place. When the carpet would be pulled up from beneath me.

I slip up with a moment of honesty. "It was like putting down roots scared her."

He raises his eyebrows. "Did it? She's about to get married."

"Yeah, I don't know. She has family money and maybe it just felt unnecessary. She wanted to see new things all the time. Like she was looking for the right life to fit her, but she couldn't quite find it."

"Well, well, well, look who the privileged one is now, Mini." He gives me a cheeky grin.

I flush. "I'm not a trust-fund baby. My mom's money isn't mine."

This isn't strictly true. I do have a trust fund out there. But I've never touched it. It's become a matter of principle.

"Mm-hmm." He raises a brow. "I definitely believe you."

I let my head fall into my hands, laughing. "I swear it's true!"

"Sounds really true, Mini." He then changes the subject. "Should we have dessert?"

I'm stuffed, but I'm not ready to stop talking to this man whom I barely know, so I nod. "Definitely."

After dinner, and an extremely decadent slice of custard cake, Charlie insists on taking the bill, and then we get up and cross the lobby. He's taller than me, but not overly tall. Rob was well over six feet, and he always joked that kissing me was giving him a neck problem.

As we walk, I feel Charlie's hand graze my lower back. Light, gentle pressure, leading me to the elevators. My stomach clenches; my pulse quickens. His hand is broad and warm through the thin fabric of my dress. He's close enough for me to catch his scent, warm spices and clean soap. When he hits the elevator button my heart jumps. We look at each other, a question in both of our eyes. His tongue darts from his mouth, wetting his very nice lips. The doors open and we walk in.

"Floor?" he asks.

"Four."

He hits the button. Just the one.

We rise, and anticipation builds in me with the tick of each floor we pass.

The doors slide open again, and I proceed down the hallway, hyper aware of his presence right behind me. He might be following me to my room, and if he is, it's rather forward of him. But I don't care. He should kiss me. He should ask if he can come in. He has done neither.

We get closer to my room, and my pulse increases, thrumming in my throat like a hummingbird.

Then, "This is me," he says. We're standing outside of his door. The door next to mine.

"I'm here." I gesture towards my room.

He looks at the door, and then his own.

"Well, isn't life just a strange series of coincidences? Seat mates, and now roommates, of a sort." His eyes are warm, and glimmer at me.

He smiles, and now, I think, is when he'll lean in. When he'll tuck my hair behind my ear and brush his lips against mine. I'm tilting up, nearly lifting my heels off the floor, waiting for him, every nerve ending in my body ready for him.

"Goodnight, Mini," he says, and my stomach plunges into ice water.

I've misread this thing entirely. I swallow, hiding my disappointment, and then smile back at him. "Goodnight, Beamer."

He swipes his keycard and then he's gone, behind the dark wood door of his room, and I'm left standing in the hall, wondering how I could have misread his signals so grossly.

Maybe he has a girlfriend back in Denver. Maybe he's gay. *Or, maybe, Daisy, he's just not interested and you're acting crazy.*

Regardless, I feel an urgent need to get to the bottom of Charlie Bond. So, naturally, when I'm inside my room, I get to work and start googling to find out what the deal is. Internet sleuthing is *not* the same as snooping, I reason with myself. People put this information out there, for the whole world to see. It's completely fair game.

Charles Bond

The search results populate. There are a surprising number of Charles Bonds in this world. A Charles Bond in New England runs a boat repair company. There's a Charles Bond in Mississippi who won a skeet shooting contest. In Portland, Charles Bond is the owner of Bond Bakery and Books.

I scroll and huff impatiently.

New search.

Charles Bond Denver Colorado

This narrows things down quite a bit. My Charlie's work profile is the first search result. I click on the link, leaning into my phone screen like a detective on the cusp of solving a case.

A picture of Charlie in a dark suit and a dignified, dark red tie, hair parted on the side, pops up. He's wearing a benign smile—not so big as to be considered *bright,* but enough of one that he doesn't look off-putting. It's a smile that says, "I'm competent, I'll solve your legal problems, and I promise not to rip you off while I'm doing it."

There's a brief bio underneath the photo—law school details, his work on the law journal, a few published papers, and the areas in which he specializes.

I hit the back button and scroll down. There are links to a few blog posts, also on his law firm's website, written by Charlie on behalf of the firm. And then the links deteriorate back to the other Charles Bonds, who, I must admit, seem to have far more interesting lives than Charlie's.

I, for one, wouldn't mind dating a bookstore slash bakery owner. Unfortunately, that particular Charles Bond appears to be in his early seventies. Still, it might be worth it for the fresh bread and unlimited access to hardbacks.

I adjust myself where I'm sitting, cross-legged on the enormous bed and try again. Maybe he uses an alias. I should definitely try Charlie, and maybe… Chuck?

I type both in, and still, nothing.

This guy either doesn't use social media *at all,* or he's got his social media locked down so tight I'd need to hire a hacker to unearth it.

Through the wall behind me, I hear his television flip on. I tiptoe closer to the source of the sound for no reason. I'm alone. But eavesdropping seems to call for tiptoes. I press my ear against the grasscloth wallpaper. It sounds like he's watching… *Shark Week*? A narrator seems to be talking about great whites as dramatic music plays.

It doesn't tell me much, but at least he's not watching cable news pundits.

I decide that that's enough for tonight. Perhaps the mystery of Charlie Bond is simply one that will remain unsolved.

Chapter 5

The following morning, I wake up on a mission. I need to find a replacement dress, and it needs to happen today. I leave the hotel with a freshly scrubbed face, wearing a linen shift dress that my mother will approve of when I see her later. I'm ready to go at the exact moment the stores open. I head down the uneven brick sidewalk at a brisk pace. Antique shops displaying silver platters and mahogany furniture sit squashed between high-end stores with mannequins wearing beautiful clothing and restaurants with dark awnings promising thoroughly air-conditioned interiors.

I scour Georgetown, rummaging through racks of clothes in expensive boutiques, searching for something that will fit and will dazzle everyone. It's nearly eleven o'clock by the time I find it, after two hours of hunting. It's a little bit on the short side and probably meant more for a nightclub than a wedding, but at least it's not encrusted in rhinestones, and it doesn't dwarf me. It's dark green and has a fluttery skirt that will be great for dancing, a high halter neckline, and a low-cut back, which meant I had to go hunt for nipple pasties to go with it as a bra is not an option. By the time I'm finished, the sun is nearing its apex in the sky, and I'm sweaty from the heat.

I skipped breakfast, so I decide to stop at a greasy spoon sort of place and treat myself to a heavily fried lunch. I slurp a cold soda and scroll through my phone, dragging French fries through ketchup. This morning, Rob's new girlfriend posted a picture on Instagram of herself and Rob, posed with suitcases by their feet. It's the first time he's featured in one of her posts, and the sudden, unexpected sight of him gives me a jolt. She looks happy and relaxed; Rob's face isn't fully visible because he's looking right at her, as though he can't bear to take his eyes off her. It's captioned *Couples that play together stay together—flying off for the weekend to celebrate love!* with an airplane emoji and a heart.

It's bizarre, seeing someone's life from the outside, knowing that soon you'll be in it. Like watching a play, and then suddenly being cast as a side character. And I most definitely will be nothing more than a side character in her life. She's an *influencer*. She has nearly a million followers, and the likes are pouring in on this post, people commenting about her outfit and how beautiful they look together. Without question, she's the star. In fact, this Instagram post is actually an ad. The hashtag denoting the fact that the luggage company has paid her to make this post makes my stomach churn. This weekend is the culmination of the thing that brought my life crashing down around me, and for her it's an opportunity to make money.

Around me, people chat, read novels, type on laptops as they eat. The doors are propped open to let in a breeze. Despite the heat, it's a lovely day, and I've solved my dress crisis. I should feel relaxed, but I feel anything but. Instead, I'm stress-eating and wondering how much time I'll be forced to spend in the company of the happy couple today.

My mother will be arriving with Michael soon, and tonight will be a *family dinner*—perhaps a chance to smooth things over before the lovebirds tie the knot. Tomorrow, there's a cocktail hour at the hotel bar and a rehearsal dinner at a rooftop restaurant downtown. The guests will be driven in a fleet of town cars, and I'm meant to give a toast, as though nothing is wrong and everything about this wedding is entirely typical. This isn't so much a wedding weekend as it is an entire wedding week, because after the wedding itself there's going to be a big brunch, and then a spa day for my mom's closest friends (of which I am counted) so that she can depart on her honeymoon fresh-faced and freshly waxed.

Cara was not happy with me being here. She thinks I should have issued a silent protest by refusing to attend, but I just can't do that to my mom. For all her flaws, this woman raised me on her own. She put me to bed each night, even if she had an event to attend. She would sit by my bedside, smelling like Chanel No°5, the diamonds in her ears glittering, her elegant tennis bracelet brushing my cheek as she ran her hand down the side of my face. My mom did date, but she never brought a man home to meet me. She kept everyone at arm's length, except for her Buttercup. Her own flower—Daisy.

My parents were divorced while I was still an infant, and all I know of my father is that he gave my mother a sum of money so enormous that it generates its own income, and he set up a trust fund for me that I have never looked at. Getting my mom to talk about my dad is like trying to pry open a vault with a plastic fork. But I've come to terms with it. He doesn't want us, so why should we spend any of our time thinking about him? As far as I'm concerned, the money belongs to my future children, if I ever have any. I don't want it. It's my father's only legacy to me, and it's not a gift. It's a payoff. A bribe in exchange for a promise that my mother and I would never disturb his new life—whatever that may be.

My phone dings.

On our way! So excited to see you, Buttercup!

A sense of dread crawls over my skin, cold and boney-fingered. I don't know if I can do this. I don't know if I can face any of it, but I have to. I'm in it now. Too late to take anything back.

I type out a message to Cara as I sip my Coke.

Hope your Nana is doing better. I miss you! Wish me luck today!

She replies right away. *She's improving! How are you holding up?*

I consider mentioning the man from the airplane, but Cara will just get excited, and it wasn't anything. I was just a dinner companion on a business trip, and whatever I thought it might be, I was wrong. But the feeling of disappointment from last night lingers. I haven't actually sparked with anyone since Rob and I broke up, and I could have sworn there was a spark with Charlie. There was definitely a spark, right?

I'm currently eating fries and wondering if all the flights back to Denver are booked up.

Just as I send the message, I bring a French fry to my mouth and watch as a slow-motion glob of ketchup falls through space and lands in my lap, where I have failed to place a napkin. It's like in a movie, when you see the horror unfold on the protagonist's face in half time as disaster strikes.

I'm instantly flustered. Shit. *Shit, shit, shit.* I'm supposed to meet my mom in the lobby of the hotel. I glare at the napkin lying helplessly next to my plate, as though it ought to have done something to prevent this. There's no way my mom won't notice the stain. I'm going to have to make a run for it back to my room to change before she gets here.

I grab my stuff and then dash down the sidewalk. The hotel isn't far. I just make it through the glass doors, and halfway to the elevator bank when I hear it. My mom's voice, coming from the check-in desk. I freeze, and then turn. The red ketchup smear glows from the white linen like a bullseye. It's right over my crotch, of all places.

"Buttercup!" She dances towards me, her arms thrown out, ready for an embrace. She's wearing all white, and the sound of her high heels echoes on the lobby floor. I move my little cross-body bag in an attempt to cover the stain.

"Hi, Mom," I say as she wraps her arms around me. I close my eyes and inhale her scent. My body relaxes, as though it remembers what I don't. Even though I don't have a hometown, my mom has been my home for my entire life.

When she releases me, she holds me by the shoulders to take a look at my face. "Oh, sweetheart, I've missed you!"

Then she scans my body, inspecting me, in the way that mothers do with their offspring. I see the moment her eyes land on the offending stain, which my purse is failing to conceal. Her lips make a little downward twitch, and my stomach twists like it's being wrung out. My lunch suddenly feels too heavy in my stomach. She releases me without saying anything, but I know exactly what she's thinking.

Michael is standing next to her, looking vaguely uncomfortable. He's tall enough for me to have to look up at him, and his blond hair has tinges of gray mixed in. But he's handsome, and his blue eyes are kind. There's really nothing to dislike about Michael. As a person, he's difficult to object to.

"Hi, Daisy," he says and gives me a side hug. "You look good."

"Thanks," I say, then remember to add, "Congratulations."

My mom moves to wrap her arms around one of his, leaning her head on his shoulder. "Isn't this exciting? A city wedding, in Georgetown!"

"*Super* exciting." I nod. "It's going to be great." I'm not sure if

I'm agreeing with her, or just trying to convince myself of that fact.

I shuffle my feet awkwardly, shifting my weight from one foot to the other.

"Maybe you should go change," my mom says lightly.

"Yeah, I was just going to do that," I answer, and she nods. The pearls in her ears glow in the soft lighting. When the silence stretches for too long, Michael suggests that they head upstairs to unpack, and my mom promises to give me a call before dinner this evening, and they vanish up the elevators.

I turn, about to do the same when, just as I'm standing in the lobby by myself, Rob walks in, holding hands with *her*. Gabrielle. She's as lithe and beautiful as she is on the internet. They each wheel black suitcases behind them, and she's wearing effortlessly cool jeans and a white relaxed T-shirt that says *I woke up like this*. Her hair is long and falls in tousled waves over her shoulders.

I should have known I would run into them just after spilling food on myself, while Gabby is arriving from the airport looking freshly ironed and made up. This isn't how I was supposed to meet her. I was supposed to meet her at dinner this evening, wearing a cool outfit and very high heels. But the jolt of discomfort that I experience as I take in my replacement is nothing compared to the sadness that falls over me when I look at Rob.

It's been a year since I've seen him in person, and he's just as handsome as he was when I met him. When he bought me a drink that came in a fake coconut at a cheesy tiki bar and asked me to dance, and impressed me by the fact that he actually *could* dance. Cara had been with me that night with a group of girls from work, and she'd winked at me when she left but made me promise up and down that I would text her the second I was home safely. Only, I didn't end up home. I texted her from Rob's apartment after we had passionate drunk sex and I was hiding in his bathroom, unsure of whether I should leave or not. One-night-stand protocol is not my forte.

Rob had finally knocked on the door to ask if I was okay, and because the possibility that he thought I might be pooping was worse than the prospect of the awkwardness of the walk of shame, I opened the door so fast he almost fell through it right onto me. It turned out that my worries had been entirely unfounded, because he dragged me back into his bed and slept with his arms wrapped around me. His mattress was too hard and his pillows were lumpy, but I loved the smell of him and the feel of his body against mine, and I slept nestled up against his chest, my knees curled up into my stomach.

"You're like a koala," he'd joked in the morning. "Or like… a rabbit, or something. What sleeps curled up like that?"

"A dog?" I suggested.

"A puppy," he'd countered, and we'd agreed that puppy was a much better comparison than dog.

We'd been together for six months before he proposed, my mom and his parents became close friends, and a year after that everything fell apart. Fell spectacularly to pieces.

I'm not hung up on him anymore. I'm really not. And I'm not under any delusion that he might be perfect or that our relationship was. He was uptight about things. Picky about restaurants and fine wine, a meticulous planner. He was obsessed with hiking and golf, neither of which I enjoy. We argued needlessly about mundane things—if we had to do the dishes directly after dinner, or if we could leave it until morning. My tendency to leave my laundry unfolded made him climb the walls.

But deep down, he was good, and a future with him was something I could easily imagine. I could see our happy family, holidays, kids toddling around and driving us crazy, and us loving them so much. Taking them to school in the morning and sitting down to dinner every evening as a family. All the things I didn't have growing up.

But none of that happened, and now I'm standing in the lobby of a lovely hotel watching my former fiancé approach me while holding hands with a woman who is unarguably more beautiful than I am.

When he sees me, he stops walking. He doesn't approach me, he just stops, at least ten feet from where I'm standing.

"Oh," he says.

His girlfriend picks up where he fails, striding forward, with her hand out. "Hi, I'm Gabby. You must be Daisy. It's so nice to finally meet you." She gives me a bright smile. "I recognized you from your picture."

From my picture? I wonder if Gabby has been doing her own internet research, or if Rob has talked about me and shown her pictures of our former life.

"It's nice to meet you too," I say and conjure a smile from some unknown place.

Rob has collected himself and come over. He wraps an arm around Gabby's waist, which he can do without a problem because she's a tall golden goddess who matches his height. I was always tucked under his armpit like an orphan seeking shelter. However, he seems to have become a mute, and so Gabby and I are going to have to carry this whole thing off ourselves.

Seeing the two of them sets my fight-or-flight system leaping into action. I can either run through them, slide between their legs towards the elevators and hide in my room, or I can stand my ground and be gracious and carefree, like I haven't been dreading this moment. Given the choice, I go with the latter.

"It's going to be a great weekend," I say brightly.

"I think so too," Gabby says, laying her hand flat against Rob's abdomen, rubbing in slow, absentminded circles. This is their thing. This is how they stand when they are in a group of friends, or when they go for a walk and stop to admire something.

I swallow hard, my heart beginning to race. Everything about this is wrong. The wrongness is so strong I start to feel dizzy and sweat beads across my forehead. I'm going to have a panic attack. I have to get out of here. I thought I could do it, but I can't. I absolutely cannot deal with this. This small talk and pretending that everything is fine and we are all a big happy family.

"Okay, well, I'm going to go to the ladies' room," I say abruptly, and a look of relief falls over Rob's face as I turn to leave.

I don't go back to my room. Instead, I walk out of the hotel and go down the street where I see a bar with darkened windows and a neon beer sign that signals to the world that you don't have to check the prices before you order a drink. I no longer care about my stained dress—the damage is done. I just need to get away from that hotel.

Chapter 6

I swing the door open to the dark, cool interior. I stand in the doorway for a moment, allowing my eyes to adjust to the lack of light. I blink a few times. Leather booths line the wall on my right, and on my left a long dark bar stretches back with brass fixtures that gleam under the overhead lighting.

"Well, look what the cat dragged in."

I recognize the deep, masculine voice right away. Charlie Bond is sitting in a booth, his laptop open in front of him, a half-eaten sandwich by his side with a glass of iced tea. I approach him slowly, apprehensive after my intuition's abject failure last night. He's wearing an easy smile that says he's happy to see me.

"You rely a lot on scripted lines, you know that?" I say.

He stretches his arms up over his head, arching his back and shaking out his shoulders, like he's been here for a while. His white Oxford tightens around his biceps. The shirtsleeves are rolled up in that way men do, blithely unaware of what effect that has on women.

"It's all part of my charm. Take a seat." He motions to the bench across from him.

"What are you doing here?" I ask as I sit on the red leather. I drop my bag next to me and resist the urge to slump.

He sweeps his hand in front of him, because it's obvious he's working. "No rest for the weary."

When he sees the look on my face, his smile falters. "What's wrong?"

I must look pretty torn up for him to have noticed in this light. No point in mincing words. There's something so disarming about Charlie. Maybe it's the knowledge that he isn't interested that's letting me relax around him. Whatever the reason, I tell him the truth. "I just saw my ex-fiancé and his new girlfriend."

Realization dawns on Charlie's face, his eyebrows raising in understanding.

"Ooh, so that's the thing I was sensing last night. You're seeing your ex at this wedding."

If only that was the whole problem. If that were all, I think I could handle it.

"Indeed." I nod and gratefully accept a glass of water from the server. "And she's stunning. I mean, really, really beautiful."

Charlie gives me a skeptical look and closes his computer, sliding it into his laptop case. "That might be the case, Daisy, but so what?"

"What do you mean so what? She's my replacement. He upgraded." I set about dabbing at my stain with a wet napkin.

Charlie shakes his head and gives a rueful chuckle, resting his elbows on the table in front of him as he leans in. "Women compare themselves to each other too much."

"What's that supposed to mean?" I ask in an offended voice, looking up at him, napkin still pressed to the linen.

"It means," he says, "that this guy proposed to you, did he not?"

"Yeah. And?"

"So, he must think you're beautiful too. It doesn't matter what the new girlfriend looks like." He leans back, like he just closed a case.

I huff, "It just doesn't make it any easier, you know? If he'd come dragging a troll behind him I might have felt less… inadequate." I'm starting to make progress on this stain. The red has lightened to a diluted pink.

"Don't call women trolls," Charlie scolds me lightly. "And don't feel inadequate." Like it's just that easy.

I squint at him. "Have you ever actually spoken with a woman before, Beamer? I mean, are we a completely alien species to you? Inadequacy is baked into us. Well, maybe not Gabby because legs that long don't come without a lifetime of praise, but for the rest of us, we're introduced to our insecurities when we're practically still in the cradle."

He leans forward again, and this time he plants his hands on the table. Large hands, with fingers pressed into the wood so that the tips turn white. He looks at me with dark eyes. "Daisy. I mean this in the most appropriate way possible. As your friend who has actively been trying to get your goat for at least twenty-four hours, you have nothing to feel inadequate about." He shakes his head. "Just the opposite, in fact."

Goosebumps wash down my arms, and all memory of Rob or Gabby evaporates on the spot. "Really?" I say in a small voice that sounds too much like myself. Too shy, too needy. I might as well be jumping up and down like a circus dog, asking for praise.

"Yes."

I sigh and abandon my wet napkin and take a drink of water through the straw. "Well, I have to have dinner with them tonight, and it's going to be awful."

He nods. "I'm sure it won't be your favorite part of your mom's wedding. But you're going to get through it, and you'll be just fine."

Something about his words sends warmth straight to my chest. It's the pep talk I would have gotten if Cara had been here, and I didn't realize how sorely I needed it until I was standing in that lobby looking at Rob's tormented face. I thought I was ready, but I just wasn't.

"When is this dinner planned for?" he asks.

I check my phone for the time. "In five hours. And counting."

He narrows his eyes at me. "And were you just planning on sitting here, drinking away your sorrows during that whole time?"

"*Maaaybe*," I say, fiddling with the straw in my drink, moving the ice cubes around so that they bob and bounce together against the glass.

"So you can say all the things you really don't want to say out loud, but your filter will be gone so you'll *definitely* say them?"

I look up and sigh. "You have a point."

He slaps his hand down on the table, "I know what you need, Daisy."

"The same pill that lady on the plane took?"

"If it were an option? Possibly. We could tell them all you slipped into an unexpected coma. But since it's not, you need a tour. And you're lucky, because I happen to be an excellent tour guide."

His use of the word *we* does something to me. Like he, who has known me for little more than a day, is in my corner for whatever reason. And it feels good.

Ten minutes later, we're sitting in the back of a yellow cab and Charlie is directing the driver towards the waterfront.

The dark linoleum seats stick to the backs of my legs, and I wiggle a bit, adjusting to the heat. The driver is playing a funk station that's barely muffled by the plastic barrier between him and us. Charlie rolls the windows down so the smudged glass doesn't mar the view.

"Is this your first time in the city?"

I nod, gazing out the window as we leave Georgetown.

"Excellent. I've got you as a virgin."

I wince at his word choice and can't help but laugh. "You're here a lot?"

"All the time. Half of my clients are in DC." He points out the window. "This is Dupont Circle. They mention it a lot in the movie *The American President*."

"The one about the president who's dating? You know that one?"

"I do," he says happily.

My curiosity is genuinely piqued. "Do you watch a lot of romantic comedies?"

He grins. "They happen to be among my favorites. And down here we are going to get to K Street, and that's where the bad guys work."

The taxi driver must have heard him because he barks a laugh from the front seat.

"Politicians?" I ask.

"Worse."

"The mafia?"

"Lobbyists," he answers in an ominous voice.

"Oh no!" I say in mock horror. "Is that where your clients live?"

He sighs, running his hand through his messy hair. "Some of them. But most of my work happens after the lobbyists have done their jobs."

The street widens, and the buildings grow taller. The sidewalks are full of people in work attire, hustling to meetings. There's enough space here for café patrons to spill out onto the sidewalks. Tables with parasols host young couples and bunches of friends, and a group of enviably slender, athletic types spill out of a SoulCycle studio.

The traffic crawls along. Cars honk whenever someone tries to change lanes, huffing their fumes like frustrated bulls, and pedestrians jaywalk with impunity.

"There's a piece of policy I've been working on for ages," I tell him. "There's a company trying to purchase a giant piece of land in an area near Matchless Mountain that's been set aside for conservation for decades. The owner died, and now the heirs are selling it to a developer. They want to mow it all down and build yet another ski resort."

"Is that so?" Charlie says, looking out the window. I can't tell if he's uninterested or just distracted.

"We wanted to get the governor to designate it as protected land, but no such luck."

Charlie doesn't look at all uninterested now. His eyes pierce me. "What kind of work have you been doing on that project?"

I look down from his sharp gaze and pick at my nails. "It was the first project that I was the lead on, actually. I was the one who took notice of the situation and presented it to my boss, and she let me take the ball and run with it." I look up to meet his gaze again. "I was so determined to save that land. I seriously thought we could do it." I look down again, reminding myself not to get too worked up. "But it's over now. The developers win, we lose, and so it goes. The cycle continues."

My attempt to sound cool isn't fooling him at all.

"You sound pretty crushed." His eyebrows have dipped over his intense eyes, furrowing his brow.

"Maybe just a little bit crushed." I give him a small smile. "It really hurt when I found out the land was being sold, but you have to develop a pretty thick skin in my field. There's more losing than winning, unfortunately." I sigh. "I think you just get used to the understanding that we're fighting a losing battle, you know? Every year it feels like we lose ground, and the bears lose habitat."

If it weren't for the fact that Charlie looks interested I would have already stopped talking. But he's still, watching me and listening, so I continue.

"Bear-to-human conflict keeps increasing, and the pressure on the remaining wilderness keeps going up, but for humans, there just doesn't seem to be an upper limit to the concept of *enough.*"

"I could never do that," he remarks.

"Lose all the time? Of course you can't, you're a lawyer. I'm guessing you have a competitive streak a mile wide."

"I do, but that's not what I meant. I meant seeing things I care about being destroyed like that. Not being able to protect them. Wanting to stop something so badly and being forced to watch it disappear."

He has a look that makes me think he might be speaking from experience.

"Yeah, it's not fun. I used to cry after work, almost every day," I answer.

I have never told anyone this truth. I don't know why I'm letting it out now. But maybe it's the fact that Charlie has become my vacation friend—the sort of person you bump into while traveling and have a short-lived connection with, free from the entanglements of real life, and then you get to part ways, carrying each other's stories and secrets, and they vanish into the ether, or into the internet, where you occasionally look them up, just to make sure they're still alive. It's low-commitment honesty.

"Is your workplace at least supportive of you all? The staff?" he asks. "I mean, in terms of mental health and all that?"

"They are."

My boss is an extremely laid-back woman named Donna who brings her wife and son to every office party and encourages us to bring our partners along as well. She likes for us to be friends. She encourages a live-and-let-live attitude, and she is extremely competent. She rules over an office composed almost entirely of women, and because the work is so emotionally taxing, she keeps a bottle of bourbon in her desk (strictly for special occasions) but also lets us slack off in between the big pushes.

We just lost one, so she's giving us all a break, letting us take days off and work remotely, until she decides it's time to buckle down again. While she's an understanding, granola-eating, vegetarian reformed hippie, she gets shit done, and she's damned good at her job. I think half the reason most of us accept our terrible salaries is because we get to work for Donna. I'm able to go to an excessively long wedding celebration because I put the hours in and poured my passion into my work, and she knows that when it's time for me to be on my A-game next time, I'll be there, no questions asked.

In response to my remark, Charlie presses his lips together and looks back out the window. The hot air ruffles his dark hair and makes him look tousled and free in a way that I wouldn't have been able to imagine when I saw him for the first time yesterday.

"How did you get so interested in conservation work?" he asks me.

I rifle through my purse for a moment, hunting for a ChapStick, as I answer him. "When I went to college, I went camping for the first time, and it was just unbelievable."

"Camping was?" he asks.

"It really was." I nod enthusiastically. "I've always lived in cities. I'd never seen the stars the way they look without city lights, or heard the sound of the forest at night. I just became sort of obsessed with it, and with wanting to protect it." I laugh a little, self-deprecating. As though the fact that my mom's opinion that my work isn't "serious" has seeped into my bones, and I need to stave off criticism before it comes my way.

"That sounds incredible," Charlie answers sincerely. "It must be wonderful doing something so fulfilling."

"Do you really work for the bad guys, Charlie?"

He puts his hands up, as if to show that he is unarmed. "I just take orders. But yes, sometimes I have to work for people I'm not terribly fond of."

"Is it hard? Doing that?"

I can't imagine doing something I'm not passionate about, but I also have the unbelievable good fortune of knowing that, should something ever go horribly, tragically wrong in my life, there is money someplace that would save me.

"It can be." The car turns, and then he points ahead of us where the Capitol building looms, large and imposing with its tall cupola. It's a building I've seen a thousand times on the news, but seeing it in person makes it look more grand, more important. "Look, the other bad guys!" he says.

"Oh no." I feign a shudder. "Should I cover my eyes?"

"You may want to. Old white guys in rumpled suits everywhere."

I grimace theatrically. "Maybe we should skip this sight."

Finally, we emerge at the National Mall, and he pays the cabbie while I hop out and dust myself off.

We walk south, across the hot expanse of thin, scraggly grass and gravel. Hot dog vendors pull wet plastic bottles of water from chest coolers to sell to exhausted tourists, pink-cheeked and soaked in sweat. The sun is still high, and its rays threaten to smother us until we become listless, limp-bodied victims of heat stroke.

Charlie points out the museums of the Smithsonian—the American History Museum, the Natural History Museum, the Air and Space Museum. At the far end of the mall, the Washington Monument rises, tall and proud.

"Do you see the color halfway up? How it changes?"

I squint at it in the distance. "Yeah."

"They had to stop building it at one point, and when they finally finished, they used stone from a different quarry, so it's not quite the same," he explains.

"Well, aren't you just full of facts?"

"I told you I'm a great tour guide. Stick with me, kid, and you'll be an expert in no time."

When we reach the water of the Potomac the air is blessedly cooler, and a breeze lifts Charlie's hair and makes it dance about. Joggers pass us, and a section of volleyball courts host groups of people playing, picnicking, drinking out of plastic cups. We walk along the water with the sort of casual swaying motion of people who aren't really going for a walk as much as doing something to occupy their bodies while they talk.

"These are the famous cherry trees," he says. "It's beautiful in the spring. The whole city goes crazy for them."

The trees are lush and full, and some of their branches hang out over the water. I imagine it must be lovely when they are in bloom.

"What's that?" I point across the water.

"The Jefferson Memorial."

The white, round building rises on the opposite bank, reflecting in the blue of the river. It looks serene. Like something picked right up out of Athens and placed there.

"I love it," I say.

He nods, his hands in his pockets as he strolls. His shirtsleeves are rolled up, displaying those beautifully lean and strong forearms, and I spend too long looking at them and not enough time on the scenery.

"It's my favorite of the monuments," he says. "It really is stunning."

I think about this city of politics, and my bleeding heart. I think about my mom, and her fixation on wealth, and how she needs me, even when she pretends she doesn't, and the fact that for most of my life, she was all I had. I think about the rift that has grown between us. I hate it.

The truth is, I miss my mom. I miss feeling like I came in first place for her, even when I didn't. She never made me feel like a burden, or like she wished she was free. When I was in high school, she took me out for pedicures and to lunch at nice restaurants, and she told me she'd been waiting for years to get to do these things with me. That she had been so happy when she found out she was having a girl, because it meant she would have a baby, and then she would have a friend for life. And then I grew up and went to college and decided to stay in Colorado, and I'm not sure she's ever really forgiven me for choosing a different sort of life from hers.

The sun is lower in the sky, and I need to get back.

"I have to shower and change for dinner."

"Where are you eating?" Charlie asks casually.

"It's going to be a busy week, so we're just eating in the hotel tonight. Keeping it low-key."

He nods. "Just wear that, then." He motions to my stained and wrinkled dress.

"I can't wear this!" I protest. "I look disgusting. I look like I spent the day finger-painting with kindergartners." I point at the pink smear, and then realize I'm point directly at my crotch and drop my hand.

Charlie stops walking and turns to look at me. "Daisy, you couldn't look disgusting even if I tossed you in that muddy bank over there, so stop putting yourself down, okay? Please?"

Something passes between us. His intensity when he looks at me tells every cell of my body that it's time for him to touch me. But we're friends. I have lots of handsome guy friends. So why does the way he looks at me send heat down to the pit of my stomach and between my legs, and why do I want to touch his lips so badly?

I break the gaze and start walking back up towards the street. "You're right. Girl power. All women are beautiful. Got it."

"That's the spirit, Mini."

We walk back up towards the street to hail a cab, but something occurs to me, and I stop and spin on my heel to face Charlie.

"Wait!" I say.

His body stiffens in alarm. "What is it?"

"I need a spoon!"

His face twists into one of confusion. "You need…a spoon?"

I nod eagerly. "You know those little silver souvenir spoons? I need to get one."

"Daisy. Why do you need a little silver spoon? Do you have a grandmother back in Denver that you didn't mention?"

"No." I laugh. "I collect them."

He slaps a head to his forehead. "Of course you do. I can't believe I almost forgot that you're a secret grandma."

"Har har. I've been collecting them since I was a kid, and I don't have a DC spoon yet."

Charlie walks up next to me and flings an arm over my shoulder, like we've been friends for years. "Alright, Mini, let's get you a spoon."

The feeling of his arm around me, relaxed and casual but noticeably firm, sets the butterflies in my stomach to work, flapping madly.

We trudge across the ungodly hot National Mall, which I am starting to appreciate less and less.

"Instead of monuments, this thing should be mounted with fans," I say through panted breaths.

He points at the Air and Space Museum. "I bet they have some jet engines in there. We could put in a suggestion."

"I wish I had enough time to actually *see* all of these museums," I say wistfully.

We cross Constitution Avenue, and leave the mall behind us. It's Friday afternoon, and the tourists wielding selfie sticks give way to actual Washingtonians walking at fast clips, in and out of rotating glass doors, in dark suits and shoes that click on the pavement. A man swinging a briefcase passes us, giving my shoulder a shove with his own as he goes, talking into his cellphone in an angry, staccato voice.

"Charming people," I say.

"You weren't familiar with DC's famous reputation as the friendliest town in America?" Charlie places a hand at the small of my back, just like last night, guiding me forward through the pedestrians. The easy, casual way he touches me isn't off-putting at all. It feels natural and protective, and a sensation like melting ice cream runs down my back as I relax into this feeling, even as the zip of attraction I've been fighting almost makes me shiver.

A store called *AMERICA!* sits on the corner ahead of us. The storefront is decorated in big white stars over blue draping.

"Do you think this place will have your silver spoon?" Charlie asks.

The aisles of the shop are filled with political kitsch of every variety. On one side there's a section clearly designated for Republicans, while the other side caters to Democrats, and in the center the shelves are filled with politically neutral merchandise.

"What do you think? Too much?" Charlie holds up a T-Shirt that says *Home Of The Brave* in bold red letters over a man in overalls carrying two machine guns, sitting on top of a cartoon pickup truck.

"Just the opposite," I answer. "I think you should wear that to your next meeting."

Charlie's head falls back in laughter as I mosey towards the back of the store, suppressing my own smile.

I've been collecting these little silver spoons since I was a girl. I have a shelf full of them at home. My mom bought one for me when we left New York, and in every city after that, I would buy one and bring it with me when we left. It was the sort of souvenir my mother approved of, and the metaphor of the silver spoon does not escape me. Nevertheless, any time I visit a new place, I get one to add to my collection.

Before we catch a cab back to the hotel, Charlie grips my shoulders and looks at me in the face. He's not as tall as Rob, but he still has to lean down to reach my eye level.

"You got this, Mini Cooper. Don't let the girl with the long legs scare you, and don't let Rob think you regret him, because he's clearly an idiot for losing you, and he probably knows it."

He looks so earnest, so sincere, that it startles me. From this vantage point, I can see the gold flecks in his eyes against the green, and the shadow of his beard coming in. His face is not the hard one I thought it was when I saw him frowning at his phone yesterday. When he's not concentrating, it's warm. And despite his square jaw, it's gentle. We've been sweating all afternoon, but he still smells good. Like his natural smell is pleasant, regardless of cologne or spray or any other grooming product.

I nod mutely at him, lost for words. "Alright," is all I manage.

Chapter 7

Despite Charlie's urging me to abandon personal hygiene, I still shower and change for dinner, and I come downstairs with fresh makeup, an outfit picked out three weeks ago with Cara, and the tallest heels I'm capable of walking in. It's not unlike wearing armor.

Standing in my hotel room with the TV playing a rerun of *The Bachelor*, I shoot her a text.

It's dinner time. Rob is here. The new girlfriend is just as hot as I thought she was. I'm going to die.

My phone rings as soon as the text goes through.

"I can't talk about this over text." Cara doesn't even bother with a greeting.

I sit on the end of the bed, on top of the feather duvet that a housekeeper must have labored over to get as smooth and crisp as it is.

"How are you feeling?" she asks.

I take a quick inventory. "My heart is pounding, and I think I'm going to throw up."

"Okay." I can practically hear Cara pacing a circle, the way she always does when she's ready to set a game plan. It doesn't matter if we are discussing which bar to go to before dinner, or if we're talking out how to launch a new policy proposal at work, she's a pacer. "Do you have a minibar?"

"At this hotel?"

"Good point. Okay, you go to the minibar, and you down one of those tiny airplane-sized bottles of vodka. And then you go into the bathroom, and you say out loud, 'I am a hot bitch.'"

I laugh, the knot in my stomach loosening just from the sound of her voice.

I wish I had her innate self-confidence. I think it's born of her life in a large and loving family, with siblings that heckle one another but are ultimately deeply supportive and steadfast.

Cara has no problem with the fact that she's wonderful—she accepts and believes in her own worth with gracious comfort, and she's hell-bent on getting me to do the same. She's always attempting to convince me that I am, in fact, wonderful too. Oftentimes, her efforts are effective. When it's something tangible. A lack of action on my part, something in which she can intervene and rectify. At work, I once found out someone was taking my ideas and presenting them to Donna as their own, and I didn't say anything until Cara heard about it, and she was the one who prodded me to put my foot down.

"I mean it, Daisy. I want to hear that bottle open, and then I want to hear your self-affirmation."

I stand up, as if she can see me. "Seriously?"

"Yes, seriously!"

I hear what sounds like a voice over a loudspeaker in the background.

"Where are you right now, Cara?" I ask suspiciously.

"I'm in the hall outside of Nana's hospital room."

"You're calling me and telling me to swig alcohol from your grandmother's hospital room?"

"The hall," she corrects. "And yes, I am. Now go on. I'm waiting. Nana doesn't have all night."

I sigh, shaking my head and laughing, and walk over to the mini bar where I take out a $15 miniature bottle of Svedka and sling it back.

"Aaahhh," I grunt out. "Oh, that burns."

"Good job, Daisy Cakes!" Cara cheers me on. "Now go to the bathroom."

"I can't believe you're making me do this," I grumble. Even though I can. This is so completely Cara, I shouldn't be surprised in the slightest. I walk into the bathroom, all beige marble, with a giant soaking tub and an all-glass walk-in shower, and position myself in front of the vanity mirror.

"Alright, I'm here. I'm a hot bitch," I say in a voice that even I must admit is pretty lame.

"Nope. No way you made anyone believe that, least of all yourself." I see her shaking her head in my mind's eye, her dark curls bobbing around her face. "Again."

"I am a hot bitch," I repeat with more conviction this time.

"Louder!" she demands.

I sigh, shaking my head at myself in the mirror, and then take a great big inhalation.

"I! AM! A! HOT! BITCH!" I yell at the top of my lungs, my voice echoing against the polished stone.

"Yes, you are! Yes, girl! You are a hot bitch!" Cara is yelling now too, and I can't forget the fact that she is in a hospital corridor.

"Cara, keep it down!" I cry with dismay.

She laughs. "You're not even here to feel embarrassed!"

"Still. Your nana can't take you shouting in her condition."

"Nana is doing great. She's going to outlive us all," she answers.

"Now, go to that dinner. Tell Rob to go fuck himself, tell his new girlfriend that he has episodic erectile dysfunction, and tell your mom that you're skipping the wedding."

"I'm not skipping the wedding." I wish I could skip the wedding.

"I know, and I forgive you for that, and I love you forever."

"I love you forever," I answer in our routine goodbye, and I hang up the phone.

By now, the vodka has hit my bloodstream, and I have actually relaxed a little bit, and the clock says that I'm already five minutes late, so I grab my key card, and I walk out into the hallway where a grey-haired woman wearing a strand of gumball-sized pearls looks like she's ready to clutch them. I wonder how long she's been standing out here.

Chapter 8

Walking into the hotel restaurant feels like walking onto an entirely different planet than the one I was on last night when I ate here with Charlie. Last night I was relaxed and loose and remarkably myself. Tonight, despite the vodka shot and the bathroom pep talk, I'm sweating with clammy hands. The heels I'm wearing might be just a smidge too high, because I'm not able to stop my knees from shaking, even as I totter towards the table.

Because I'm late, everyone has already been seated and served drinks. They are at a round table near the center of the dining room. The same white candles dance, giving the same warm ambience as last night, and the open door to the patio lets in the pleasant evening air, but the adrenaline pumping through my body means I'm freezing cold in my spaghetti-strap silk camisole and cigarette pants. I clutch my bag in a tight fist as I approach.

My mom sees me first. "There she is!" she says. "Hi, Buttercup!"

The table turns to look at me, all their heads swiveling in unison as I approach, like an interview panel seeing a new candidate for the first time.

Rob's eyes skim up the length of my body, and Michael looks awkward as he rises to greet me. Gabby is holding Rob's hand on the white tablecloth, a red drink in a martini glass in front of her. I see the knot of Rob's throat move up and down as he swallows. I meet his blue eyes, and they dart away.

I plaster a smile onto my face, "Hi, Mom!" I say as she reaches for me, and I give her a hug. My mom is wearing all white again. Her elegant blouse is tucked into a pencil skirt, and her ears twinkle with sapphires.

"Hi Michael… everyone." I bob my head up and down like a doll as I greet the table. And then I sit.

I'm placed between Rob and my mom, with Michael and Gabby on either side of them. The words *fifth wheel* swim through my head as I look at them all with my rictus smile. This is bordering on ridiculous. Has surpassed ridiculous, actually. We are into absurdist territory. Mockery. Farce.

"Well." My mom clasps her hands in front of her, and her princess-cut engagement ring sparkles at me. Mine was round-cut. "Now that we're all here, I just want to say it is just so good to have all of us together, isn't it?"

The discomfort around the table might as well be a sixth person seated right there with us, leaning over and slurping soup with its elbows planted on the table.

"It is, Diane. It's so nice." Michael rubs her back supportively.

"You have always been like a son to me, Rob, and I am just so thrilled that you're here," Mom says, "And, Gabby, it's so great to finally meet you."

"I'm thrilled too, Diane." Gabby gives her a charming smile that I immediately dislike. "Rob just adores you. I'm so glad to be a part of all of this."

"Well, I adore Rob right back," my mom says to Gabby, and then winks at Rob.

"I think it's safe to say we all adore Rob." Michael chuckles uncomfortably.

Rob lifts his glass and takes a large gulp in response. It occurs to me now that the only word I've heard Rob speak thus far is the *"Oh"* he uttered when he ran into me in the lobby this afternoon. And now he's seated next to me, with his new girlfriend on the other side, thus far refusing to make eye contact or acknowledge me.

He's drinking a martini, dirty. I know this without even looking. Dirty martinis are what he drinks when he needs something strong and the occasion is formal. Coronas when out with friends, red wine when cooking dinner at home, and when he's hiking he fills a CamelBak with water and hydration powder and brings a can of Coors along for when he reaches the top. I rarely hiked with Rob, but when he forced me out on the trail, he always packed one for me too.

My mom has her usual glass of white wine in front of her, and Michael is drinking what looks like a Manhattan. A server comes to take my order, a lovely middle-aged woman who seems to have already picked up on the tension tonight, and so I have my gin and tonic in front of me in a matter of moments.

"So how was everyone's flight in?" Mom asks, her eyes bright and lively.

"Good," I say as I take a much-needed drink.

"It was terrific, Diane," Gabby chirps.

A little bubble of resentment slides up my throat. Gabby really is perfect. She's wearing an elegant black cocktail dress that I haven't been able to scrutinize properly because she's sitting down, but I just know it looks amazing on her. The pearls at her throat look real, and she has a dainty little cocktail ring on her right ring finger that seems to say, *"Wouldn't a ring on her left hand look great too?"*

I'm now regretting not wearing a dress. I wanted to keep it cool, like I'm here but I don't *need* to be here, and a dress felt like it would be a display of too much effort. But now, in this moment, all I can think is that Gabby is the daughter my mother wished she had. Tall and swan-like, expensively dressed, and charming enough that if any real conversation is going to come out of this dinner, it's going to be coming from her.

Gabby reaches across the back of Rob's chair and rubs between his shoulder blades. I pull my lips between my teeth and clench the napkin in my lap.

"The airport wasn't too crazy?" Michael asks. "We knew having the wedding over Labor Day weekend might put some pressure on the out-of-towners, but we couldn't help ourselves. It just seemed like a great excuse to stretch the party."

My mom beams at him.

"It wasn't too bad," Rob says. It's good to know that his vocal cords are in full working order, at least.

I consider telling the story about giving the car in front of me the finger, and then sitting next to the driver of said car for three and a half hours, just to watch my mom fall off her chair. For all the shit I gave Charlie, the truth is my mom offered to fly me out in business class, but I refused. I was happy to accept the hotel accommodations, because, quite frankly, I can't afford a DC hotel for this many nights, but I put my foot down at business class. I'm not too good for economy. I wonder if Rob and Gabby took her up on that offer though. If they were sipping champagne and stretching their legs out when they took off from Denver Airport.

My mom loves Rob. He was like a son to her. She told me that she felt like she had a "real family" when she was together with Rob and me and his parents. "*This* is what I've always wanted," she'd said.

I wondered, at the time, that if that was what she always wanted, then why did she spend my whole childhood wandering from city to city, refusing to allow herself to make any meaningful connections? Why wasn't anything ever enough for her? Why wasn't *I* enough?

When Rob and I broke up, she claimed to be genuinely crushed for me. But she never expressed anything beyond that hurt. She never really *apologized* for her part in it. At least, not in a satisfactory way. And as everyone peruses the menus, I begin to truly feel, for the first time, that being here was a genuine mistake. But I also know that if I wasn't here, the guilt would have absolutely crushed me.

Our server returns to take our orders. I exhale in the first time in what feels like an hour. The tension at the table has my spine ramrod straight, and I'm in dire need of this reprieve.

"So, what's everyone having?" she asks, holding a pad in one hand, a pen in the other.

Please God, no one order appetizers, I think.

Last night I lost myself in a bowl of pasta, but tonight I order a grilled shrimp salad, dressing on the side. I'll dip the tines of my fork in the dressing, like my mom taught me to do, rather than pour it over the lettuce.

The server finishes taking orders, and we all look around the table at each other again, blinking as though we're surprised to find ourselves here.

Rob clears his throat and adjusts himself in his seat, and he reaches over and grips Gabby's hand in his own. I'm certain no one else notices, but the look she gives me is smug. *I win,* it says. It's the first actual reason I've gotten to dislike her, which is oddly satisfying. Until now, my resentment towards her has been unfair, but now that I've gotten that look my mind is free to unspool imaginings of her spilling her soup in her lap or smiling at the table with spinach stuck in her teeth.

"How's work been, Rob?" Michael asks. It's a safe, man-to-man sort of question, and everyone at the table latches on like it's a life raft.

"Rob actually got a promotion last week!" Gabby chimes in and smiles at Michael as she holds her cocktail in one hand, Rob's hand in the other.

"Is that so?" Michael says with a pleased expression. "Well, then let's celebrate that!"

"Yes!" Mom agrees enthusiastically. "Congratulations, Rob!" And she raises her glass, and we all toast to Rob's success in financial management.

We struggle through dinner. The conversation is stilted and awkward, and does not improve. By the time we are halfway through the entrée, everyone has been extremely well plied with alcohol, and my mom has developed a pleading look in her eyes. I've seen this look many times, and I know it's my turn to take up the baton.

"So," I say, turning towards Rob and Gabby between bites of shrimp and bitter lettuce, "how did you two meet?"

Rob twitches in his seat and turns to look at me wordlessly. This is when I notice his face is coated in a light sheen of sweat. I'd failed to consider the fact that this is just as painful for him as it is for me. Possibly more. A small pang of sympathy runs through me.

"We met at the park," he says like it's a question he'd forgotten the answer to and he's only just remembering. He twists his drink—the second martini—by the stem, back and forth.

"He was playing frisbee and he hit me in the head. My dog, Molly, almost bit him," Gabby adds.

"Oh, what a nice meet-cute!" my mom exclaims. "What kind of dog do you have, Gabby?"

"She's a labradoodle—half Labrador, half poodle," she explains as if we haven't all heard of a labradoodle before. "And she's so smart. She *totally* knew that Rob threw that frisbee when he came up to apologize, and then she lunged at him, but he handled it so well I knew he was a keeper. I don't trust anyone who's not good with dogs, but he was just a natural, so I asked for his number."

"Oh, so you made the first move, huh?" Michael asks. "I like a woman with some confidence, right, sweetheart?" He glances at my mom and shoots her a wink. If Donna were here, I would be demanding her bottle of bourbon right this instant.

"Anyway, after that it was just really natural," Gabby continues. "He took me to Pastore's—this cute little Italian place right by his apartment, and the rest is history."

And this, right here, is the moment their relationship really feels *real.* My fork stops on its way to my mouth like I'm in a freeze frame. Pastore's was *our spot.* It was the place we walked to when we felt too lazy to cook. It was the place that made my favorite pasta primavera that I could never go to again after we broke up. I spent countless nights sitting across from Rob over Pastore's cheesy checkered tablecloths, eating breadsticks and then shoving the basket away because I can't control myself, sipping wine and laughing, and stealing bites from his tiramisu. The thought of them there together actually makes my stomach turn, and my pathetically inadequate dinner doesn't seem so insubstantial anymore.

I turn my head slowly to look at Rob next to me. His face has taken on a distinct pallor, like he knows exactly what I'm thinking. That Gabby stepped into the life we shared and took my seat across the table from him. And yet, I know there's some irrationality to this. It's not like restaurants can be claimed by a relationship. But when relationships end, there is this natural way in which each party sort of knows which spot belongs to them, and which spot belongs to the other. Pastore's was Rob's spot, and of course I knew, without actually thinking about it, that eventually another girl would be there with him. But regardless, it still hurts, and I can see that Rob knows that and is fully aware of me looking at him.

"Did *you* ever go to Pastore's, Daisy?" Gabby asks.

My eyes shift from Rob to her, and she is wearing a look that reads false, innocent sweetness that wouldn't fool even a child. She knows exactly what she's doing. Her eyes are a little bit glassy, probably from all the drinks. People say and do stupid things when they're drunk, but I don't care. This question, clearly intended to do nothing but hurt me—to point out that now *she* is the one going to dinner with him—is a measure too far. I think about what Cara would tell me to do. Her voice is in my head, telling me to fight fire with fire, and I take a deep breath before I speak, steeling myself.

"Lots of times," I say, and take a sip of wine, as though I'm feeling completely comfortable. "Actually, the first time Rob and I made out was in the hallway between the coat rack and the dining room. You know the hallway, right, Gabby? It's really dark and sort of mysterious. You can really lose yourself in there. Like no one else is watching. I was hanging up my coat, and Rob just couldn't help himself, I guess. He just pulled me in."

Gabby blanches, and Michael coughs into his drink, and my mom's knuckles turn white on her silverware. Then Mom laughs, the high, forced falsetto laugh that she uses when she's with strangers and not really herself. "Let's not overshare, Daisy. We're at dinner."

"Oh," I say innocently, "I'm sorry, Mom. I don't mean to make anyone uncomfortable."

Dinner wraps up pretty quickly after that. Michael gets the check, and no one protests. But, as we file out, awkwardly saying goodnight, my mom pulls me aside to a small room off the lobby where guests can read the paper or perhaps a Dickens novel, picked from the tall dark bookshelves lining the walls, filled with gorgeous leather-bound volumes. Cushy blue velvet sofas sit opposite one another beside robust palms and reading lamps glow with welcoming light. I barely have time to take any of this in as my mother stands in her tall brown leather wedge sandals, planted shoulder width apart on the carpet, with her hands fisted firmly on her hips.

"What was *that*, Daisy?" she asks in a tone reserved specifically for making me shrink away from her. The impulse to hide is still there, and I feel a familiar pang of shame at having disappointed her, but I stand my ground.

"What was what, Mom?"

"You know exactly what," she spits. "That performance at dinner. Gabby looked like she was going to cry."

I scoff, turning away and staring at the rows of books. "Oh, I highly doubt that."

"Do you? How do you think she felt—the fifth wheel at a table full of family, next to her boyfriend's ex?"

It hasn't occurred to me until right now that Gabby probably felt pretty damn awkward. But after this monumentally uncomfortable mockery of a family dinner, I don't care.

I turn back to her, gripping my little bag hard in my right hand by my side. "We aren't family, Mom. As much as you want to make us pretend like we're all one big happy family, we aren't, okay? It's not real, and you forcing everyone to pretend is not helping."

My mother looks momentarily stricken by my uncharacteristic outburst, but I ignore it, and continue. "Never mind Gabby. She knew what she was walking into, and believe me, she can handle herself. She, at least, has someone's hand to hold, you know? How do you think *I* felt, sitting there next to Rob, who *dumped* me?"

"You *promised* me that you were okay with all of this," she says angrily. "You promised not to make a scene this weekend. I need to be able to count on you, Daisy."

Guilt slithers through my gut like a muddy eel. I did promise that.

"You understand, don't you? I need you this weekend. I need you to be my Buttercup."

"I am… I am your Buttercup, Mom," I say. My voice is small now, all my self-righteous bluster gone. "You can count on me. You always can. I'm sorry I upset you." And there it is. Another apology, even when my heart isn't entirely in it.

Through this whole conversation, neither one of us has addressed the elephant in the room. The thing that we're aware of, and that I know she's counting on me not to mention. So, I don't.

Her face softens then, and she nods. "Thank you, Daisy," she says, sounding like my mom again. "You know how much I love you. What would I do without you?"

I've heard that refrain my entire life. *What would I do without you?* As though I'm the parent, and she's the one relying on me for support.

"I don't know, Mom," I say, and then give her a cheeky smile that I know she loves. "You'd probably be living in a yoga ashram in Bali with some guy named Apollo or something."

My joke finally cuts the tension, and my mom pulls me into her for a hug. Her perfume surrounds me, and I let my shoulders drop. *She's my mom,* I think. Despite everything, she's still my mom, and I need to get this resentment under control.

When she leaves to go to her room, I sink down into a sofa. It's so deep my feet don't reach the floor when I lean back into the cushions. With the sigh of the long-suffering, I unbuckle my heels and let them drop onto the carpet. I curl into the sofa, leaning into the back and arm rest, tucked in like a child with a blankie, and burrow my head down into my knees. *Deep breaths,* I think as my heart rate slows. The first night is over with. I never have to do that again. Just keep looking forward.

It's still too early for me to go to bed, and if I go to my room, I can lose myself in *Real Housewives* reruns, but I know I'll also be lonely. The lobby is still and quiet, but the sounds of the restaurant bar filter in and make me feel, if not like I have company, then at least like I'm not the only person in the universe.

I relive dinner in my head. Gabby's smug look, Rob's discomfort, Michael's attempts to smooth things over, my mom's disappointment in me, and my own outburst born of a fit of jealousy. Finally, the urge to cry overcomes me, and the tears wet the knees of my pants, leaving dark spots and, I'm sure, smudging my mascara down my face. I suppress a full-blown sob and take deep, slow breaths.

"Dinner was that bad, huh?"

I look up at Charlie from my knees. I imagine I look rather pathetic, sitting here curled up like a child hiding under a table after having a tantrum.

"What are you doing here?" I say, swiping beneath my eyes for runny makeup.

He sits down on the far end of my sofa. "I'm not saying I was spying on you. But we *are* at the same hotel, and I did happen to know that this was going to be a tough night for you, so maybe I was spying on you just a little. I was at the patio bar. I saw your family leave."

"So, in other words, you were totally spying on us," I grumble at him even though I'm starting to smile.

He raises his hands in a gesture that says *I mean no harm.* "I couldn't hear anything that you guys were saying. I just didn't want you to be alone, in case…" He drifts off. "You know, the ex turned out to be a complete twat about things.

I shake my head. "He was fine. He hated it as much as I did. I could tell. And he didn't do anything wrong."

"You mean besides being the idiot who broke up with you?"

I laugh a little through my tears. "I guess besides that. Yeah."

"And the girlfriend?"

"She sucks," I answer. "And I ended up acting like a bitch and my mom is totally upset."

"How long have you guys been broken up?"

"A year."

He sighs. "You know, when my girlfriend dumped me, I barely functioned for a year. For the first six months I didn't do anything besides go to work and go hiking. And then I started actually seeing people again, and started putting my life back together. But even after a year, I would have hated running into her. There's no way I could have sat through a whole dinner with her new boyfriend.

"I think you were really courageous, and I don't know the whole story, but to be frank, I think your mom was kind of an asshole for inviting him."

He looks at me with his warm, disarming eyes. He's facing me on the sofa, one polished shoe on the floor, the other hanging off the edge. He has his arm across the back of the couch.

He's wearing the same clothes he was wearing earlier today. The shirtsleeves are still rolled up, and the veins running down the inside of his forearm are clearly, enticingly visible. My eyes drift there, and want to linger, but I force them back to his face, which is tilted in concern. It's impossible not to notice how handsome he is. Even when I'm this sad and stressed out, I'm still a heterosexual woman who hasn't really been touched by a man since Rob kissed me on the forehead the last time he left my apartment. I don't know why Charlie has decided to care, or why he has gotten so invested in my problems, but I'm glad he's here.

"It's not like that." I shake my head. "She didn't have a choice in the matter. She just wants us all to be happy again."

His brows dip in confusion. "What do you mean, she didn't have a choice? She couldn't have chosen *not* to invite your ex-fiancé to dinner with you and her future husband, and force you to sit through a whole night with the new girlfriend? I know I'm overstepping here, but that seems kind of selfish, Daisy."

I look at him and say nothing. The silence stretches between us, unspooling like a ball of yarn rolling across my living room floor. I chase after it, trying to think of *something* to say. Some explanation that will answer the question in his eyes, *what's really going on?*

But nothing comes to mind. I haven't volunteered this information to a single soul, except Cara. I've never talked about it with anyone. The shame and embarrassment has been like an anvil on my chest for over a year, squeezing the life from my lungs and limbs, and I've been trying frantically to hold back my feelings about it. It's been like sitting on the hatch to the cargo hold of a ship in a grisly storm, attempting to keep the encroaching water down, even as the vessel comes apart all around me with crashing waves.

I swallow hard. My hands clench around my knees, still tucked up against my chest. I look at him. He looks back at me, his gaze steady and unwavering. I'm still a little bit loopy from the alcohol. My guard is down. And suddenly, the urge to tell the truth is immediate and overwhelming.

I rub at the corner of my mouth with clammy fingers. My heart drums a heavy beat in my chest.

"The thing is, Charlie," I begin slowly, "My mom's fiancé, Michael, is a great guy. And Rob is a great guy. But Michael is Rob's dad."

Hearing it said out loud like that—the truth that I've been hiding for so long—makes me want to go into hysterics all over again.

"Michael was my fiancé's dad. And he and my mom, like, fell in love, I guess, and they had an affair. And Michael ended up leaving his wife—Rob's mom—and now he's marrying my mother."

Charlie's face is blank with astonishment, then shock. His mouth falls partly open. "You're kidding me, Daisy."

I shake my head. And then drop it back into my knees, hiding from the judgement I know is about to radiate off him. This is so fucked up. This is *so. Fucked. Up.*

Chapter 9

The day Rob and I found out is seared into my brain in one of those memories that's so clear it's like you could take snapshots of it and lay them out in sequential order. This is the moment Rob was on the phone with his mom when she told him. This is the moment Rob started laughing in disbelief, because he thought she was playing some kind of sick joke on him. This is the moment he put the phone down and looked at me, and told me. This is the moment his face transformed from shock to horror. This is the moment the resentment boiled up in his eyes and I could feel him judging *me* for what my mom did to his parents' marriage—like a piece of rotten fruit that fell from a bad tree.

His mom had called him around nine o'clock in the evening, distraught. I could hear her voice through the phone. Hysterical babbling that I couldn't quite make out. I'd thought someone had died. That there'd been a horrific accident, and I was bracing myself for tragedy. Already thinking about my project at work, explaining to Donna that I needed emergency time off, considering the cost of plane tickets to get out to Maryland, where his family lived.

But when Rob put the phone down, no news of a family member dying in a car wreck materialized, and instead he tilted his head back and stared at the ceiling for a moment, before he started to chuckle, and then laugh. Hysterical, manic laughter, like the sound you imagine a psychiatric patient makes when he's been in the room with the padded walls for too long. Rob laughed, and I sat next to him, saying *what? What happened?* I knew something was terribly *off*. Something was wrong, but I couldn't possibly fathom what it might be.

I jostled his shoulder to get him to stop laughing and look at me and tell me what the fuck was going on. Then Rob had stopped laughing, and he'd straightened, his lip curling like he had a mouthful of spoiled milk.

He looked me square in the face. "Your mom's been fucking my dad."

The way he said it itself felt like an insult. *Your mom, my dad.* Like my mom was definitely the one squarely at fault in all this. Like she was the perpetrator, the seductress, who had lured his innocent father in. Like it didn't take two people to carry on an affair.

I'd like to say I didn't believe him. That I laughed too, at the absurdity of what must be a joke. But I did believe him. I knew the moment he said it that he was telling the truth. It wasn't just his reaction that made me know it. Images came pouring back to me from the time Rob and I had been dating. How our parents—his parents and my mom—had hit it off so quickly. Rob and I had flown out to the East Coast, and my mom had come down from New York on the train to Maryland, and everyone had been introduced.

That weekend had been fun. Idyllic, almost. Rob and I had been over the moon about how natural it felt. Our parents hit it off from the first moment. My mom has this easy, charming way about her with new people. She's funny and quick to laugh, and she helps out at a dinner party—offering to clean up and help the host cook, always bringing a bottle of wine. She'd shown up to meet them with wine and flowers and a little Tiffany box with a crystal figurine inside.

By the end of dinner on Friday night, Rob's mom was insisting that she go get her luggage from her hotel and stay in their second spare room, and we'd all spent the weekend dining out, the women shopping together, Rob and his dad getting in a game of golf at the Congressional Country Club where Michael is a member. When Rob and I flew back to Denver on Sunday night, my mom had agreed to stay through the end of Monday so that she and Pam—Rob's mom— could go to the National Art Gallery before she left.

After that, it was like the three of them no longer even wanted Rob and me around. Not that we weren't welcome—they would have loved to have us. But they had formed their own friendship, and they were so thrilled to like each other. That their potential in-laws would be people they could enjoy spending time with, and that holidays wouldn't have to be split. Holidays, naturally, would be shared, they had all agreed. Soon they were vacationing together—at Rob's parents' house in Maine, and at my mom's place on Block Island.

The next time Rob and I came out to Maryland, my mom came too, and it was just as fun and easy as before. For the first time in my life, I felt what real home life was like. Rob is an only child, like me, and everyone seemed to be enjoying the company of a larger gathering. His parents embraced me with so much enthusiasm and affection that I thought I might just float off on a cloud of love.

But I noticed something. I'd never said a word about it, but my mom and Michael had inside jokes. A lot of inside jokes. Pam was in on them too, but they always seemed to be born of something my mom and Michael had done together. And a little flicker of fear had passed through my body like a frisson of static. I'd brushed it off.

The notion that they might be flirting was ridiculous. Michael doted on Pam like she'd hung the moon. He was always touching her. He put his hand on her arm as he passed in the kitchen when she was chopping onions. He rubbed her shoulders, standing behind her chair, after she set breakfast on the table. Their affection was almost too much for someone like me, who grew up without two parents.

One evening, back in Denver, Rob and I had gotten a FaceTime from my mom. I accepted the call to see three heads squished into the screen. My mom, Michael, and Pam, all together on the deck of my mom's summer house, wine glasses in hand, red-cheeked from drinking and suntanning. They were laughing and shouting over each other to tell us that they loved us, and they missed us, and then Michael had said something that made my mom break into hysterics and we couldn't understand a word of what was being said as they got distracted and delved back into their own conversation, and the call ended.

"So, I guess they're friends now," Rob had chuckled when he hung up the phone.

"It's nice, right? That they get along so well."

"It is." He nodded, and his eyes were bright and pleased, and I'd snuggled into the couch with him to finish watching our movie.

Not long after that, Rob proposed at the edge of a lookout point that displayed the Rocky Mountains in all their majestic glory, and after he slid the round, blinking diamond onto my left ring finger, I'd leapt into his arms. We called his parents, who cheered, and I called my mom, who squealed with delight that her daughter was marrying just the right sort of man from just the sort of family she approved of. "Congratulations, Buttercup," she'd said. "You did really well." My heart had felt so full, like there was nothing else in the world that I needed, and my future suddenly seemed so secure, so safe, in a way I'm not sure I'd ever experienced before. I felt like I'd been gifted something I didn't even know I was missing.

I've been staring off into space, and Charlie says my name with a note of concern. "Daisy? Are you okay?"

I give my head a shake. "Yeah, I'm fine." I release my knees and tuck them underneath me and turn the palms of my hands up in my lap, like I'm letting go of something. "So, now you know all my dirty laundry."

"I wouldn't exactly call it *your* dirty laundry," he says. "But I have to admit, that is truly one of the most insane things I think I've ever heard."

I nod, "I know. It's like… Jerry Springer level. Like, I think Jerry would probably have *paid* us to come on his show. Although"—I tilt my head—"maybe he already did pay people. Maybe that's how he got them. I don't know." A strange little bubble of laughter comes up from where my stomach is still knotted together. "But, if Rob and I had stayed together, we would have been *stepsiblings* in addition to husband and wife."

"God yeah, I didn't even think about that." Charlie rubs a hand down his face and then looks at me again. "Jesus. No wonder you're so freaked out by this whole thing."

Charlie isn't giving me the look of judgement I was expecting. He doesn't look weirded out, or like I'm not the girl I've been pretending to be—an imposter, playing at a normal life. A normal family. Instead, there's empathy written all over his face.

"I cannot imagine what you're going through," he says sincerely. "I mean, the ex-fiancé thing was a lot, but it was… I don't know, something a lot of people have to deal with, you know? Like, there's a playbook for that. And you were doing it. You were muscling up and facing the new girlfriend and being there for your mom. But this…" He trails off. "I don't really know what to say."

He's scooted closer to me on the sofa, so that his arm stretched out on the back rest nearly reaches my shoulder.

"You don't have to say anything." I shake my head. "It's just been a really tough year. My engagement ended because of the thing with my mom, and then I just lost that campaign to have that land put into conservation, and now I'm here at this wedding…"

Charlie nods and then looks down, thinking. He sucks his very good bottom lip between his teeth and worries it for a minute. Then he looks back at me, his eyes meeting mine with an open expression.

"I really don't want to pry, Daisy. So please tell me if I'm overstepping, or tell me to piss off or whatever, but why are you here?"

I don't really have an answer to that question, except that it's my mom, and she needs me.

"I'm not really sure. I thought about not coming." I shrug a shoulder. "But I just felt like I had to, you know?"

He shakes his head slowly. "Actually, I don't really know. I can't imagine a family member doing that to me. I don't even know what that would feel like."

I snort a cynical sort of laugh. "I don't think I would have been able to imagine it either, until it happened."

"And you're going through all this alone." He doesn't say it as a question.

I feel suddenly shy, like I should perhaps be embarrassed about this fact. I give a small nod and pick at my bare pinky toe, polished in pink from the pedicure I got in preparation for this trip. More armor.

"My best friend Cara was supposed to come with me, but her grandmother got sick."

Charlie nods quietly, seeming to need a moment to take all this in. I don't blame him. It took me weeks to really absorb the fact that Michael and my mom had started carrying on an affair. He scratches at a spot on his dark slacks, where a thread has come up out of the weave. It's the first sign of any sort of dishevelment I've seen on him.

"I couldn't do this if I were in your shoes, Daisy. You should be proud of yourself."

"Proud of myself?"

"Yeah." He nods. "For being the bigger person. The biggest person."

"There's nothing big about me." I don't mean literally, but he takes up the invitation anyway. It's like teasing each other is becoming a language.

"Yes, you are thimble-sized," he agrees, "but I mean your heart. You've got a big heart. You spend your time saving the bears, and when you're not doing that, you're propping up your mom, even when she might not deserve it, and taking all this on your shoulders."

I flush at the compliment and continue picking at my toenail, which cannot be an appealing sight for a guy as polished as Charlie is.

"So, what are you going to do with the rest of your night?" he asks.

I look at him askance. "Go to bed?"

He shakes his head. "Nah, not like this. You'll end up sitting on the floor of your shower."

How did he know?

"I was headed out to meet a friend. Why don't you come along? You can give yourself another story to mark this day, instead of that awful dinner."

My lips turn up into a smile. The first real one since we shared a cab back to the hotel. "Why not?"

He glances down at my high heels discarded on the floor in front of us. "You may want to change your shoes, though." He grins.

Chapter 10

I meet Charlie back in the lobby wearing pair of nude flats.

He nods when he sees me. "Much better."

We leave the hotel and swing right.

"Where are we going?" I ask.

"Dupont," he says. "It's my favorite neighborhood."

He places his broad hand at my back, as seems to be his habit, and leads me along down the brick sidewalk. A pleasant shiver runs through me at the warmth through the silk of my camisole.

The city's nightlife is out and in full swing. Girls walk in packs down the street clutching handbags at their sides, and preppy guys roam in khaki chinos and boat shoes. Even at night, when nightclubs open their doors and unfurl their awnings, the city's character stays put. The young people—the ones going out at this hour—are wearing things that wouldn't look out of place in closets full of business attire. It's like a more relaxed version of a congressional hearing.

The streets have emptied out significantly, and we cross intersections even when the light is red. Charlie walks in long strides, and I struggle to keep pace without calling attention to how short my legs are. Eventually, we emerge on the expansive traffic circle. Dupont. In the center there's a tall fountain, and couples sit chatting on the benches that line the perimeter. A scruffy man gives a paper cup a shake as we pass. Charlie drops a dollar bill in, and I scramble to follow suit, rifling through my little bag for loose change.

We pass through the circle, cross a street, and then arrive at a deep red awning with the words *The Mad Hatter* written in bold letters. A heavily built guy stands out front smoking a cigarette.

"ID," he says in a monotone drawl, and we both produce our Colorado driver's licenses.

I stop in my tracks when we step inside. The whole place is *Alice in Wonderland*-themed. The floor is black and white checks, and above the bar an enormous and somewhat disturbing Cheshire cat grins down at us with hypnotic eyes.

"There he is." Charlie points through the dim, red light at a guy hanging on the end of the bar. As we approach, I gaze around myself, somewhat in awe, and notice a grouping of furniture—a long table with mismatched chairs around it—mounted upside down on the ceiling. The table is set for a tea party.

"This is amazing," I say with a smile.

"It's cool, right?" Charlie grins at me over his shoulder. "Good drinks too."

"Hey, man!" his friend greets him. He's a guy with dark blond hair that's thinning on top, and he's wearing a similar uniform to Charlie's—white Oxford, dark slacks, polished shoes. His suit jacket is slung over the back of his bar chair. He and Charlie lean in for the handshake-hug-backslap that men always do, and then the guy looks at me, his eyes gliding up my body.

He turns back to Charlie with raised eyebrows. "Who's your friend?"

"Mark, this is Daisy. Daisy, meet Mark. He used to work in the Denver office, but he couldn't cut it and now he's exiled here."

Mark rolls his eyes and laughs. "It's nice to meet you, Daisy." He offers me his hand to shake.

"You too," I say. "And I highly doubt this place is exile."

"Nah, just a swamp full of sea monsters." He gives me spooky eyes, and I do something between a chuckle and a snort, and my hand darts up to cover my nose.

"Cute," Mark says, looking at Charlie, and I flush so hard I can feel it past my collarbone. "How'd you two meet?"

"Daisy gave me the finger on the way to the airport," Charlie says happily with his hands in his pockets as he leans back on his heels.

"Charlie almost killed me with his douchey BMW," I retort, and Mark looks like he's not quite sure whether to believe us or not.

We both take bar stools. Charlie pulls the one out next to Mark for me, and then takes the one on the other side, so I'm between the two of them. The way he does that, placing me so that I won't be pushed out of the conversation while he and Mark catch up, strikes me as exceptionally considerate.

"How did the meetings go?" Mark asks Charlie with a serious expression.

"Complete shit," Charlie says, motioning to get the bartender's attention. "McGovern won't budge an inch."

The bartender is pouring what looks like a thousand shots and nods impatiently at him, like, *I see you, buddy, you don't need to wave a flag.*

"That guy's a jackass," Mark says, taking a sip from a sweaty glass of beer. Then he looks at me. "Charlie's been working on this contract with—"

"Let's not talk about work," Charlie interrupts. "We all know it's boring, and if Daisy falls asleep, I have to carry her all the way back to Georgetown over my shoulder."

Mark laughs. "So, Daisy, what do you do?"

"I save bears," I say with a straight face, because for some reason I think it sounds funny and I want to be the charming, witty Daisy right now.

"Are you a zookeeper?" Mark asks.

"She works for a conservation nonprofit," Charlie clarifies.

Mark's eyes widen, then dart between Charlie and me. "Ah. And you do know our friend here is a bloodsucking leech on humanity?"

"Aw, don't be so hard on yourselves. You lawyers are vampires, at least."

Mark points at me and looks at Charlie. "I like her."

Charlie rolls his eyes with a chuckle, and the bartender finally comes over to take our drinks order, laying her hand on the bar top like she needs to catch her breath.

Charlie gets an IPA for himself, and I ask for a soda water and lime, because I can still feel the alcohol from dinner, and I don't want to wake up with a crushing headache.

A moment later we have drinks in front of us, and Charlie takes a swig from his dark bottle and lays his hand across the back of my chair. He doesn't touch me, but the awareness that his hand is there is like a magnet pulling at me. He slides it back and forth slowly, across the wood of the backrest, and goosebumps raise across my skin. The hair at the back of my neck rises up like it's reaching for him.

Mark asks what I'm in town for, and I tell him about my mom's wedding, and Charlie nods along, without giving any hint of the complete clusterfuck the whole thing is.

"And did you really flip him off at the airport?"

"I did." I laugh. "But he flipped me off too."

"Only after!" Charlie protests, and then looks back to Mark. "And I did not mean to cut her off, and I gave her the courtesy wave, so retaliation felt warranted."

"You didn't accept the courtesy wave?" Mark says in mock astonishment. "That's like, a law, isn't it? You *have to* accept the courtesy wave."

"It is." Charlie nods and then looks to me. "We're lawyers. We know these things."

"How could you *not* have seen me?" I say pointedly as I swivel in my seat to face him. Thus far, it's been me talking to Mark, with Charlie leaning forward, his hand on the back of my chair, just inches from my bare skin, almost like he has his arm around me. Almost, but not quite.

"Because," he says. Our faces are close. Closer than necessary. "You drive a go-kart. And it was in my blind spot."

I roll my eyes. "It's not *that* small."

"It shouldn't be street legal." He shakes his head, leaning back determinedly. "But it is *just* the right size for you."

"And then you just… became friends?" Mark looks suspiciously between us.

"More or less," Charlie says, spinning his beer on the bar. "She was so feisty I just couldn't resist."

What is this version of me that Charlie sees? It's like being with him, who I don't know at all and who has no context in my real life, is making it possible for me to explore different versions of myself. In Charlie's company, I feel like my whole personality is allowed to exist freely, without being encumbered by my own anxiety.

Mark nods slowly at us, like we're both lunatics. And he then challenges me to a game of pool.

"Let's see what you got," he goads me.

"I don't think you know what you're in for." I raise a sassy eyebrow at him. "I happen to be an *expert* at pool." I hop off my seat and cock a hip. I'm lying. I couldn't hit a cue ball with a tennis racket. But I let

Mark think that I'm about to shark him off the table anyways.

We head across the crowded bar, through an arched doorway, into a back room where two tables are lined up and we grab one.

Mark lines the balls up in that triangle thing I don't know the name of. Maybe it doesn't even have a name. Maybe it's just "the triangle." Charlie leans back against the wall with his legs crossed and a small smile playing across his lips as I grab a stick from the wall and rub blue chalk on the end of it like I've seen my friends do. I line up in front of the white ball and prop the stick in one hand. I have to stand up on my toes to reach as I bend over. I close one eye in a dramatic squint.

"Alright, boys, get ready to be impressed." And I haul back and then let the stick shoot forward, slamming into the white ball, which veers off at a steep angle and bounces lamely off the felt.

Mark's head falls back in a roar of laughter, and Charlie is looking at me, chuckling helplessly, holding his arms out like, *what?*

"So, you don't play pool then," Mark says, and saunters over to me. "Want to learn?"

Tonight, I decide I'm up for anything.

We start over.

He stands behind me and positions my arm on the lawn of the table, showing me how to properly hold a pool cue, and his other hand is over mine as he shows me how to slide the cue forward. His shoulders envelop me, and as I look forward, to where I'm meant to be aiming, I catch Charlie's expression. He's still leaning casually against the wall, but his eyes are dark, almost angry. It's the expression he wore when he was focusing on his phone in the airport, and I assumed he must be an asshole. He holds my gaze for a moment, as Mark talks into my ear about angles and technique, but all I hear is a buzzing sound when Charlie's tongue glides over his bottom lip.

When I release the cue this time I miss entirely, but it has nothing to do with Mark's lesson.

"Aw, you'll get the hang of it." Mark laughs, blithely unaware that I'm dizzy with lust over his friend, and he goes ahead and shoots first.

I stand, looking at Charlie, whose eyes now sweep my body, and my stomach fizzes like I just drank an entire bottle of champagne.

"I'm gonna get a drink," I say vacantly and walk past him.

My breath is coming in quick, shallow clips, and my knees feel week. The rush of attraction that just passed through me was nearly enough to knock me unconscious, right on top of the pool table. The way Charlie's eyes had gone all dark and hooded when he looked at me, studied me, almost predatory, calls to every female part of my body. I need to get away. It's bad enough that I'm already wildly attracted to him. He made it pretty clear that he's not interested in going *there*. I *cannot* develop a raging, full-blown crush on a guy I'm going to know for a few days and then likely never see again.

I push myself into the crush of people, winding through, towards the bar. The place was full when we came in, but now it's packed. However, one of the few perks of being fun-sized is that I'm able to sneak through crowds with the stealth of a spy.

At the bar I ask for a light beer, and then change it to a gin and tonic. The drinks from dinner have burned off, and I'm in need of something to blunt my overstimulated senses.

"Are you okay, Daisy?" Charlie's voice is behind me, close enough that I feel his breath against the back of my neck. The crowd pushes him forward, jostling him into me, until he's touching me, my back pressed to his chest. I feel the hard edge of his belt buckle through the fabric of my top. I flinch, and he presses his hands firmly on the bar on either side of me, so that his body fully ensconces mine, and he pushes off, back against the crowd, creating space between us, and forming a sort of protective circle around me with his arms.

I turn on my heel to face him. "I'm fine," I say. I have to tilt my head back to see his eyes. "I just realized my buzz is gone, and the Cheshire Cat and upside-down furniture is starting to freak me out."

One side of his beautiful mouth lifts into a smile, and he studies my face with his intense, dark eyes. The spotlights over the bar highlight a dimple. An extremely cute, sweet, kissable dimple. The dimple, and the urge to brush my lips against it, sends a surge of alarm through me, and I turn back to the bartender and slide my credit card across the wood. Charlie stops me and puts his own card down instead.

"You don't have to do that," I protest over my shoulder. "You already got the cab today."

"I know I don't have to. I *want* to," he says into my ear. He's so close that his warmth is sinking into me. Drowning me. I take a shaky inhalation and fill my lungs with air, trying to steady myself.

My drink arrives, and I grasp on to it like a life raft. Charlie's arm is around my shoulders, leading me back towards the pool table, but as we approach he steers me left, and my traitorous legs with their Jell-O knees obey him rather than me, and he takes me through a doorway, into a dark hall with a concrete floor and painted black walls. The overhead lights are sharp and cast his face into shadow, and a thin dagger of fear slices through me.

What if I've misread him entirely? What if he really is a serial killer and he's been grooming me? The intensity in his face makes me take a step back, until I'm against the cold cinderblocks. He places his hands on my shoulders, his touch so light it's like the brush of a moth's wing.

"Daisy." He lowers his head until he's at eye level with me. "Are you okay? Do you want me to take you home? I mean, back to the hotel?"

I exhale relief as the moment of panic vanishes, but that just leaves more room in my chest for a flood of tenderness. I don't know why he's doing this. Why are we friends? Why does he even care?

"I'm fine," I say, and it comes out defensively.

His brow creases in reaction. "Okay." He nods. "It's just that you left all of a sudden, and with the night you've had, I was worried that maybe it was all a bit much."

"Playing pool?" I say, as though I don't know what he's talking about.

"No, I mean…" He pushes a hand through his hair. "Just maybe you're tired or you were thinking about your whole"—he waves a hand in the air in a vague gesture, and I can tell he's searching for a word besides *dumpster fire*—"your whole situation," he finishes.

I shake my head again. "Really, I'm fine. I'm having fun."

I *am* having fun. I'm having more fun right now than I've had in months. I haven't even thought about Rob, or my mom, or Gabby, or anyone else since we walked in here. I've been too busy enjoying myself being fun, sassy Daisy, who makes snarky remarks and pretends to be a pool shark.

"You're sure?" he asks. "Just let me know, and we'll go."

I bite my bottom lip, and his eyes dart there, and then back up to mine. Heat pools deep in my belly. He brushes his bottom lip with his tongue, and I fight back the urge to lean up and bite him there, to feel that tender flesh against my own mouth. We look at each other for a moment that stretches, longer and longer, like the hallway is expanding indefinitely. We're alone. And he's here, taking care of me, when he could be partying with his buddy and picking up girls.

"You'd really take me back? If I wanted to leave?"

His brow furrows like it's obvious. "Of course I would."

I swallow a lump like a billiard ball at the emotion that wells up inside of me. The feeling of being cared for is so comforting that I could curl up against his chest and live there forever.

"I don't want to go back," I say. "I want to stay."

The corners of his mouth lift, his eyes lighten from concern to pleasure, and he takes me by the hand to lead me back out into the crowd. His long fingers twist with mine, and it feels so natural that I might not have noticed except the place where his skin touches mine sears me like a branding iron, sending heat shooting up my arm and into my chest cavity.

Charlie clears a path for us, and I follow, walking in a dream, being led by a handsome man through a surreal bar in a surreal city. I'm so outside of myself I feel like I could float up to the ceiling and have tea with Alice. He leads us back to the pool table that Mark has given up to another group.

"Sorry, guys." Mark says. "I couldn't really hold it when you both just *disappeared*." But his annoyance is all show, and his eyebrows bounce suggestively as he looks between the two of us.

Charlie releases my hand and I grip my purse awkwardly, ignoring the little pang of disappointment that he wasn't *really* holding my hand. Not in the way I'd *want* him to hold my hand.

"The bar was crowded," Charlie says. "Getting Daisy's drink took a while."

Chapter 11

As the night wears on, I have a second drink. The bar is hot and musky with the sweat of too many bodies pressed together. Mark meets a girl named Florence with a bouncy ponytail and a group of friends who cheer them on when they take shots, and then I get pulled in and I'm downing something called a Brain Damage that tastes like its name.

The lights in the room grow brighter, the music louder. I feel loopy and happy and completely free. It's '80s Night, and Florence I are dancing, and when 'Word Up' comes on over the speakers and Cameo instructs us to *Wave your hands in the air, like you don't care,* I do it. And I don't care. I don't care about anything but this night. The laughter and the ease with which it comes. There's no tension left in me. No thought about tomorrow or the day after that, or returning to Colorado, back to my empty apartment and alienation from my mother's new family.

Florence grabs my hands and we spin, and when she lets me go I twirl across the floor and bump into Charlie, my chest pressed against his. He catches me. I look up at him, and he's smiling, like seeing me this happy, laughing, losing myself, fills him with joy. I lay my head on his shoulder and inhale his spicy scent.

"You're really nice, you know that?" I slur. "You're not a douchebag at *aaalll*. Like, not even a little bit. The first time I saw you, I thought you would be *such* a douchebag."

He laughs, and I feel it vibrate through me as holds me against him.

"And you smell, like, really good," I add.

A small voice tells me that I'm going to regret this. But the voice is coming from somewhere far away, and I don't have time for it right now. I'm having too much fun.

I wobble a little, and Charlie steadies me. "Maybe that's enough Brain Damage for you tonight."

"I'll damage *your* brain," I say.

"I'm sure you will, Mini."

He ushers me over to the bar and asks for a glass of water, which he makes me drink. And then he asks for another, and he makes me drink that too.

I make it halfway through the second glass before setting it down on the bar with a heavy clunk. My motor skills aren't operating at full capacity. "I can't. Too full."

In the far corner, Florence is now sitting in Mark's lap with her tongue down his throat, and he's eagerly reciprocating.

"It's late," Charlie says. "Maybe we should go back."

He's looking at me with some concern as I wipe my mouth with the back of my hand. I'm suddenly very, very tired. "*Mmmkay*," I answer, just happy to be here with him steadying me.

He takes me by the shoulder, an arm wrapped around me, tucking me into him, and we head towards the door.

"We're out!" he calls to Mark.

Mark unplasters himself from Florence just long enough to nod and give a thumbs-up before returning to her mouth.

The cool air of the night contrasts so strongly against the sweltering heat of the bar that I shiver when we step outside, and Charlie tucks me deeper against his side as we walk. There's a dull ringing in my ears from the loud music, and when I talk it's too loud.

"Thank you so much for taking me with you tonight!" I yell at him.

"I'm glad you had fun." I can hear the smile in his voice, even though I can't see his face from this angle.

"You're just…. you're special, Charlie." *Stop talking,* the voice in my head commands, and it's louder now. More insistent. Loud enough that soon I'll have to start paying attention to it. But not yet.

We wander up the street at a leisurely pace. The water in my system is doing its job, and I begin to sober up. We reach the circle and cross the street. We walk the path with the benches. Someone is asleep on one, and Charlie tucks a bill beneath their boot.

"And you're so nice." I add to my inventory of his qualities. I blink. "I already said that."

Charlie stops walking and pulls me down onto a bench next to him.

"You're probably too drunk for me to ask this, but how are you feeling about tomorrow?"

"Tomorrow?" It takes me a moment to remember why I'm here. And then the heavy stone in my stomach returns. "Oh. Tomorrow." I scowl. "Tomorrow sucks."

"I'm sorry," Charlie says quickly. "I shouldn't have brought it up."

I sigh heavily, leaning into him because while my head is slowly clearing up, my inhibitions are still totally collapsed.

I sigh, "It's okay."

A man and woman walking a dog pass us. I wonder idly, through the drunken fog, why they are walking a dog in the middle of the night.

"I don't care about tomorrow," I declare. "Fuck tomorrow."

Charlie chuckles, and his stomach tightens under my hand where I have it placed. I'm totally indiscreetly checking out his abs.

He looks down at me, and I catch his eyes. I'm fully prepared for him to lean in and kiss me. This is it. Here we go. I tilt my head up.

"I was thinking," he says.

"Yeah?" I answer in my best husky half-whisper.

"What if I came as your date? To the wedding."

I sit up abruptly. The voice in my head is now yelling at me at full force.

"You want to be my date?"

Charlie sits up straighter. "I'm not trying to come on to you or anything."

I manage to stop myself from pouting at him in disappointment, but just barely. The voice in my head relaxes a little, but not much. It's very concerned that I'm embarrassing myself.

"I was just thinking that, dealing with all of it—with your ex and your mom and the whole debacle—might be easier if you had someone in your corner."

"You're in my corner?"

He grins and nods. "I'm definitely in your corner."

I chew my lip. I obviously want to bring a handsome, well-dressed man with me to the wedding. But I don't want to use him to make Rob jealous, and I don't want to make him go out of his way for me.

"Aren't you here working?" I give him a suspicious look that makes him laugh.

"Tomorrow is Saturday, Daisy. And even in my profession, we're allowed to go eat dinner. And then there's Sunday. All I have to do tomorrow is go over some documents and reply to my emails."

"Very, very boring documents," I add.

"Yes, very, very boring documents. But the boring meetings don't resume until Monday."

"On Labor Day?"

He chuckles. "And surrender all those billable hours? Unthinkable. But I'm free and clear and fully available as a plus-one until then, if you'll have me."

I give him a very sober look now. "You're being serious?"

"I am."

"You want to put on a suit and talk to a bunch of stuck-up strangers so that I don't feel uncomfortable?"

"I want to do all those things so that you don't feel uncomfortable, and so that you don't have a total breakdown. You should have seen the look on your face after your dinner tonight."

I stare at the ground for a minute, my blurry thoughts attempting to weigh the pros and cons of this proposition.

Charlie is hot as hell: definite pro.

I'm developing a crush on Charlie that will almost definitely get worse if I spend more time with him: con. I think.

I won't have to stand there talking Rob and Gabby alone: big pro.

When the couples' dance is called, I won't be sitting in a chair by myself: another big pro.

"You're sure?" I ask, looking back up at him.

He nods, totally serious.

I nod back. "Okay."

Charlie gives me an easy smile and gets up from the bench and pulls me up with him. "Alright, it's a deal. Beamer and Mini are going to tear that wedding up, and you won't even remember that Rob is there with his hot new girlfriend."

"Hey!" I protest and give his chest a playful slap.

"I didn't say *you're* not hot, Daisy! There can be more than one hot woman in a room."

"Ugh." I grumble. "You just don't understand women."

He laughs. "I already knew that. You all are totally crazy."

We walk back to the hotel mostly in silence. It's a comfortable silence. Like we are just both here, together, thinking our own thoughts, and that's completely okay.

When he hits the button for the elevator I don't freak out, because I know now he's not going to put the moves on me, and when we reach our doors, we grin at each other as we each swipe our key cards.

"Goodnight, Mini," he says.

"Goodnight, Beamer," I answer.

And we both vanish into our rooms.

Chapter 12

I wake up with sand in my mouth, and there's someone outside using a jackhammer that's making my head pound.

No.

There's no sand, no jackhammer. Just my own head attempting to explode itself, and my mouth so dry I can barely manage to swallow.

I grope around on my nightstand, where it seems I had the foresight to leave a glass of water for future Daisy, and chug. I stagger out of bed. I'm wearing my underwear and the camisole from last night, which is now a wrinkled mess. My bra is flung over the top of the television screen.

The first order of business is to address my bladder which is so full it may start leaking at any moment. I sit on the toilet, holding my head in my hands with my elbows resting on my knees. The drumbeat of pain continues unabated.

My God, what have I done to myself?

The rehearsal dinner is tonight, and I'm going to have to find some way to get myself back into working order before then. I rummage through the landfill of makeup on my vanity, and unearth my bottle of Advil. I take two and fill the toothbrush glass and swallow them.

Then I fill it a second time and drink that. And then a third.

Back in the bedroom I peel the sticky silk from my body and, for some reason unknown to me, I sniff it and gag. It smells like old beer and sweat and possibly… rotten eggs? At this point, I've completely lost control of the endless personal belongings I decided to drag along with me, and I have to rummage through a pile on the ground to find a T-shirt, which I then pull onto my clammy body. I lie down in bed, pulling a pillow over my head in an attempt to smother the pain. It doesn't work. I need coffee, and a big bowl of fruit, and eggs. I barely have the strength to make it back to the bathroom in the event that I need to pee again, and a hopeless groan escapes my lips. And then I remember where I am. And on whose dime.

Seized with new motivation, I scramble over to the desk where the room service menu sits untouched, and I dial them up and order myself a feast. Then I go back to bed and wake up thirty minutes later to a knock, and a very nice gentleman rolls a table into my room and begins lifting cloches from plates of various sizes. A decadent bowl of fresh berries is unveiled, as well as a plate of poached eggs over the avocado toast of my dreams. He sets up a French press of coffee and lays out silverware and a mug. A glass of fresh squeezed orange juice appears, and a basket of pastries.

"Is there anything else I can get for you, miss?" he asks me politely, after I've signed for the food and left an exceptionally generous tip (thanks, Michael), all while keeping his eyes carefully averted from my crotch region, because I've completely forgotten that I'm not wearing any pajama bottoms.

"Oh," I say, pulling a sheet over my lap. "No, nothing… I mean, this is beautiful. You're so kind. Thank you. Thanks so much." The words continue to spill from my lips as he nods his head up and down, backing towards the door.

The food is delicious. I mean, really, really good. Good enough that I'm going to be thinking about this avocado toast for the rest of my life. And no, I'm not being dramatic.

When I'm stuffed and heavily caffeinated, I start to feel somewhat human again.

It's eleven-thirty, and I know that if I exercise, I will feel better. The thought is as appealing to me as the notion of lying on a bed of nails, but I need the endorphins to counteract the damage I did to myself last night. I pull my hair up into a bun, squeeze myself into a sports bra and leggings, and head to the hotel gym.

The space is sleek and minimalist with light wood floors and frosted glass windows. The equipment is polished to the point of appearing unused, and I imagine someone labors over it every evening to keep it looking pristine. The same cucumber water from the lobby is stationed here as well, in addition to glass reusable water bottles for guests to take and fill to our heart's content. Cool damp towels scented with lavender wait in a small glass refrigerator. At home I work out at the Y in a not-so-nice neighborhood, and the greatest luxury there is when I manage to avoid the plastic shower curtain sticking to my butt when I bend over to wash my feet.

Forty minutes and about a gallon of cucumber water later, I'm a new woman. I pat my forehead with a lavender towel. It's undeniable—life really is easier with money. But for a reason I have yet to fully untangle, I'm still not interested. I'll exercise at the Y for as long as my legs can carry me on a treadmill.

Despite the luxurious amenities offered in the gym, when I walk into the swanky, softly lit halls of the hotel, I look like a demon. Exercising with a hangover seems to have exacerbated my usual state of post-workout dishevelment. My face is as red as a stoplight from the high intensity cardio, I'm soaked in sweat and with the frizzy hair sticking up around my head, I might scare children. So, I do what any reasonable person does in this situation, and I book it to the elevator. When it arrives, it is mercifully empty, and I walk in and slouch against the wall as it carries me up to the fourth floor. How ironic that spending an hour working on my health makes me look like I'm dying.

The doors slide open, and I turn the corner down to my stretch of hall, and finally, I reach my room—so close to safety. So close to being tucked away alone with my shower and a robe. But, of course, due to the ongoing curse that seems to be haunting me, the next door down swings open, and Charlie comes striding out, dressed casually in slim-fit khakis and a dark polo shirt. He freezes when he sees me. My hand is on the door handle to my room. The door is two inches ajar. I could bolt in and slam it shut. But instead, I stand like a mannequin before him in all my tomatoey glory.

His eyes drop to my midriff and stay there for a moment before they dart back up to my very, very red face. "Good afternoon, Daisy," he says lightly, and his lips twitch just a little.

"Hi," I say chirpily. "Just got back from the gym."

He's starting to really smile. Like he doesn't want to, but he can't help it. "I can see that. You look… worked out." I see the gears turning in his head. He wants to make fun of me. He wants to so badly he's having a hard time holding it back.

"My face is red," I say, and then want to slam my head in the wall for saying something *that* inane.

"It is." He nods. "You must go pretty hard."

"I do what I can," I say, attempting to affect a casual air.

"So, I'm glad I ran into you," he begins, as though I'm not trying to stealthily sneak my way into my room one inch at a time.

"Why's that?" I back into the doorway.

"Well, I figured that since I'm going to be your date tonight, I should probably get some details, and we should probably come up with a backstory and that sort of thing."

My date?

Oh. My. God. Of all the details to forget about from last night, how, *how* could I have forgotten one so important? Me hanging on him, telling him how great he is, mooning over him—it all comes rushing back to me in a humiliating rip tide. The park bench, sitting up against him, letting him offer to be my date, and then actually accepting.

I'm standing with my jaw open and then remember to close my mouth. "Right," I say gamely, as though I didn't agree to this while nearly blacked out. "All of that makes sense."

"Should we just do it now?" he suggests.

"Um. Now? Like right now?" I desperately need to go and hide, and maybe also sit on the floor of my shower.

"Sure," he says with a shrug. "Why don't I just come in for a second, and we can talk it through?"

I stare at him for a moment as I grasp about for a reasonable excuse. My room looks like a bomb went off in a department store, but how do I explain to a man that he can't come in because there's a bra hanging over the TV?

The moment stretches on until time has run out, and the word "Alright" comes out of my mouth of its own volition. *I told you so,* says the voice from last night and I snap back at it to do a better job next time.

I open the door all the way and walk in. Charlie follows me.

Seeing it through his eyes, it's worse than I remember. Piles of clothes litter the bed and are strewn across the floor from me hunting for outfits that suit DC's tropical climate. The overabundance of shoes that I packed lie in a heap inside of the open closet doors. The purple monstrosity is in the corner, overwhelming a luggage stand, with the lid hanging open limply, like it just gave up and vomited its contents all over the place.

I walk across the room, rigidly stepping over an upturned pair of stilettos in an attempt to pretend that nothing is amiss here, and set myself on the edge of a chaise situated in the corner with as much dignity as I can muster.

When Charlie is in the room, he covers his mouth with a hand.

He's in shock. He's seen this and he's so shocked that he's going to leave and he might just notify the front desk of a fire hazard.

His shoulders shake, and a snort escapes his nose, and then he's buckling over in a full-on, gut-splitting belly laugh. "Oh, Daisy," he says through tears, "I knew when I saw you hauling that thing out of the airport that it was unreasonably big." He throws an arm up to point in the direction of my suitcase. "But I honestly never imagined how much could really fit in there."

It's time to defend myself. "Look. I was panic-packing, okay? You know what kind of pressure I'm under."

"There's a purple bra on your television set," he says through hiccupping breaths and tears. "You have more shoes in this hotel room than I even *own*."

"Okay, that's enough. I realize it's a gigantic mess, Okay? That's why I didn't want you to come in."

It takes him a minute, but he sobers, and then he looks at me seriously. "Daisy. Are you a hoarder?"

"Go to hell," I answer. I have now officially decided not to care, which seems to be a new skill I've developed that exclusively applies to Charlie.

"There's treatment, you know. Therapy. Medications. There are answers out there for you."

I fling a throw pillow at him which he catches in one hand, and then sits at the foot end of the chaise, facing me.

"Alright. I'm finished. I promise."

I look at him skeptically.

"Really finished. Honestly."

"Okay," I answer.

"So, what's the plan for tonight?"

I explain about the cocktail reception and the town cars to the fancy rooftop restaurant.

He lights up. "Oh, I know that place! Great oysters."

And then I tell him which of Rob's aunts and uncles to look out for, what Rob looks like, and the way my mother likes to give my boyfriends a thorough once-over when she meets them, to make sure they pass muster.

"Are there any, like, skeletons in closets that I should know about? Touchy subjects?" I give him a frank look, and he presses his lips together. "Right."

"Yeah, I think you already know about the touchiest subject of all time. You would have to try pretty hard to stick your foot in your mouth."

"Okay, well, in that case, I'll come pick you up before the cocktails, and we'll go down together?"

I experience a moment of disbelief that he's actually agreeing to do this. That I'm allowing him to do this. But at that moment, as the plan is laid, a flood of gratitude pours through me.

"Thank you for doing this, Charlie."

"It's my pleasure," he says with the wave of a hand.

"No, I really mean it. Thank you."

"Daisy," he says in that way he has of using my name to signal something very sincere. "I told you. It's my pleasure."

His tone sends a wash of heat through me, and if my face weren't already scarlet, it would be now.

I usher Charlie Bond out of my room as quickly as I can after that, shoving on his back as he goes as slowly as possible so he can examine the contents of my various piles. He stops to pluck my bra off the TV and tosses it at me with an evil grin. But eventually, I manage to maneuver him out the door so that I can peel my sweaty clothes from my body and finally get in the shower and wash last night and this morning off of me.

Chapter 13

I'm out of the shower and dressed when there's a knock on my door. I wonder what Charlie is up to now, and am seriously questioning my overall judgement in men, but it's not Charlie. I find my mom standing in the carpeted hallway.

Without saying anything I step to the side, and she saunters in. She's carrying on the all-white theme with a fluttery sundress and white sun hat. She's really leaning into this bridal thing.

She steps carefully into the room, examining the disaster zone with obvious distaste. "Daisy, this is horrible. I raised you better than this." I ignore the comment as she removes her sunglasses and sits down in the armchair with a huff.

I think she wants to talk about what happened last night. The insanely uncomfortable dinner and my outburst, but no. It appears she's moved past it.

"Michael is golfing!" she says with dismay. She looks as though she might have just said, *Michael went to prison.*

"O…kay?" I'm standing in front of her in bare feet. "I'm guessing that's a problem?"

"He didn't even tell me until this morning! He said he forgot."

I sit down on the end of the chaise opposite her, "Mom, I don't think this is a big deal. He probably just wants some time to relax before all the festivities."

"He didn't even bring Rob," she says with despair. "Rob and Gabby are going for a city tour. So he's just going by himself! Who golfs alone, Daisy?"

I don't know anything about golf. Is that not something you do alone?

"Mom, I think you're overreacting."

She scoffs, and falls back into the seat. "I'm not overreacting. This is inconsiderate."

Inconsiderate? I could tell her a few things about inconsiderate. But instead, I reach over and put my hand on hers consolingly. Her skin is baby soft, and her nails are freshly manicured, painted in a tasteful nude color.

"Should we hang out today, Mom?" I suggest. I had planned to go to the Smithsonian National Zoo, which I've read is supposed to be excellent, but my mom lights up at the suggestion.

"Yes! Let's go do lunch before everyone arrives!" Her mood brightens considerably.

"Okay, let's do that."

Mom gets out her phone and starts tapping away. "There's a fabulous restaurant just down the street that got a Michelin star last year, but it's so nice out today. Have you been out yet?" She doesn't wait for me to answer. "So maybe we should find something with outdoor seating."

I'm nodding along with her, willing to do whatever she wants to do.

"Here it is." She holds her phone out to me so I can see the Yelp reviews. "I'll call them."

Thirty minutes later we're seated on a comfortable patio

overlooking the water. Ivy climbs the brick walls on either side of us, and a glass balcony gives us an unobstructed view of the river. The sky drifts with puffy white clouds, and some of the humidity seems to have lifted, so we can sit outside without sweating through our clothes.

My mom's hat protects her fair, unlined skin from any unwelcome sun exposure, and she has her hands folded in front of her. If there's one thing my mom always is, it's the picture of tasteful, understated elegance.

Our server arrives and introduces himself as Ray. He's a tall, handsome man with a tattoo that peeks out at the wrist of his uniform's tuxedo shirt.

"Sisters?" he quips.

"Oh, stop." My mother waves her hand, utterly delighted. "I'm her mother, of course."

"You can't be." He feigns surprise, and my mom giggles and then leans in conspiratorially.

"It's actually my wedding weekend!"

"Congratulations!" he says. "That's terrific! So," he says to me, "are you Mom's maid of honor?"

I fidget with my cloth napkin. "Um, I—"

"I asked her!" my mom interjects. "But she didn't want to be. She said she didn't want to stand in front of everyone. Can you imagine? Not being in your own mother's wedding?"

My teeth clench, and when the server disappears to go get our iced teas, I don't say anything.

"Oh, I wish you had been in the wedding, Daisy. It would have been so much fun." The look of disappointment on her face is genuine, and I feel a twinge of guilt, even through the undercurrent of resentment.

I can't stop myself with my mom. She's all I have. But even so, how,

how can she be saying this to me? When she had asked, over a phone call shortly after the engagement had been announced, I'd almost sprayed coffee all over my tiny kitchen. My mom's lack of self-awareness can be truly baffling, when you consider how charming and smooth she is on social occasions. It's like all those social graces extend to everyone except me. With me, my mom is the center of her own universe. Even when she coddled me as a child, it was always sort of about her.

"Mom, you know I couldn't have done that. It would just have been way too hard."

Mom sighs impatiently. "Is this thing with Rob going to be an issue forever?"

"No," I say, pushing down my annoyance, "It's okay, Mom. I can be your maid of honor in spirit tomorrow, okay? And I'm giving that toast tonight. It'll still be great," I console her.

Our salads arrive, and Mom cuts her lettuce into pieces before she spears it with her fork and puts it carefully into her mouth and then chews twenty times. This is another thing she does to maintain her figure, in addition to daily Pilates and never consuming carbohydrates.

After my monstrous breakfast this morning, I'm not very hungry, so I move my food around on my plate while she eats.

"I'm glad you're taking care of yourself," she says as I sip iced tea and don't eat. "You look better than the last time I saw you. You've lost weight."

"Thanks," I say, not mentioning the fact that I was a fine weight the last time she saw me, and the reason for the weight loss is a protracted episode of post-breakup depression.

"Have you been exercising?"

"Yep, three times a week," I answer.

"Good." She nods in approval. "You know women lose muscle mass as they age."

"I'm twenty-six, mom. I'm not exactly shopping for nursing homes."

"Nevertheless, Daisy," she says. "It's good to keep up these habits."

We sit in an awkward silence. I'm struggling to bounce the conversational ball.

"So," she goes on, "is there anyone special in your life? It's been a while since you dated."

My lip tries to curl, but I maintain my composure. *I haven't dated because my engagement ended, and I haven't really been up for it, Mom.*

I'm about to say no, and then pause. I don't have to say no. Thanks to Charlie, I can say yes, in fact I am dating someone, and he happens to be terribly handsome.

"Actually," I begin, "I was meaning to ask, is it alright if I bring a date to the rehearsal tonight? And to the wedding? I know it's really last-minute but—"

"Oh my goodness, Daisy!" My mom lights up. "Of course it's alright! It's more than alright! I'll let the wedding planner know, right now." She gets her phone out of her little Chanel bag and taps at it as she speaks. "Who is he? Tell me everything! Why didn't you tell me before?" She looks pointedly at me. "Why didn't he attend last night's dinner?"

A flicker of uncertainty passes through her eyes. So subtle that only I would notice it. The only person who has been a constant in her life for the last twenty-six years.

"It was sort of last-minute," I answer. "He had some work stuff to deal with. But he was going to be in DC anyway for some meetings, so I figured, why not?"

Inside, I take a moment to send a mental apology to the wedding planner who is no doubt going to be spending the rest of the day rearranging seating charts and notifying caterers to accommodate Charlie.

"What's his name? What does he do?" She leans in as she asks.

"His name is Charlie. He's an attorney."

"An attorney!" she repeats happily. My mom has stars in her eyes already. Attorney is an approved profession as far as my mom is concerned. In college I dated a guy, Ryan, who was studying Environmental Science, and she said she wasn't interested in meeting him because "it couldn't go anywhere, anyway." Environmental science was *not* an approved profession. The joke's on her though, because Ryan founded a tech startup dealing with upstream plastics production and he was recently listed in a BuzzFeed 30 under 30 list, which labeled him as the *Future CEO to look out for*.

"How did you two meet?" Mom is asking me.

"Um…" Charlie and I forgot to rehearse this bit. "On an airplane. We were seat mates."

"That's a great meet-cute." She points her fork at me. "Is he from Denver too?"

"He is." I nod. I'm going to have to get a detailed backstory together with Charlie before tonight. And fill him in on whatever I come up with during this lunch.

"How long have you been seeing each other?"

I press my lips together as I try to work out what to tell her. It can't be too long, because then I would have added him as my plus-one on the invitation. But it can't be too new, or I wouldn't have invited him at all. "I guess it's been, like, six weeks?"

"Well," Mom says as she brings a bit of endive to her lips, "I can't wait to meet him. I wasn't looking forward to introducing you as single."

My stomach drops although I'm not sure why I'm even surprised by this sentiment. Of course Mom has been worried about introducing me to her friends as single. It's utterly predictable.

"Does he know what you do for a living?" she asks.

"Of course."

"Well that's good, I suppose," she says. "Not everyone would be comfortable with a spouse in a not-for-profit job."

"Non-profit job," I correct her. "Saying not-for-profit job makes it sound like I'm working for free."

She gives me an arch look that says, *you might as well be.*

"I like my job. Money isn't the only thing that matters, you know. It's important work."

I'm feeling an edge of irritation now, and I take another sip of my tea, like the cold will also cool my temper. We've had variations of this exchange over and over again. Her little barbs, my attempts at defending myself. Sometimes the urge to grab my mother by the shoulders and tell her to wake up is overwhelming. *Earth to Diane. Please reply if you are receiving transmission!*

"Sometimes I don't know if it's me you're trying to punish, Daisy, or just yourself," she says after she's finished chewing another lettuce leaf.

"You think I'm trying to punish you?" I ask, baffled.

"I'm only saying that I hate the thought of you not living up to your potential. You could be whatever you want to be, Buttercup."

"I think I am fulfilling my potential," I say, feeling incredibly small.

"Please, darling, don't sell yourself short. You can still be active in charities. You know I am, don't you? I sit on several boards. You could take advantage of the circumstances I've provided you with. It's quite frankly a little bit strange that you don't. What do I tell people when they ask about my daughter?"

My jaw tightens at her words. At the reminder that I'm not the person she thinks I ought to be. I'm less than.

"You mean the money my father left me?" The way I say it makes it sound like he's dead, but he may as well be.

She nods. "I don't know why you're so recalcitrant about it. You weren't always. You let me buy you that car of yours in college."

"I'm not recalcitrant," I say. "I just don't need that money. It's not really mine, and I have a job that pays me. I never knew my dad and I don't want to, and—"

I stop myself. If I were to finish that sentence, I would tell her that half of the reason I don't acknowledge the money is because I don't want to live a life like hers. The sort of life that my father's money has paid for. I've seen enough ennui and restlessness among the wealthy to know that money is not a panacea. It won't give you a purpose, or a family, or a sense of self. I want to do more than float— I want roots, and a life with meaning. Things that money can't buy.

But I can never tell my mother that. It would crush her. Even the thought alone makes me crumple with shame—that I'm not grateful to her for raising me, that I'm not loyal to her, when for my entire life it's been only the two of us. She would never understand that it's not about her. It's about me having the choice to be who I am. All she would see is rejection. And so, I hedge and plead for her to try to understand that we are just different. And that it's okay—it doesn't mean I don't love her. I just wish she would love me as I am, rather than attempt to mold me into the girl she wanted me to become.

"And what, Daisy?" she asks, looking at me intently.

I lick my lips nervously, "I'm just happy with the way things are," I say. "You should just tell your friends that I'm happy. It's all that matters, right?"

She sighs. "I suppose so, but I will never understand how it makes you happy. You could have such a wonderful life. An easy life. There's no reason for you to work so hard."

I close my eyes for a brief moment and center myself, and then change the subject to wedding decorations, and my private moment of agony is over.

When lunch is finished, my mom decides we should go see the Natural History Museum. I mention the zoo as an option, but she vetoes it.

"Oh no," she says, "I don't want to ruin my hair."

She gets us an Uber to the National Mall, and we walk into the tall atrium of the museum where a large, proud elephant greets us. Architecturally, the space is beautiful. Around the perimeter of the circular room, several stories high, arched doorways each lead to different exhibits.

"Come on, Daisy, let's go see the Hope Diamond." My mom takes me by the wrist, leading the way.

We walk through a doorway marked Halls of Gems and Minerals. The exhibit is dark, with sharp spotlights directed at glass cases displaying rainbows of colored gems and crystals. A glowing purple geode the size of a small refrigerator stands proudly in the front, and jewels of historical significance lie on velvet, glimmering enticingly.

"God, would you look at this one?" Mom says in front of a case displaying a necklace of rubies and diamonds with a matching tiara. "Can you imagine opening your closet and putting this on before the opera?"

Then, we get to the main event—the Hope Diamond, circulating slowly, within its own freestanding case. The enormous blue diamond glimmers and twinkles, luring us in as we gaze into its depths. It's remarkably beautiful and, with its dangerous past, a little bit frightening. Every owner has come to a bad end. It's said to be cursed, supposedly even worn by Marie Antoinette before she met Madame Guillotine.

My mom continues to fawn over the jewels, and I wander over to the geodes. I'm fascinated by how such ordinary-looking rocks can be cracked open to reveal such immense beauty. That the things around us aren't what they appear to be, and that something the world might write off can harbor secrets that no one would ever suspect.

I wonder if I've ever passed a geode without even knowing it, on the occasions when I do go out on the trail. If I've ever stumbled across something precious and failed to even appreciate it.

Chapter 14

My mom and I return to the hotel in time to change for cocktails. The out-of-town guests have begun arriving, and in the lobby friends and family greet one another with hugs and back slaps and handshakes. My mom dazzles in the center of a group congratulating her and is busy air-kissing friends. I sneak past unnoticed.

When I get to my floor, I beeline it for Charlie's room and knock. I'm starting to get nervous about this charade we've planned, but after seeing everyone downstairs I'm more grateful than ever. Facing that crowd with someone next to me will make everything so much easier. I hope.

Charlie swings the door open and smiles when he sees it's me. I ignore the little swoop in my stomach at the sight of him. "I wasn't expecting to see you until later," he says. "What's up?"

"We need to get our story straight," I say, like we're on the lam, running from the cops. "My mom interrogated me about our relationship at lunch, and I need to fill you in."

"Sure. Come on in."

He steps to the side, and I walk into a hotel room that is identical to mine, except for the fact that it looks almost unused.

He watches me as I look around myself. "Yes, Daisy. This is how people without mental health problems live in hotel rooms. Notice that you are able to walk freely across this room without fear of getting a pair of underwear wrapped around your ankle."

"Hilarious." I roll my eyes at him.

The bed is made, and his clothes and suitcase must be tucked neatly away, because the only personal belongings I see are his laptop and some papers spread out on the desk. On his nightstand is a half-full water glass, a prescription pill bottle, and a pair of folded eyeglasses.

He grins back at me as his eyes glimmer.

"You wear contacts?" I ask and then feel a little bit embarrassed. It's very strange standing in the personal space of someone you hardly know. Seeing little glimpses of their private life. Things you don't ordinarily learn until later. I feel like I'm snooping through his medicine cabinet.

"I'm afraid so," he says. "These eyes just couldn't handle law school."

"I don't blame them."

A smile slides across his mouth. "I can't say that I do, either."

He leads me to the foot end of the bed where he sits and turns to face me. I'm sitting on a bed with Charlie. And he's about to be my pretend date. Okay. This isn't weird. And I don't want to fall back into the bed with him. Not at all.

"Alright, so, game plan," I say like a sports coach. "We met on an airplane."

"A little on the nose there, Daisy. Did you tell her about calling me Beamer, too?

"No, I failed to mention that part." I laugh. "But she knows you're a lawyer, and that you're from Denver."

"Okay." He nods along.

"We've been dating for six weeks."

"Alright," he says. "But you should know, eight weeks is my upper limit. I'm afraid of commitment. What else?"

"Nothing else, but I thought we should probably come up with some stuff so that if people ask us, we have the same answers. And… I should probably know a little bit about you."

"Sounds like a good idea." His face is totally relaxed, like this is completely normal.

"So," I say like I'm interviewing him for a job, "tell me about yourself."

He laughs. "There's not much to tell. I'm a lawyer, which you already know. I grew up in Denver with my dad. I have a kid sister named Susan who raises cocker spaniels and has two daughters, Lucy and Ava."

"Is she in Denver too?"

"Nope, she lives in San Francisco with her husband. He works in tech."

"Okay. That's good for me to know. And Mom will approve of tech."

He quirks a brow curiously at that remark, but lets it pass.

"What else?" He rubs his chin, thinking.

"What's your favorite food? Your favorite color?" I ask.

"You think people are going to ask you what my favorite color is?" He looks at me skeptically.

"Okay, just food then."

"Well, this is a pretty big question, Daisy. I'm not sure I can boil it down to just one thing."

"You don't have a favorite food?" I ask in disbelief. "My favorite food is easy: chocolate chip cookie dough ice cream."

"Well, isn't that just adorable," he says and boops my nose. My eyes cross where his finger landed. "You have the palate of a child."

I roll my eyes although I'm smiling. "Do you at least have a favorite food *genre*?"

He thinks for a minute. "French."

"French?"

'What's wrong with French food?"

"There's nothing *wrong* with French food, but… it's just, like, the basis for all other Western food. You might as well say, 'I like food.'"

"The Italians would take exception to that statement," he says sagely.

"You don't have like, something you ate as a kid a lot? Or like, something weird that you like to eat?"

"I like mustard on steak," he offers.

"You're a monster," I say plainly.

"It's good!" he protests through laughter as he rocks back. "No one ever believes me!" He shakes a fist at the heavens.

I cross my arms over my chest. "I absolutely do not believe you. Plus, not only do you eat innocent animals, but you put mustard on them." I shake my head. "It's a double insult."

He's laughing helplessly. "I guess it's good that I already know you're a vegetarian. And that you like ice cream."

We swap notes—he went to college at the University of Colorado, Boulder. Same as me, but he was three years ahead, which means he's twenty-nine. His dad has arthritis, and he visits his sister whenever he can, because it's hard for her to travel with young girls. His favorite movie is *Animal House*, and he loves watching vintage episodes of *Saturday Night Live*.

I tell him about moving all over the country, that New York was always my favorite because it's such a transient city that I felt like I belonged there. I talk about Cara and how she's the one who chose me for friendship. It was like she singled me out and decided that we were going to be friends, and then we were. And the fact that she's been such a support throughout the various stages of my life falling apart.

"Do you think anyone is going to bring up the…" He doesn't finish the sentence.

"No, I highly doubt it. I'm sure everyone knows, but I can't imagine anyone bringing it up."

He nods. "Okay. But if they do, should I…?"

"Feign ignorance," I say. "Make for an exit. Pretend I haven't told you."

He looks at me. "You *did* tell me."

I pause for a minute. "I did. But that doesn't count. I don't know you. You're like, just my vacation buddy."

"You know I like mustard steak."

"I do know that." I start laughing again, "And I really wish I didn't."

"So, what's a vacation buddy, anyway?"

I look at him, "You know what a vacation buddy is. It's someone you make friends with on vacation, and then when vacation is over," I shrug, "You Facebook-request them and you just sort of move on with your life, you know?"

He stills and looks at me. "Is that what you plan to do, Daisy? Are you going to Facebook-friend-request me?" He looks vaguely insulted. Like I just gave him a fake number.

I should probably tell him that I can't find him on Facebook, but he really doesn't need to know that I already tried to spy on his life.

"I don't know," I say. "I just assumed because…"

Why did I actually assume that we would disappear from each other's lives back in Denver? We've been having fun. He took me out to meet his friend and made sure I got home safely. Surely he's a friend worth hanging on to?

"Do you mean you want to be real friends?" I ask.

He lifts a shoulder. "I sort of thought that we might be real friends, yeah."

He's looking right into my eyes. They're browner now, in the shadowy blue light of the room, soft and deep. My heart rate kicks up a notch in response. "Okay. Well, then, we're friends," I say and give him a little smile.

The corners of his mouth lift. "Good. I like making new friends."

We look at each other in silence for a minute. I take a deep breath as a tingle runs up my spine at those words. Every interaction with him starts out easy and then begins to feel heavy, and my body won't seem to stop reacting.

"Okay," I say finally. "Well, I'm going to go get dressed."

He checks his expensive watch. "There's still an hour and a half before we need to be downstairs," he says, confused.

"Ah shit, I'm running late," I say and head for the door to the sound of him chuckling.

––––––––––––

When I get dressed this evening, I'm much calmer than I was yesterday, with the knowledge that I don't have to do this alone tonight. Everyone is going to be looking at me, and I can only imagine what they'll be thinking, about me, about Rob, about our parents. But I'll have Charlie there, and I know beyond doubt that he will be in my corner, and if I need to escape, he'll be there too.

I shower, wash, and condition my hair. I shave every inch of my body and exfoliate, and then moisturize. I blow dry my hair and then curl it so that it falls in loose waves around my face. I spend at least half an hour on my makeup, dabbing concealer and creating a smoky look that Cara agreed make my eyes look sexy and feline. Finally, I put on the underwear I bought for this evening. It doesn't make sense to have bought special underwear, but I need every ounce of confidence I can get and wearing something expensive and sexy under my clothes won't hurt. Then, I pull a deep red silk cocktail dress out of my closet (one of the items I carefully hung, as opposed to most of my other clothes) and step into it. It was selected for this evening because of its sophistication, but it wasn't an option for the wedding, because there's no way I could dance in it.

It's narrow and cut just below my knees and has a slit up the side to give it a little oomph, and it has slender spaghetti straps that crisscross at the back. It's undeniably sexy, and I hope I pull it off. I pair it with a pair of black stilettos and gold earrings, and I'm ready with five minutes to spare.

I can't sit down, or the dress will crease, so I stand in the center of my room, clutching my little black bag in one hand, and wait. Charlie is due to be here any minute. I strain my ears to listen for any sounds coming from his side of the wall, but it's silent. A group of people walk past in the hallway and their voices echo as laughter bounces from the walls. My nerves have been steadily increasing as I've gone through the process of getting myself ready. I feel like I'm about to walk into a court room as a defendant. My palms sweat, and I wipe them on the duvet cover of my bed. My speech for tonight is folded up on a piece of paper tucked into my bag, and I rehearse it in my head, over and over again, as my heart begins pounding. Then, after what feels like a lifetime, there's a soft knock on the door. I walk across the room and open it.

Charlie is standing in the hallway waiting for me, wearing a sleek navy suit that's cut so well I think it has to be custom. His shoulders are broad, his waist tapered. His legs are long and lean, except for, I can't help but notice, very well-toned thighs.

"Hi." I smile at him. "Thanks again for doing this."

Charlie's smile falls a little when he sees me, and I panic. The dress is awful. The makeup is wrong. I look like a hooker. He stares at me like he just got a piece of bad news. His eyes are dark and fixed on my face, then they sweep my body, and goosebumps rise everywhere they fall. The knot of his Adam's apple bobs up and down with a swallow. He gives his head a little shake, and his mouth turns into an easy lopsided grin.

"Wow, Daisy. You really are one. Hot. Bitch."

"Oh my God, you heard that?" My whole body turns red with mortification. I bring my hands up to hide behind them, and then stop myself to save my makeup.

"Daisy, I think the President probably heard you all the way from the White House," he says lightly and then laughs at my horrified expression.

"Why didn't you tell me you heard?" I nearly gasp.

"I didn't want to embarrass you," he says, leaning against my door frame.

"But you wanted to embarrass me now?" In my head, I curse Cara for her relentless supportiveness.

He laughs easily, that damn dimple appearing on his right cheek. "Don't worry, Mini. It was adorable listening to you hype yourself up. You ready to go?"

I nod and step forward, letting the door click shut behind me.

Charlie leads me down the hallway, his hand on my lower back in that way of his, and as we ride the elevator down, he sees my hands tremble.

"Deep breaths, Mini. You got this," he says, looking at me seriously,

"I'm going to be right here the whole time, okay? And if you need to get out just say something weird. Like, say banana."

"Banana?" I give him a sideways look.

"Yeah, like a code word. If you say banana, I know we need to get you out of there."

I grin at him, getting into the idea, "Okay. Banana it is."

We step out of the elevators and walk across the lobby to the hotel bar, which has been closed for tonight. Corded off with a red velvet rope and a sign that tells us there is a private event in progress. A man in a hotel uniform checks our names against a list, like there's a risk that people might try to crash this thing.

This is a society wedding. It's not going to be a small and cozy affair. The space is already crowded with guests. I recognize Rob's aunts and uncles catching up while holding drinks, and people I've never seen before stand in tight circles talking and laughing. There must be at least fifty people here already, maybe more. If this is the rehearsal dinner, what will the wedding be like?

A woman with a champagne-colored lace dress and matching heels tilts her head together with a woman in black as they share a joke. Their jewels glimmer in the soft light. Everyone has a cocktail glass in hand, and servers mill about carrying trays of hors d'oeuvres. Charlie grabs a piece of shrimp toast and pops it into his mouth, flashing me a grin. He's so relaxed in nearly every situation, it seems. The only time I've seen him be really serious is when he's looking at his work.

As we move through the room, his hand doesn't leave my back, and it's a warm, comforting presence that keeps my legs from falling out from under me. We order drinks—champagne for me, a martini straight up for him, and stand facing each other.

"I don't know what to say to anyone," I whisper.

He dips his head towards mine. "Well, then, it's good you don't have to say anything if you don't want to," he whispers back with a raised eyebrow. His breath is minty and clean, with just a hint of the alcohol from his drink.

"You really do look beautiful, Daisy. I'm sorry I didn't say so earlier. I shouldn't have joked with you then."

My eyes raise to his, locking in place. "I do?"

"Stunning," he says, and my heart leaps up into my throat while my stomach feels like I'm on a rollercoaster.

Right then, Rob and Gabby walk into the room. Gabby is elegant in a robin's-egg blue cocktail dress that matches Rob's tie. The color suits her blond hair and brings out her tan. Rob's eyes meet mine, and then widen a bit at Charlie by my side. They dart away as Gabby says something and he nods at her, and they go to the bar.

"Daisy." Rob's uncle from Connecticut approaches. He's a big-time hedge fund manager who commutes into the city every day. His hair has thinned out more since the last time I saw him, and he's a bit thicker around the middle. His black suit jacket is open, and he's holding a glass of dark liquor with an ice cube floating in it. "It's been a while." He takes my hand and, to my dismay, leans over and kisses it. "You look as beautiful as ever."

"Hi, Uncle Jack," I say, and then feel awkward, because Uncle Jack is what he told me to call him when Rob and I were still a couple and I'm not sure that I'm really entitled to that name anymore. And I have no idea how Jack feels about my mom, and the relationship between his brother and my mom, but he's here, so he must be supportive of his brother, at least.

That's why Rob is here, I'm certain. Rob is here to support his father. He hates what happened, maybe even more than me. He grew up in a home with two loving parents who doted on one another, and when the affair happened and then the divorce, he was utterly devastated. Gutted. The rug was pulled out from under him. This was something he'd never experienced before, whereas I was raised getting used to moving from one thing to the next, both figuratively and literally. It came as a shock to me, but I was brought up handling shocks, sudden departures, disruptions. Before he finally broke things off between us, he'd told me that it felt like he'd lost his whole childhood. That everything had been a lie. But Rob is nothing if not loyal to his family, and he and his dad were close. Eventually, I suppose, he found a way to move forward with him, just like I did with my mom.

"Who's your friend?" Uncle Jack's eyes shift to Charlie next to me.

"Charles Bond." Charlie proffers his hand, and the two men give a firm shake. "Daisy's boyfriend."

Boyfriend? We hadn't actually agreed on that particular title. I thought we were just going with "date."

Then, Charlie wraps his arm around me and gives my shoulder a squeeze, pulling me into him so that my shoulder is tucked snugly under his. From the corner of my eye, I see Rob look our way, his eyebrows dipped together curiously. Smug satisfaction sparks through me at that look, and I place my hand on Charlie's chest in intimate affection.

"Charlie works in contract law," I say. "He's in and out of DC a lot." It comes out rather more proudly than I expected, but why not? Charlie is obviously successful, and he's handsome as the devil himself. Why not indulge in feeling proud to have him by my side tonight, even if it's just for show?

Mom and Michael come in, and everyone turns to them in greeting. The happy couple smiles and hold hands, and then Michael takes her by the waist and tilts her backwards and dips her into a kiss, and the room breaks into a round of applause. Someone wolf-whistles from the back corner. My mother is flushed, and her eyes are bright. She's stunning in a floor-length ivory slip dress that hugs her body and displays her Pilates-toned figure to its greatest advantage.

Charlie shifts so that he stands behind me and brushes his fingers up my arms with a little nudge so that I'm tipped back against him. The top of my head is at his cheekbone. The heat of his chest, firm and broad, sinks into my body. "You okay?" he asks softly into my ear and his breath skates along the side of my neck. My own breath comes with a shudder, and my thighs squeeze together at the pleasure of his closeness. My mom and Michael and this whole uncomfortable evening seem to vanish for just a moment. My awareness narrows, my vision clouds, until all I feel, all I can think about is Charlie holding me by my arms, his finger brushing up and down in delicate strokes, his steady, strong body behind mine. Static fills my ears as his smell envelops me—the blend of warm spices and soap.

I nod my head, though the pleasure coursing through me has made me limp and rubbery all over, and I worry the nod might be more of a bobble. "Yeah, I'm fine," I reply.

We mill about, making small talk as relations approach and congratulate me—as if the truth of what has happened isn't known by everyone in the room—and strangers introduce themselves and ask the same questions over and over again: *what do you do for a living? How do you like Denver? Aren't you just so thrilled for your mom?*

The last question hits like a barb each time it comes. As though they aren't perfectly aware of how my mother met Michael. Perhaps some of them aren't, but gossip like this rarely stays put for long, and I would be shocked if there wasn't a buzz of it floating around right now, discreetly shared behind hands and cocktail napkins.

Throughout the evening, Charlie never stops touching me. He keeps his hand around my shoulder, he brushes my back with light fingertips, he slides his fingers down to lace with mine. He's the picture of well-mannered congeniality, happily introducing himself, making people laugh with his charming demeanor. At one point, while talking to a woman named Carol who is leaning into him and touching his arm, he traces the length of my spine, down to the place where my dress meets my lower back, causing me to shiver so hard I'm sure he notices, and Carol looks at me with envy written all over her face.

Eventually, as my mom circulates with Michael, greeting and thanking guests, she makes her way over to Charlie and me, holding a half-finished glass of wine in her left hand. Her engagement ring is displayed to full sparkling effect.

"You must be Charlie," she says with a charming smile. "Daisy has told me *so* much about you. I'm thrilled to finally be meeting you."

I've told her exactly three things about Charlie, but my mom knows what she's doing at a party. She's an expert in the art of both flattery and small talk.

"It's nice to meet you too, Ms. Thomas," Charlie says politely. "And congratulations. I know Daisy is just thrilled for you both."

"Is that right? Oh, I'm so glad to hear that." A surprising flicker of relief passes through her eyes. As though she doubted what I might have told Charlie about her.

"Michael," Michael says somewhat gruffly. I wonder if seeing me next to someone besides his son is strange for him. If he feels any remorse for how things unfolded after his affair with my mother came to light. I've only spoken to my mom about it, and even then, it was very broad strokes. It was clear that Rob and I weren't going to stand in the way of her happiness, and she'd been convinced that it didn't need to stand in the way of Rob and me either.

"So, Daisy tells me you're an attorney," Mom says.

"That's right. Contract law. Very boring." Charlie nods.

"Well, the world needs lawyers," Michael says.

"Very true," Mom says. "And it's a great profession. Very cerebral. I can't imagine that I'd ever understand all those complicated documents." She titters sweetly.

"I'm sure you'd do just fine, Ms. Thomas. They put you through the wringer in law school, but after that it turns into routine."

"Oh, I can't imagine that being the case. I'm sure you find your work fascinating."

"It has its moments," Charlie concedes. "What do you do for a living, Michael?"

"Michael is chief surgeon at the Potomac Center for Oncology," Mom says proudly. "He's very in demand."

Michael swallows uncomfortably and adjusts his tie. "Oncology surgeons tend to be in demand, unfortunately."

"Oh." Mom swats his arm playfully. "Well, of course they are, and it's very sad, but Michael is *the best*. There's even a waiting list."

"Your patients must be very grateful," Charlie answers.

Finally, after my second glass of champagne, the cocktail portion of the evening winds down, and we are ushered into a fleet of sleek limousines that will whisk us downtown. Charlie and I slide in along the black leather seats, smooth on the backs of my legs, opposite an older couple with coordinated outfits and matching white hair.

"Walter." The man nods at us by way of greeting. He has an enormous, full mustache over his upper lip.

"And I'm Peg." The woman holds her hand out, palm down, like she's expecting me to bring my lips to it, and I take it awkwardly and sort of bob it up and down in a limp handshake.

"Classy event. Really classy," Walter keeps repeating. "I mean, this is class. The way it's supposed to be done."

Peg nods along with Walter. "What a gorgeous night. And Diane looks so stunning in that dress. I can't wait to see what she wears tomorrow. And the flowers! I'm sure the flowers are going to be spectacular."

"It's gonna be a doozy," Walter says, like he's talking about an incoming hurricane. "Nothing like what kids are doing nowadays, with all those things in tents and cottages. Do you remember Katherine's wedding, Peg?"

"Oh, how could I forget?" Peg exclaims.

"I was slopping around in mud up to my ankles. A bunch of hippie nonsense, if you ask me." Walter turns to us. "Katherine's our niece. She married a forest ranger. Can you believe it? Making a living wandering around the forest? No career for a man."

Charlie and I both stare at them as they go on like this, and then Charlie turns to me and widens his eyes in quiet acknowledgement that we are both thinking about what an asshole Walter is.

"So, how do the two of you know Mike and Diane?" Peg asks us, as Walter mutters on under his breath about all the class.

"I'm Diane's daughter, Daisy."

Walter's eyes cut to mine. "You're Diane's daughter?"

"I am." I shift uncomfortably on the leather seat.

"Well," Peg says on a breath. "Congratulations, Daisy. Your mother is a lovely woman."

I smile at her.

"I'm Charles," Charlie offers, "Daisy's boyfriend."

Walter shakes his hand across the expanse of the limo. "Good to meet you, Charles."

"Likewise," Charlie says.

"So, Daisy," Peg says, "Diane has mentioned that you live out in Colorado. What do you do there?"

I take a breath, and there's a moment's hesitation as I consider lying. There's no way Walter and Peg will be impressed by my choice of career. "I work for a non-profit dedicated to wildlife conservation."

Walter frowns.

"Well, isn't that just lovely," Peg says politely. "Isn't that lovely, Walter?"

"A job like that must not pay well," he says through the frown.

"I do alright," I say, not that it's any of his business.

"And what do you do, Charles?" Walter looks to Charlie, like he's waiting for him to reassure us all that he's going to be the breadwinner.

"I'm a yoga instructor," Charlie says happily.

My head swivels as I stare at him in astonishment. His eyes have that sparkling sheen they get when he's about to really mess with someone. The same look he had on the airplane with me.

"Really?" Peg's eyes widen with fascination, and Walter's frown deepens. With his great big mustache, his face is beginning to look startlingly like a walrus. The effect is somewhat disconcerting.

"Oh yeah, I love it!" Charlie nods enthusiastically. "I started off in law school—my father wanted me to be a corporate attorney. You know how fathers are." He laughs. "But I took my first yoga class, and I tell you, it changed. My. Life. I actually felt my third eye *open*."

Charlie makes a motion with his hand to demonstrate how an eye opens.

"Third eye," Walter says flatly.

"I do some yoga at a studio in the city," Peg says. "It's great for flexibility."

"You're telling me!" Charlie quips. "So, anyway, after my third eye opened, I started meditating and found a guru who helped me balance my chakra, and I just *knew* that this was my calling. So I dropped out of law school. I was *so* close too. In my third year. Top of my class. But when the universe calls, you just can't ignore it, you know?"

I'm gripping my handbag and struggling not to laugh, and Walter is now rubbing at the corner of his mouth in agitation. "Your father couldn't have been too pleased about that."

"Oh no! It turns out, my dad *loves* it. You should see his downward dog! He can get his legs behind his head!"

"He can?" Peg says, leaning forward in interest.

"He's very advanced," Charlie says.

"Is that how the two of you met? Was Daisy in your yoga class?" Peg asks.

"Oh no. Although Daisy is *very* flexible too," He gives Peg a wink, and she blushes. "No, I actually went on an ayahuasca retreat—"

"What is that?" Peg interjects, rapt.

"It's a sort of hallucinogenic tea," Charlie answers smoothly. "Very good for the spirit."

"Drugs," Walter grunts.

Charlie continues, undeterred. "When I was in the sweat lodge, after the tea, an enormous bear appeared and told me that he was my spirit guide. So, then I knew without a doubt what I had to do."

Walter's frown has turned into a scowl, and he's gone from walrus to English bulldog. "What was that?"

"I had to start doing everything I could to protect the bears," he says sincerely. "And so when I turned twenty-five and I came into my trust fund, I donated it to Daisy's nonprofit, and that's how we met. They invited me to an event at a local park, and Daisy was there, and her aura was so full of kindness. I fell in love with her on the spot."

"You… donated… your trust fund?" Walter is aghast at the notion.

"The whole kit and caboodle," Charlie says, pleased with himself. He reaches over and gives my hand a squeeze.

"How do the two of you live?" Walter wants to know.

"Just like everyone else," Charlie says. "But I have to admit, Daisy is the real breadwinner in our household, which is fine, because I'm committed to being a stay-at-home dad when the time comes." He turns to me. "Right, sweetheart?"

I take up the story gamely, deeply invested in this now. "Oh, that's right. I would never leave my job, and Charlie is just *so* nurturing." I give them a dreamy look.

"Well, I think it's lovely that the two of you found each other. What a unique story," Peg says.

"A stay-at-home dad." Walter is struggling. His mouth wavering between a frown and a grimace. Walrus and bulldog.

"I can't wait," Charlie says. "I keep trying to convince Daisy that we should shift to communal living."

He's really running away with this now, and I can see the story unspooling in his eyes. "Really start living with nature, you know? Pool our resources with other families. I mean, we are both so dedicated to bears, and there's this encampment in the mountains…"

"Encampment." It appears Walter has resorted to just repeating things that Charlie says.

"And I would love to start growing our own food," Charlie finishes. "So, what do you do, Walter?"

My lips are trembling with the effort it takes not to laugh at Walter's facial expressions. He's cycling through various shades of color—white to red, back to white again.

"Walter works in finance," Peg says kindly when Walter fails to answer. "But what the two of you are doing is lovely."

"Is it?" Walter says.

"It *is*, Walter," Peg says firmly. "Can't you see? They're *soul mates*."

"We are actually," Charlie replies with confidence. "Our root chakras are so aligned that sometimes they feel like they've merged."

"Oh, honey." Peg turns to Walter. "Maybe we should work on our chakras!"

Walter looks at his wife with alarm. "There's nothing wrong with our chakras, dear. Our chakras are perfectly fine as they are."

"Are you sure? We've never looked into it." She tilts her head in thought.

"I'm *very* sure," Walter barks. "My chakra is exceptional. Best chakra out there."

"If you're interested, I can give you a blessing," Charlie offers, and then scratches his chin. "Although I'm not qualified yet. Maybe you should see my guru. I can give you his card." He starts patting his breast pockets theatrically.

"That won't be necessary," Walter says at the same time Peg exclaims, "Oh, I would *love* that, Charles! You're so kind!"

"Ah," he says with disappointment in his voice, "I don't have his card on me."

"Thank goodness," Walter mumbles, relieved.

"Oh." Peg's face falls. "Well, maybe tomorrow."

Charlie nods. "Yes. Definitely tomorrow. Come and find me. I'll be up at dawn engaging in my gratitude ritual to Mother Gaia, so you can just ask the hotel for my room and knock on my door."

I'm trembling with suppressed mirth now, and Charlie squeezes my hand again, begging me not to give him up.

"I'll be with him, of course," I say. "We both like to greet the sun with a gratitude ritual and a micro-dose."

Charlie looks over at me like I'm a genius. "That's right. We mix it into our tea."

"A micro-dose?" Peg asks while Walter looks alarmed.

"Mushrooms," I say. "The magic kind."

"We collect them in the forest," Charlie adds with enthusiasm. "It gives you a nice boost, and it helps us maintain our enlightenment and connection to the Goddess while we're in the city, away from nature."

"That's fascinating," Peg says, intrigued. "Could maybe we try some—"

"Peg," Walter cuts her off. "We're not taking magic mushrooms."

Peg's face falls, and I feel a little bit sorry for her. Maybe Peg *should* try some magic mushrooms. Not that I ever have. But still. She might like it.

At that moment, the limo comes to a stop, and when the driver opens the door, Walter drags Peg out while she scrambles to scribble her number on an old receipt that she pulled from her purse to pass on to Charlie.

When Walter has gotten Peg out of the car to safety, I finally release the gut-splitting laughter I've been holding in, and Charlie is hunched over, his shoulders shaking.

I turn to him. "Oh my God, where did that come from?"

He's laughing harder now. "I don't know." He's shaking his head, talking through bouts of laughter. "Walter just seemed like such a prick. I couldn't help myself."

"Did you see his face when Peg wanted to deal with their chakras?" I'm crying and holding my fingers under my eyes so my mascara doesn't run.

"And the mushrooms!" Charlie falls back on the seat. "You're completely brilliant. She wants to do them with Walter!"

"Oh," I gasp. "Poor Walter."

As our laughter fades, I look at Charlie and his face grows serious as he looks back at me. "Thank you for that," I say sincerely.

"You needed it," Charlie says. "You looked so uncomfortable when you told them what you do for a living."

"It's kind of hard when I know all of these people disapprove."

"Why would you think they disapprove?"

"All these people are all about money," I say, rubbing the satin of my clutch with a thumb. The smooth texture is soothing against my anxiety.

"You should be proud of what you do, Daisy. You don't have anything to be ashamed of. People like Walter should feel ashamed. Finance is just about the least helpful profession I can think of, short of oil baron."

"I bet Walter would love to be an oil baron."

"It's what keeps him up at night. He never struck oil."

"What if we're seated next to them at dinner?" I ask, suddenly worried.

Charlie shrugs a shoulder, unconcerned. "Then I guess you're dating a yogi."

I laugh at the idea that Peg might get the chance to interview Charlie some more about his psychedelic experiences, and Charlie takes my hand and helps me out of the car. My ankles wobble a little when my four-and-a-half inch heels hit the pavement, and he steadies me by my shoulders. "You got it?" he asks.

"Got it," I say.

"You're really determined not to be mini tonight."

Usually the jokes about my small stature grate on me, but Charlie is so genuinely kind that I know his jokes aren't mean-spirited. I smile and shoot him a wink. "Well, I was planning on looking into people's faces tonight, so it's really more a matter of practicality."

He grins and leads me into the restaurant.

We're on the twelfth floor, and tall glass windows give us a panoramic view of the city. The Washington Monument is visible, its white marble lit up like a beacon.

The entire restaurant has been closed for this event, and the guests are grouped at round tables spread out through the room.

We're seated across from Rob and Gabby, of course, because my mother seems hell-bent on making us all embrace each other, and we're joined by Rob's cousin Tyler and his wife Astrid.

Rob shifts in his seat uncomfortably when Charlie pulls my chair out across from him.

"I'm Gabby," Gabby says to Charlie as she checks him out.

"Charlie," he replies. "I'm Daisy's boyfriend."

My stomach flips again at the terminology, and I smile across the table at Rob whose eyes have lit in alarm. "You didn't say you have a boyfriend."

"It's newish," I answer.

"Daisy's a terrific girl," Charlie says and takes my hand on top of the tablecloth.

Rob's eyes dart there and then back to the two of us, and Gabby grabs Rob's hand too.

"How did you meet?" Rob asks. He's already said more to me tonight than he has during the entirety of the weekend thus far.

"On an airplane," Charlie answers, like we rehearsed. "She was crocheting a baby blanket for her best friend." I glance over at Charlie, surprised that he remembers that it's crochet, not knitting, and what I was making.

"Cara had a baby?" Rob asks, surprised.

"She's three months along," I say with pleasure.

"That's exciting," Rob says with genuine interest. "Does she know the sex?"

I shake my head. "No, she wants it to be a surprise. I can't wait to be an aunt, though. It's going to be amazing."

Charlie's hand has crept up my arm until it's lying across the back of my chair, and he gives my shoulder an affectionate squeeze.

"Daisy is going to be a terrific aunt," Charlie says. "I can't imagine how loved that baby is going to be."

"She's very warm." Rob nods and his eyes have a strange sort of far-off look. Like he's not really here anymore.

"Rob is also so affectionate," Gabby says, "He's always doting on babies out in public."

"Is he?" I ask. I've personally never seen Rob dote on a baby, but maybe he does. I haven't spoken to him in a year. Maybe he turned into a baby person. I suddenly realize I don't really care one way or the other.

"Oh yeah," Gabby says, "a totally natural nurturer. Molly is obsessed with him."

"Molly?" Charlie asks.

"My dog."

"I thought you said Molly tried to bite him?" I ask.

"She did," Rob says. "And she still sits on the other side of the room when I come over."

Gabby presses her lips together.

"Our dog is a jerk too," Astrid says, jumping into the conversation.

"Molly isn't a jerk. She's just shy," Gabby says defensively.

"Our dog tries to bite people's ankles when they come into the house," Astrid tells her. "We put this collar on her that squirts her in the face with water whenever she barks."

Gabby looks taken aback. "They make those?"

"Oh, they make everything for pets," Tyler says. "You can get a vest thing that gives your dog a back massage."

"That's kind of cool," Charlie says, suddenly interested. "My dad has this really old arthritic Blue Tick Hound. Maybe I'll get him one. My dad has a massage chair so the two of them can sit there together getting massages."

The table laughs.

"Well, I would never squirt Molly with water," Gabby says with disapproval in her voice.

The air of amicability that was forming around us floats away like fog lifting.

"Anyway, dogs are great," Tyler says finally. And everyone agrees on that, at least.

Wedge salads are carried out on large trays by servers wearing tuxedos.

I pick the bacon off mine carefully and slide it to the side of the plate. "Any takers?" I ask the table at large.

All hands shoot up, but Charlie has already snatched the plate and is shoveling the bacon onto his own.

"Boyfriend perk," Charlie declares, and I try to keep the flush down at his words.

"The kitchen must have forgotten not to put bacon on yours." Astrid makes a sad face.

"So." Tyler looks over at Gabby. "What do you do out in Denver?"

"I'm an influencer," she says in the same tone one would reference a totally normal job. Like, *I'm an accountant.*

Astrid stops her fork mid-air. "Wait. You mean, like, a social media influencer?"

"Yep," Gabby says happily.

"What's an influencer?" Tyler asks.

"An influencer," Astrid says, "is the best job in the world. You just take pictures of your life and then companies give you money."

Gabby laughs. "It's actually not as great as it seems."

"It's really not," Rob says, but not in irritation. More like in support. "She puts a ton of work into it."

"How did you start doing it?" Astrid asks.

"I still don't understand," Tyler says.

Gabby's eyes tick over to Tyler. "Basically, I have a lot of followers on Instagram and a few other social media platforms, and because I have so much reach, companies will sponsor me to post about their products, or to feature them in whatever I'm doing."

"Like a celebrity?" Tyler says in disbelief.

"I'm not a celebrity," Gabby protests, just as Astrid says, "Exactly like that."

"How did it start?" Charlie asks, his curiosity piqued.

"Well," Gabby begins, "I had this blog about traveling as a single woman. And it started to get some followers, and I opened an Instagram account to catalogue pictures from my trips. And then it just started to pick up some steam, and now"—she shrugs her shoulders—"I started getting approached for sponsorships and deals and stuff, and I was able to quit my job and start doing it full-time. And I include other things too—like lifestyle stuff and home décor."

"Are you going to be posting about this?" Astrid asks with excitement. Her salad has been completely abandoned in her fascination. Tyler looks like he still doesn't quite get that this can actually be a career.

"No." Gabby looks at Rob affectionately. "This is private."

Rob smiles at her and his arm reaches over under the table, and I know he's holding her hand. Charlie gives my knee a squeeze that's meant to be supportive but sends sparks way up to the tops of my thighs.

"That is just… so cool," Astrid says.

"What were you doing before you became an… influencer?" Tyler asks carefully, like he's testing out this new word on his tongue.

"I worked in brand merchandising. I helped companies create identities that consumers could easily understand and hopefully be interested in."

"Well, you must have been good at it," Astrid says. "You made yourself into a brand!"

Tyler's brow is furrowed. "How many followers do you have on Instagram?"

"A million," Rob replies before Gabby can answer. "She has a million goddamn followers."

Gabby blushes deeply, like she's sort of embarrassed or shy. Something tells me that, in a different world, I might like Gabby. She's explained this whole thing without sounding conceited at all. But instead of being gracious, I shove a giant piece of iceberg lettuce into my mouth and munch like a cow.

Astrid continues asking Gabby about all the places she's been. A list I could probably recite from memory because I've obviously read all her blog posts and examined every picture in detail.

And then the main course arrives.

A large steak is placed in front of me, with a side of green beans and potatoes. I look at the plate with disappointment. My mom knows very well that I don't eat meat, but she refuses to acknowledge it. She thinks it's too hippie-ish of me and has told me she'd *prefer* it if I ate meat. Everyone's eyes land on my plate, and without saying anything, Charlie scoots his plate over to mine and slides all of his vegetables and potatoes next to the giant hunk of beef.

My heart does a little squeeze, and I look at him with gratitude.

As the table conversation continues, Charlie repeats all the pertinent details about his life for the hundredth time this evening.

Questions are peppered in politely between the continued interrogation of Gabby's career. He's being exceptionally patient, and I wonder again at the fact that he's doing this for me. Being the guest at a wedding where you know exactly no one is horrible. I've done it before, and it's painful making the same small talk over and over again. And he's going to have repeat it all tomorrow.

Dinner is coming to a close, and it will be time to give my toast soon. I'm full of green beans and mashed potatoes, and Charlie has eaten his entire steak and half of mine. Servers mill about, removing empty dinner plates and refilling wine and water glasses. I check my purse, hung on the back of my chair by its little gold chain, for my speech. It's folded up in the side pocket meant to hold a credit card. The creases in the paper are soft from me folding and unfolding it so many times to go over it, committing it to memory.

I agonized over this. Over what I was going to say. My mom asked me to talk at the wedding, but I begged her not to force me. I'm okay in small groups, even if I have a tendency to doubt and second-guess myself, but public speaking isn't my forte, and the thought of standing up in a ballroom, congratulating my mother, when everyone knows what happened—knows my humiliation and the fact that Rob and I split before we became stepsiblings—was a measure too far. She guilted me until I compromised on the rehearsal dinner, and that seemed to satisfy her. I had no idea that the rehearsal dinner would occupy an entire restaurant.

"You got this." Charlie leans in and whispers in my ear. "I'm here. I have you."

"Banana," I whisper back and he looks at me seriously and raises his eyebrows.

"Yeah? Banana?"

I smile and shake my head. "Just kidding. Look at me go." I give him a weak half-smile, feigning confidence that I don't feel.

And then, when all the plates have been cleared, I stand and tap my knife against my water glass so that it chimes through the space. It takes some doing, but the hum of conversation softens, and one by one, heads swivel towards me.

Okay, I tell myself as my heart kicks its heels into my chest, *I can do this.*

I smooth my skirt with damp hands. My knees tremble with nerves, my kneecaps twitching, but I take a shuddering breath, and begin.

"Mom," I say, and my mother looks at me with bright, expectant eyes. She holds a tissue in her hand at the ready.

"For my entire life, it's just been you and me. You're not just my mom, you're my best friend. You took me to the beach and built sandcastles with me. You were there when I learned to ride a bike."

This is accurate—my mom was there, though it was my nanny Violet who went running down the street after me.

"When I grew into adulthood, you taught me to be a lady."

My mother's eyes glisten as I go on. "We moved around when I was growing up—a lot. But I never felt like I didn't have a home. Because you were my home. I knew that, as long as we were together, it didn't matter where we were, because you were there. And you were what mattered."

The words are coming to me through the haze of nerves, despite the hundred eyes on me and my legs that haven't stopped trembling.

"When you fell in love with Michael, it wasn't easy for me."

A twinge of apprehension passes over her face now. Her lips tip down just a little, barely perceptible, but I know her every expression so well I almost see them before they happen. This one is disapproval. Her grip tightens on her tissue. "Because," I say, "I've never had to share you."

Her tiny frown vanishes.

"But now you've found the love of your life, and I'm so happy for you."

My throat starts to close. The lies I've dreamed up—forced myself to believe—are choking me. I'm happy that she's happy. But like this? Deep down, I wish I'd never introduced her to Rob's parents. Not because Rob and I necessarily should have ended up married, but because what happened was just so unfair to us. The emotion on my face is real as a tear escapes and trickles down my right cheek, but it's not joy. It's something complicated that I have yet to fully untangle.

"Michael." My eyes slide over to him. "You're like a father to me."

A father-in-law, I can practically *hear* everyone having the same thought, and I hope the blotchy redness I know is creeping up my neck isn't too obvious in the soft light of the dining room.

"And I know you'll take good care of my mom." And then I give him a theatrically threatening look. "*You better*."

A light rumbling of laughter arrives on cue.

"But I have no doubt that the two of you will be very happy together, and that makes me happy. I love you both. And I wish you all the joy in the world."

I raise my glass as the dinner guests clap their hands, and then we all drink a toast to my mother and soon-to-be stepfather.

My mom is smiling at me through tears, and she gives me a little nod of approval.

I take my seat with shaking breaths and a brow that's now damp from the stress, and Charlie's arm is right there, sliding around my shoulders, pulling me into him. "That was perfect, Daisy." He whispers into my ear in a low voice, "Be proud of yourself."

The tension in my body drains out of me in a rush like a dam that's burst, and I relax into him, letting my head fall sideways onto his shoulder as his hand glides up and down my arm in calming strokes. I sigh a release of anxiety.

Rob is looking at me with resentment written in his eyes that sends ice crystals through my limbs. As though he didn't make the same decision that I did—to be here and support our parents, even if we didn't want to. When Mom invited me to the wedding and I was hedging, desperately trying to think of a way to get out of it, a way to put my foot down and say no, she told me that Rob was coming.

"He's supporting his father," she'd said firmly. "Life is complicated, Daisy. Things happen, and you can't hold on to resentment. I know you're not happy, but Michael and I love each other, and you should be there for me. *I'm your mother.*"

"I know, Mom," I'd pleaded. "But it's just been such a hard year already."

My mother had scoffed at that. "Don't make this about you, Daisy. This is important. It's my wedding. I need you to be there for me."

I'd said nothing, but sighed heavily, already knowing what the outcome of the conversation was going to be.

"Can you imagine how I'll feel if Rob is there for his father, and my only daughter chooses not to show up? How… humiliating that will be?"

And that had done it. Picturing my mom, sad and bereft, because of me. Because I had disappointed her. I had finally agreed, and that afternoon I had put my RSVP in the mail.

But right now, Rob doesn't seem to be remembering any of that. The fact that his father was half of the equation that made this whole thing happen. He's looking at me like I've just betrayed him. Like I'm the woman who broke up his parents' marriage and took his childhood from him.

Charlie continues stroking my arm and then releases me, and

shifts his hand to mine, which he grips and doesn't let go even though it's clammy. He turns his hand so that our fingers lace, and when I turn to the side, he's looking at me with affection in his eyes. Tenderness. And Rob vanishes. The wedding vanishes. The room we're sitting in, and all the people fall away as I lose myself in those hazel eyes that hold mine with such ease.

Dessert is served—dark chocolate cake with raspberry sauce—and I eat all of it because even after a pile of green beans I'm still hungry, and when I'm finished, I steal bites from Charlie's plate. He swats my fork with his playfully before he relents. As soon as it's socially acceptable to leave, I look at Charlie and say, "Let's banana split."

"Let's blow this popsicle stand," he answers back smoothly, and I grin at him, slaphappy from the adrenaline mixed with dopamine that this is one more night in the books.

"Thanks for being here," I say.

"Of course."

"I guess I'm glad you're not a *sundae* driver after all." I elbow him in the ribs.

"Oh my God, Daisy." He slaps a hand over his forehead. "Did you really just say that?"

"I bet you can't *top* that!"

"Oh no." He grimaces even as he smiles. "It's painful."

I chuckle. "Sorry, couldn't help myself."

"Don't be. We're partners in *cream* now." He's wearing a mischievous grin, and my eyes light as he joins the game.

"Yes! That was a good one!"

We're in the elevator now with a group who are staring at us as we grin stupidly at each other. "*Ice cream* at your puns," I say.

"Weak," Charlie replies, goading me. "Everyone knows the ice cream pun."

"Aw, come on, it wasn't that bad." I make flirty eyes at him.

"Nope. I don't play *flavorites*." He shakes his head seriously. "You're going to have to go back to *sundae* school."

A man next to us winces. The puns are so bad they are making the people around us shifty.

"No fair! I used sundae already." I look up at his face, and he's laughing lightly.

"Don't push me, Mini. I *cone* do this all day."

The elevator dings at the ground floor, and everyone files out ahead of us. The wincing man glances over his shoulder at us with concern, like perhaps the two of us should be seen by a professional.

My head falls back in laughter, and I'm so giddy I don't even think about it when I'm the one who grabs Charlie by the hand and pulls him out onto the dark street.

"I don't want to go back," I say.

"Is that so? Another round of shots at the bar for you, Mini? More Brain Damage?"

"*Nooo.* No Brain Damage ever again. Let's walk," I say and then stumble dangerously over an uneven edge in the concrete sidewalk.

Charlie gives my high heels a dubious look.

"Or let's sit," I offer.

"Alright. Are you hungry? All you had for dinner was green beans."

"Ugh, I know. But no, I'm fine. I ate all my cake, and half of yours, remember?"

He laughs at that. "I figured you needed the calories more than I do. I'm surprised your mom didn't make a note about your dietary preferences."

"I'm not," I say. "She doesn't approve of vegetarians."

He holds my hand as we head over to a nearby bench, near a patch of grass. "No offense, Daisy, but your mom is kind of a piece of work."

I am a little bit offended, actually. I can be very defensive about my mom. It's my kryptonite. But I ignore it, because what he said is true, and because I trust him.

"I know," I say. "But she loves me."

"I believe you," he says, "but she still served you a steak dinner."

"She did indeed." I sigh. "She's just… who she is, I guess. I have to pick my battles with her."

He nods as we sit down, and he wraps his arm around me and pulls me into him, like it's the most natural thing in the world. As though the boyfriend game is still going on. I lay my head back on his shoulder and look up at the buildings of downtown DC.

"What made you decide to come this weekend?" he asks softly.

I take a breath. How to explain my relationship with my mother? The way I'm so protective of her, and feel such a strong need to please her?

"She's my only family," I answer truthfully, and I tell him about her past, my dad who's not in the picture.

"Sometimes I think that after my dad left, she just didn't know who she was anymore. Maybe she never knew who she was. She came from this dirt-poor family, and then when she made it to the place she wanted to be, she was rejected. But she had me, and I think when I was a child, she needed me as much as I needed her."

We look at each other as I explain these truths to him. The sorts of inner thoughts I only share with myself, that are saved for nighttime when I can't sleep, and I've had another phone call from my mom who has expectations of me that I just can't meet and I don't understand.

How did I grow up to become such a different person from her?

Why did I end up being this girl who ran from her mother and her whole lifestyle? Who moved to a part of the country where her only family would never live, and who refuses to accept the trust fund that sits untouched, waiting?

"You know, though, that she can't expect you to always be there, right? You're the child in the relationship. It's great that you're there for her. I really admire it. But she's the adult."

I sigh. "I know that. But part of me feels sorry for her. She's been through so much."

"So have you, Daisy," he says.

We're quiet for a moment. It's a comfortable silence, and I take the time to enjoy his warmth and the feeling of his body around mine.

"I grew up poor," Charlie says, shocking me.

"You did?"

He nods quietly.

"But you said your dad has a place in Vail."

"My dad's 'place in Vail' is really just a one-room cabin off I-70 that you can only get to on foot. He built it with his own two hands on a postage stamp of land that he inherited when I was a teenager from a great-uncle who died. It's sort of a fluke."

"Why did you let me think you were wealthy?" I ask, confused.

The night is cool around us, and the humidity has collapsed into fog. The streetlamps carry a halo of light around them as it refracts off the water in the air. This part of the city is quiet now. The offices are closed, and the few pedestrians that pass us walk dogs who sniff at the patch of grass by our bench and do their business, and then carry on.

He sucks his teeth for a second before answering my question. "I've always been sensitive about being poor, I guess. When I was a kid, I got made fun of for wearing off-brand clothes. You know, like sneakers with four stripes, instead of the Adidas three? And of course, that's not so bad. Kids always get made fun of for one thing or another. But my dad was really stubborn about not being ashamed of it. He worked hard—he's in construction—but my mom's cancer put us into a mountain of debt, and we never seemed to be able to get ahead. We lost the house and moved into a trailer when I was ten, and he only recently managed to pay that off and sell it and get into an apartment. I tried to buy him an actual house—like the one we lived in when I was born—but he wasn't having it.

"Anyway, before the house was gone, we spent a winter without heat, but we had a wood-burning stove, and my dad chopped wood every day to keep it running, and we all camped out in the living room at night. Susan and I slept on the sofa, head to foot, and my dad slept in his recliner.

"I never got to go to the dentist, and when I was sixteen I had a tooth that started hurting, and the pain just got worse and worse until my dad finally took me to the dentist and I ended up having a root canal done. My dad had to ask his sister for money, and then insisted on paying her back every cent."

"I'm so sorry," I say, shaking my head.

"Don't be," he says. "It was harder on Susan than it was on me. She never got to wear the types of clothes all the other girls were wearing, and some of her friends took pity on her and gave her their castoffs. Of course, my dad had no idea what he was doing with a girl in the house. I remember once"—he's chuckling at the memory—"she got sent home from school with a note that she needed a bath, because her hair was such a rat's nest there'd been a lollypop stick stuck in there that no one had noticed. My dad just cut her hair off, like really short. Like, I'm talking he put a bowl on her head and cut it."

"Oh my God!" I exclaim. "Poor Susan!"

"She hated him for it. She still gives him shit whenever she's home. But it's all fine now. The three of us are close."

I feel abashed now, for complaining to him about how I grew up. I never had to worry about food on the table or having a warm bed at night.

"Anyway, when I got to college, I picked the first field that I thought I could be good at that would make a lot of money. And I'm terrible at math." He shudders a little. "So I became a lawyer."

"And that's why you drive a douchey BMW and wear a fancy watch?"

He laughs. "I guess I have a weakness for nice things. I spent so long wanting things that we couldn't afford that I just went for it when I finally could." He looks at me. "Do you find it horribly cringey?"

I don't have to think about the answer. "No. If you were actually the guy I thought you were at first, it would be cringey, but not on you. You're too nice. And you deserve it, after all that."

"I've never really talked to anyone about this before," he says.

"I've never told anyone besides Cara about what my mom did," I reply.

He pulls me in closer to him, his arm tight around me. "I like how small you are."

"Oh God, not this again," I grumble.

"No, I mean it! You just fit right in here," He jiggles his arm to display how nicely I really do fit up against him. I tuck my head in, just under his chin, and inhale his smell. And then I turn my head into him and outright sniff him.

"Body odor?" he asks as he chuckles at me sniffing around his throat like a badger.

"No. The opposite. Whatever you wear smells so good."

"I don't wear anything."

I stop and lean back with my hands on his chest, which is exceptionally firm. "You don't wear anything?" I squint at him in suspicion.

He shakes his head, his arm still around me, like he wants to suck me back into him. "Nope." He laughs at my expression. "This is just what I smell like."

"*Stoppp*," I whine at him. "It's not fair!"

He laughs again, a full, hearty laugh, his face open and relaxed. "What's not fair now, Daisy?"

"You can't just smell this good. It's not fair to the rest of us! You can't just walk around the world smelling like that and expect people to think it's fine."

"I thought you liked it?" he says as he chuckles.

"I do! That's exactly the problem. Maybe if it were a cologne or something then I could say, 'Well, he has really good-smelling cologne', but instead I have to say 'He's really good-smelling.'"

Charlie is looking at me with eyes I haven't seen before. They are serious, and maybe a bit apprehensive. I've scared him. I sniffed around too much.

"Daisy," he says softly.

"Yeah?"

He swallows like he's nervous. "I'd really like to kiss you right now."

My whole body seizes, and at the flinch he begins to release me, but I stop him, putting my hand over his, where it sits at my hip.

"No." I give my head a flustered shake. "I mean, not 'no.' I mean, don't let go."

"O… kay?"

"I mean, I'd like it if you kissed me."

His eyes darken with pleasure. He uses his long arm to pull me back to him, into that space in which I fit so nicely. My heart thunders in my ears, and the butterflies in my stomach are throwing a fit. Every nerve ending in my body is on high alert, and when his hand slides up my back I shiver.

Things are moving in slow motion, and I want them to speed up so I can finally feel the lips I've been staring at since I first saw him up close, but I also want this moment to never end. To be right on the cusp of this forever. To feel this anticipation and yearning and to live inside the heavy look in his eyes as they drop to my mouth.

His other hand slides up and brushes my jaw, tilting my head back. And then his lips meet mine in a gentle slide. They're soft. Just as soft as they look. As soft as I imagined they would be, and a little whimper finds its way out of my mouth as he leans in and his tongue brushes mine.

He's a mix of sweet and bitter, chocolate cake and strong gin, but not in a bad way. In a way that makes heat pool between my legs and makes me want to climb up his body so I can get him more firmly in my grasp.

I run my hand up the back of his head, and the kiss deepens with the slide of tongues as we taste one another, exploring. His breaths quicken through his nose, so that they are nearly as fast as my own, and he runs a finger under the delicate strap of my dress. "This thing was driving me crazy all night," he says against my lips.

"My dress?" I managed to say between a shifting of our mouths.

"What the dress is hiding." He delves back to my mouth again, and we break apart just long enough for him to add, "And showing."

It's good we're sitting because I'm too weak to stand.

He slides a hand up my thigh, gripping me, his fingers digging into my flesh, and I want to straddle him, but we're on a park bench in the middle of the city, and despite the overwhelming lust that's making it hard to think, there's still a thread of restraint holding me together. So I keep kissing him and kissing him, until my mouth is bruised, and my skin feels chafed from the stubble of his evening beard.

He kisses down my neck, all the way to my clavicle, and my head tilts back as I stifle a moan.

"Oh God, Charlie," I breathe.

"I know," he says, "God, I know. I've been wanting to kiss you since I saw that stupid purple suitcase."

I giggle helplessly. "Why didn't you then?" I ask as I pant, and he teases my throat with his tongue.

"*Mmpph*," he replies into my skin.

"What?"

He wanders up to find my mouth again, and I shut up because he tastes so damn good and my head is swimming.

"There wasn't a good time," he says when we finally break apart.

"What about after dinner that first night?" I'm nuzzled into him firmly now, smelling him again, and he's rubbing his hands up my arms and down the ridge of my spine, and running his fingers lightly under the fabric at the back of my dress, sending sparks shooting all over my body.

"You'd been drinking. And you were alone in a hotel, and it just didn't seem appropriate."

I think my chest might burst, and I'll die right on this city bench. "So that explains last night too."

"Yes, it definitely does," he says as he kisses the top of my head. "But God, watching you dance and laugh and tease the hell out of Mark, who thinks you're a smoke show, by the way, made me want to drag you back to the hotel flung over my shoulder."

I know I was drunk, but I still wish he had done it. But Charlie would never have done it, because he's a *good guy*, and that makes things even better.

A cab comes down the street with its light on. The first car that's passed in five minutes, and Charlie leaps up to hail it. We slide into the backseat, and he pulls me back into him and we make out on the whole ride back to the hotel.

We walk into the hotel lobby with our hands entwined, fingers laced, and his thumb strokes mine, up and down, in slow circles.

The lobby is blessedly empty, although some members of the rehearsal dinner cackle at the bar, their laughter echoing out across the marble.

"Come on." Charlie guides me towards the elevators.

We walk down the corridor, and my body shivers. Every place he touches me catches fire, and when the doors to the elevator open and he ushers me in, touching my back, sliding his hand down until it brushes the top of my underwear, I shiver. My nipples tighten in anticipation.

I want more of Charlie. I want his hands all over my body. I want to taste him and smell him and feel him all at the same time. I want to hear his breath hitch with pleasure and agony. I want to know what he likes, if he's soft or rough. Some part of me seems to know that whatever his style is, it'll be mine too.

When the elevator doors close with a thump, then a snick, Charlie turns me and presses me against the wall. Heavy relief courses through me when his mouth lands on mine, eager and hard, nearly aggressive. Our breaths mingle as he devours me, sucking on my bottom lip, grazing me with his teeth. His hands wander, sliding up from my hips, across my breasts and sensitized nipples. I gasp at the surge of pleasure, and then I hitch my leg up shamelessly, grateful for the slit in my dress. I run my hands up strong, lean biceps, and wrap them around his neck, fisting my hands in the soft, curling hair at his nape. He groans into my mouth, and he grips my thigh as I press myself into him. Like it's nothing, he takes me by my backside and lifts me until I'm in the air, pinned between him and the wall. When he rotates his hips forward, I can feel him through his slacks, rocking into me at the same moment he lowers his head to my throat, nipping and sucking and utterly torturing me.

The elevator doors open, and we paint a pretty picture, me splayed against the wall, and Charlie pinning me there, our noses brushing and lips still grazing each other, reluctant to break apart. He presses his forehead against mine for a moment, his breath fast and heavy, before releasing me. I slide to the ground slowly, every inch of my body moving against his, and when he kisses my forehead, I feel him smell my hair.

"I like your smell too," he murmurs, and the vibration of his voice sends a long tingle down the length of my spine.

We walk down the hallway, hand in hand. I'm dreaming. Floating. I'm imagining undoing the buttons of his shirt and pushing it off his shoulders, and the tension of the moment when he unzips the back of my dress. When we get to our doors, sitting chastely next to one another, he watches me swipe my card. His eyes are so dark they might as well be black. I push the door open and step backwards into it. Charlie doesn't move. His hand still grips mine, and he pulls me back into him, his feet planted firmly in the doorway, and glides his hand down my back.

"I had a really good time tonight, Daisy."

"So did I," I breathe as I lean into him and let my lips brush his.

His nose bumps mine, and he turns his head back and forth, doing it again. It almost feels more intimate than all the groping.

I step back again and, again, try to pull him with me.

He shakes his head with a small rueful smile. "I can't, Daisy."

My heart falls down into my stomach. "You can't."

He must see my insecurity transforming my face, because he rushes to add, "I want to. God, I really want to." He runs a hand through the dark hair that I want so badly to have my own fingers in. "But I can't. I just…it's better if we wait."

I swallow, confused, but I nod. "Okay. That's okay."

I step forward, and he kisses me again, tenderly. Soft kisses that make promises he can't, or won't, keep, and then he lets me go.

"Good night, Daisy," he says, and goes to his own door, where I watch as he swipes his card and disappears inside.

Chapter 15

The following morning, I wake up after taking hours to fall asleep. I lay in bed, hyperaware of the fact that Charlie was just on the other side of the wall. It was midnight by the time we'd returned to the hotel, and at one o'clock, still awake, staring at the ceiling in the dark, I heard the hum of David Attenborough's voice coming through the wall from his room. I turned on my own television and flipped through the channels until Attenborough's voice synched up with its counterpart. At least we were doing the same thing, I thought, taking a tiny measure of solace. And finally, I fell asleep.

My room's phone ringing is what brings me to consciousness. I grope around on my nightstand feebly, struggling through the morning haze. I feel through the pile of yarn and Cara's baby blanket. I knock my book onto the floor, and my bottle of eye drops goes too, until I finally reach the phone. There's no caller ID, but I hold it up to my ear, my face still smashed into the pillow.

"Hello?" It comes out as a croak.

I clear my throat to try again. "Hello?" I say, sounding fully human this time.

"Good morning, Daisy." The smile in Charlie's voice is audible through the phone. I smile into my pillow as my stomach tightens with zippy tingles, and now I'm fully awake. Charlie should hire himself out as a wakeup call service. No one would ever be late again.

"Hi," I say, smiling back and snuggling into my blanket with giddy delight.

"Did I wake you up?" His voice is tentative.

"Sort of, but I don't mind."

"Are you in the mood for breakfast?"

I'm in the mood for anything with Charlie Bond.

"Sure," I say, and the line goes silent. "Hello?" I say. "*Hellooo?*"

The line must have cut out, so I set about trying to figure out how to call him back, but there's a knock on my door before I get there.

I stumble out of bed, and walk on tiptoes because my feet are still tender from the shoe abuse I put them through last night, and open the door to find Charlie standing on the other side, showered with rumpled wet hair still sticking up all over the place, wearing dark jeans and a white t-shirt.

His eyes rove up my body. My oversized sleep shirt comes down to the tops of my thighs.

"Donald Duck, huh?" he says as he steps past me. I look down at the cartoon duck on the front of my shirt and then blush as I follow him into the room, grinning like a golden retriever.

"Just give me a minute to get dressed and we can go," I say.

But Charlie is kicking off his shoes and clearing the clothes spread on the other half of my bed.

"Go where?" he asks, looking over at me from where he's bent over, holding an armful of cardigans.

"What are you doing?" I ask.

"Getting ready for breakfast. What are *you* doing?" He starts fluffing up the pillows against the headboard.

I pause and stare at him in confusion.

"We're in a hotel, Daisy," he says slowly, since I haven't gotten the picture yet. "Let's get room service together."

Something in my chest unfurls, like a flower opening for the sun.

"We can charge it to my room." He grins at me as he settles on the bed and pats the spot next to him.

I dive with a running leap onto the bed, and land with a whump into the fluffy blankets and pillows and warm, firm Charlie.

He wraps an arm around me as I tilt my head up to him. His lips come down, and I yelp, "Wait!"

"What?" He sits up and feels around himself frantically like there might be a landmine embedded someplace.

"I just… hang on." I dart from the bed, and scamper into the bathroom where I frantically grab my toothbrush and toothpaste and begin brushing my teeth at breakneck speed.

"You don't have to do that!" he yells from the other room.

Yes, I absolutely do. I just found Charlie. There's no way I'm scaring him off with my morning dragon breath.

I scrub my tongue, and then rinse and spit and rinse and spit again and splash some water on my face and sniff my armpits and wonder if I have time to just take a quick shower.

"Daisy, come back to bed!"

The sweetest words I've ever heard.

I walk back into the bedroom and climb onto the bed, crawling towards Charlie like a toddler. He smiles playfully and grabs my wrists when I get close and hauls me up to him. I squeal as he drags me, stretching my body out until it's next to and flush with his.

"No running this time," he says with a playful smile, and then lands a kiss on my mouth. He folds me into his body, wrapping around me like an envelope and turning me so that I'm on my back, sinking into the down, and he pulls a blanket up over us so that we are completely hidden.

He's over me. The light of morning filters through the blanket and turns everything a dark golden color. He brushes the hair away from my face. "I couldn't sleep last night, could you?"

I shake my head. "David Attenborough."

"Thank goodness for good old David," he replies and then kisses me again, deep this time, and slow, so slow. He takes his time working over my lips. My hands run up his back, feeling the ripple of muscle there, and then down to get a squeeze of his ass. It's a very nice ass. It's a very nice everything.

He pulls back and looks at me, and then kisses the tip of my nose. "The cutest nose," he says.

And then he kisses my cheek. "The cutest cheeks."

It turns out my ears are also the cutest, and my forehead. He peppers me with kisses, telling me how much he adores each part. "The most gorgeous shoulder." "The best throat." "The most perfect chin."

Each sentence makes me feel a little lighter, a little higher. If Charlie were to pull the blanket off us, I would drift away as a pink cloud of cotton candy in the wind. I'm dreaming. And any moment I'll wake up.

But I'm not dreaming, and when Charlie pulls the blanket back I don't drift away. I'm snug and warm and unbelievably turned on with my head tucked into his neck.

"What should we order?" he asks, as though he didn't just give me the hottest foreplay of all time.

"Not hungry," I say as I nuzzle his throat and kiss him and smell him and try to burrow in like a rabbit. Exactly like a rabbit, actually. I feel *very* much like a rabbit right now.

"You ate green beans and cake for dinner last night. I'm feeding you," he says. "Or the hotel kitchen is feeding you. It's the best I can do under the circumstances." He picks up the phone.

Thirty minutes later, I open the door to my room to sign for the food with bruised lips and hair that says I've been having sex all night, although I haven't. I haven't had any sex. Charlie is all mouth and tongue and hands, but it's all over the clothes and my body is throbbing in frustration. Very, very good frustration. I don't remember *ever* being this turned on. I've been grinding myself against his thigh while he tickles me just above my panties and grips my ass to get me closer to him. We've been making out like teenagers in the back seat of their parents' Ford.

The bellman wheels the cart of food into the room, navigating around my detritus, and begins to set things up, but I usher him out in a hurry.

"That's alright, we've got it from here!" I shoot him a crazed smile.

"Aw, Daisy, you should have let him set it up," Charlie says, sitting up in bed when the bellman is gone. "That's half of what you pay for."

I pounce on him, straddling him and wrapping my arms around his head.

"*Prffct brrsts,*" he muffles through my T-shirt before he nips at a tight nipple, and I squeal.

I lean back and pull his T-shirt from the waist of his jeans, but he grasps my hands. "Daisy," he says reluctantly, stopping me in my very determined tracks. "Let's take our time. Okay?"

I give him sad puppy eyes, but he's not caving, so I sit down next to him. We lift the trays off the food and pour coffee.

Since I was refusing to give Charlie my food order, due to acting like a petulant child, he was forced to guess at what I wanted. But he nailed it anyways. A yogurt parfait with berries and granola is waiting for me, as well as the heavenly avocado toast of my dreams that I had yesterday. He's eating an eggs Benedict, and when he pierces the egg, the yolk runs perfect and creamy out onto his plate and blends with his potatoes. He watches it like he's fascinated.

As we eat, Charlie continues interviewing me about my life. What do I like best about my work? What is Cara like? Her husband? Where did my mom take me traveling when I was a kid?

He's attentive. An active listener. Interjecting questions here and there, and waiting when I ramble. This is so easy. Talking to Charlie is like talking to someone I've known forever.

He tells me that his sister is worried about her youngest daughter—she's two and still not talking. His dad's arthritis in his back is getting so bad he's starting to need a walker, and Charlie is wondering if he should broach the subject of assisted living. His last girlfriend, Sarah, broke up with him after they'd been together for three years, and only a month later she was seriously dating his best friend. Two weeks after that she'd moved from her sister's place, where she'd been camping out, and into his apartment.

"I was a fucking wreck," he tells me. "He swore to me that nothing happened until she'd ended things, but I honestly don't believe either of them, and I haven't talked to him since."

"How long were you two friends?" I ask.

"Since we were in sixth grade. He was one of the kids who didn't pick on me for being poor."

Suddenly his hesitance about falling into bed with me makes more sense. He's vulnerable. Realizing that makes me want to kiss him right over his heart.

I grip his wrist, looking at him with a direct, sincere gaze. "I'm so sorry, Charlie. Losing all that at once. I can't imagine."

He gives his head a little shake, with a small, careful smile. "You *can* imagine, Daisy. You're going through it."

And then he pushes me back on the bed and climbs over me, playfully pinning my wrists above my head with his strong hands. From this angle the curve of his bicep is right in my face, and I salivate. He comes down and pecks me on the lips. "So," he says casually, and kisses me again. "What do you want to do today?" Another kiss.

"Stay here? Undress you? Watch you work naked?"

"It's Sunday, Mini."

"Is that an ice cream joke?"

He chuckles. "No work on Sundays. No meetings. No email. My boss can go fuck himself."

I decide to take him seriously and don't make a joke about fucking, because that would be crass, so instead I say, "You willing to spend some time out in the heat?"

"I'm willing to go wherever you want," he replies and kisses me on the forehead. "What were you thinking?"

I know the answer right away. "The National Zoo."

"Good choice," he says. "That sounds like fun."

He climbs off me and I give myself a second to pout at the loss of him before I gather up some clothes and go to the bathroom to change. The temptation to strip in front of him and continue my attempts at seduction are strong, but Charlie seems to want to take things slow, and I understand that I need to respect that.

I comb my hair and pull it up off my neck, and then change into a pair of comfortable, slouchy jean shorts and a loose tank top. When I've gathered the various artifacts that I need before I go out into the world, and stuff them into my purse, I throw it over my shoulder.

"Let's go."

Charlie has been lounging in the bed, eating leftover scoops of yogurt from my parfait and watching a Bob Ross rerun on the TV.

"Alright," he says and hops up.

We cab it to a neighborhood called Woodley Park where we enter the zoo. Charlie holds the door of the taxi open for me, and when I step out into the heat he takes my hand in his, entwining our fingers like it's the most natural thing. We wander down paths between exhibits, moving from one patch of shade to the next, escaping the heat as much as possible. I attempt to focus on what we're seeing, despite Charlie's hands on me, the dimple that appears when he smiles at river otters flipping about, or a cheeky lemur stealing a snack from its friend.

He seems to sense that this is important to me, because he says nothing when I spend a long time reading about the Conservation Biology Institute. So many of these animals are endangered, and the zookeepers here act as conservationists, tracking the genetic history of each animal to ensure that, should it ever be necessary, all of these creatures could be used to save their species.

Finally, we arrive at the pandas, and I'm excited enough to bounce a little bit on my toes when a large, content looking black and white bear loafs across a stretch of shaded grass and flops down on its backside and then rolls over as though preparing for a well-earned nap.

"Is this, like, the ultimate bear sighting for you?" Charlie asks.

I laugh, "It's definitely up there."

We watch the panda making itself comfortable for a while. Charlie stands just behind me, running his fingertips down the length of my arms, so that goosebumps raise across my skin and I shiver, even in the heat. I turn to look at him, my eyes heavy lidded and lips slightly parted. Charlie grips my hand and pulls me behind a tree next to the path, out of sight of the families pushing strollers and children attempting to climb the exhibit fence.

"I just need to get this out of my system." His voice is low, and I raise my head so that his lips graze mine. His body is pressed against me, and I run my hands over his shoulders as I kiss him with increasing intensity. It's almost too much. My desire for him is overwhelming and urgent. When we break apart, with swollen lips and short breaths, we decide it's time to go.

We wander out of the zoo, holding hands, in search of lunch. Every now and then Charlie tugs me into him so he can land a kiss on my head. When we take our chairs at a table under an umbrella on the sidewalk, pedestrians pass in both directions, getting on with their lives, while I sit, enraptured by Charlie's eyes on me. A waitress comes and sets down large bottles of cold water. Charlie orders a veggie wrap.

My heart must be in my eyes because he shrugs at me, "I thought I'd give your way a try."

We both dig into our food, and drink large gulps of water. I'm not sure if it's this heat or just the potently drugging effect that Charlie's presence has on me, but my limbs feel limp.

"Did you get to see everything you wanted?" he asks.

I nod happily. "Yeah. Thank you so much for going with me. I really wanted to see the pandas, obviously, but it was also just so amazing to learn about all the conservation work they do here."

He swallows a bite and takes a drink of water. "It was my pleasure. I liked seeing it too."

He sets his wrap down then, as though he has something important to say. "Speaking of educating oneself, I'm considering a job change."

I put my half-eaten wrap down as my brows go up. "Are you?"

He nods. "I'm not contributing a damn thing to the world. All I do is work for rich assholes to make them richer." The words come out rather more forcefully than perhaps he was intending, because a passing woman looks over her shoulder at him and hustles herself down the sidewalk, and I suppress a smile at the passion in his voice. "I'm envious of you, Daisy," he finishes.

"Of me? My life is so fucked up, though."

He shakes his head. "Everyone's lives are fucked up to some extent. The people around you might be fucked up, but *you* are perfectly fine. You're better than fine. You have beliefs and convictions, and you really care about the world around you." He lifts his veggie wrap as though it's proof.

I raise an eyebrow. "Being a vegetarian doesn't make me a saint, Charlie."

"I know that," he says with a smile. "I was actually thinking more about your family. Your mom is…" He trails off, not wanting to finish the sentence.

I cut him a look. "It's okay. I can handle it."

"She's taking advantage of you," he says frankly. "I don't know a single person who would have gotten up and given a toast like you did last night. That guy Walter kept talking about class in the limo. What you did, *that* was class. And I'm worried that your mom doesn't deserve it. Doesn't deserve everything you're putting yourself through *just for her*. I don't think your mom even came up to thank you. Am I wrong? Has she acknowledged what a huge gesture that was?"

I bite my lip and look at my plate, fidgeting with my napkin. "You're not wrong. She hasn't," I say.

"Why do you put yourself through so much trouble for her? After what she did?" He's leaning forward, looking at my face even as I try to hide it.

"I don't know," I say to him, "I just feel so *guilty*. She *needs* me, and I already left her and went to Colorado, and she just… I just can't stand it when I let her down."

"Let her down? How have you let her down?" Charlie's brow is creased, and he twists and untwists the cap to his water.

I'm getting frustrated. Irritated, not at Charlie, but at the conversation. That I'm in this situation. That I can't ever seem to stand up for myself, even when I want to. That my mom doesn't appreciate me, or approve of me, and I know it, and yet somehow, I still let her get away with *everything*. That I live a strange sort of double life—the person I am when I am in Denver is not the same person my mother sees. All these things—my personal beliefs, my mother's value system, the way she treats me, the way I can't seem to extricate myself from her expectations—they are all somehow bound together, and I haven't been able to parse them out. Whenever I try, all I feel is guilt.

You're a doormat, a little voice in my head says. *But she needs you,* says another. My eyes well with tears and I fight them, but one escapes and glides down and dangles from my chin. I dab at it impatiently with my napkin and attempt to explain what I'm feeling.

"It's kind of like, as I grew up, I became the parent. My mom takes fine care of herself, and she has all the resources in the world to do it, but emotionally, she's just… off. When I went to college and decided to stay out in Colorado she was devastated, like I was leaving her. And she's so incredibly worried about how people see her, and she wants me to fit this mold that I just can't fit and that I don't want to fit. And I know it bothers her. She wishes I were different. So, I try to make it up to her in other ways, but it never seems to work. Or at least, it never seems to be enough."

My mom has been pushing and pushing for years, expecting me to be there for her, expecting things from me that aren't really fair to expect from another person, worrying about the impression *my* life will make on *her* friends. It doesn't make any sense, and yet, I don't know how to stop it.

Cara sees it and has told me a thousand times to just put my foot down, but it's not that simple. You don't just abandon people you love because they don't turn out to be the sort of person you think they ought to be. My mom took good care of me as a child, and maybe it's just my turn to take care of her.

"I just think…" I start. "Maybe she just needs some looking after now, and I need to be tolerant and patient, the way parents are tolerant and patient with their children."

But the toll that tolerance and patience has taken on my life is adding up, and it's reaching a point where I don't know if there even *is* a line that can be crossed that will make me stand up for myself.

There has to be a point, right? Where you realize you need to put yourself first and you stop compromising who you are to suit other people? I don't want to live in the state of willful ignorance that my mother and her friends choose. I don't want to enjoy money if it means exploiting people more vulnerable than myself. I want to feel like I'm doing something worthwhile with my life, and I don't want to be looked down on for it.

I rub at a little spot of rust on the table in front of me, "Maybe that's what unconditional love is all about, though. Giving that person what they need to be happy, even if it comes at the expense of your own self?"

That's how it feels right now, at least. It feels like my mom expects me to bend and bend, and contort myself into the daughter she wishes she had. And then, when I finally began to figure things out for myself, to build my own life and my own future, she tried it on for size and decided that she liked it. It feels like I had something good, and she wanted it for herself, regardless of what it might cost me. And yet, I'm still here. Giving her my blessing to marry Rob's dad. Giving her my blessing to continue living her life the way she always has.

Where is the line?

Charlie's lips are pressed tightly together, and he scratches his chin. "I'm not an expert on love. But I don't think unconditional love means sacrificing yourself. And I'm not sure it's fair for you to take all of that on your shoulders, Daisy. Your mom is an adult, and you are her child," he repeats himself from last night, but I don't mind. "Those roles shouldn't be reversed. And it's not fair of her to expect you to live your life to suit her demands."

I nod sadly. "I know. I just need to figure out how to get myself out of this guilt, and then maybe I'll be able to start setting some boundaries for myself."

Boundaries. It's Cara's siren song. She is *very* into boundaries, and she wishes that I was very into boundaries. But I'm terrible at them. Once someone, or something, is in my heart, it's all the way in. No half-measures.

"Are you alright?" Charlie asks, reaching for my hand and lacing our fingers together. "Can I do anything?"

"You've already done so much, Charlie." I give him a feeble smile, and his eyes warm.

"I'm just going to say this," he says, and he looks very intense. Perhaps a little bit nervous. His fingers keep working the cap of his water bottle. "You don't need to be any different from who you already are. You're pretty spectacular." I snort, and he ignores me. "If she can't see that, then it's her failing. Not yours."

The words are simple, but they floor me nonetheless. For a brief stretch of time, I allow myself to sink into his gaze. I study his soft eyes and mouth, his lovely nose and jaw. He's beautiful and thoughtful and he's filling up my heart which has been so empty, broken to pieces and put back together again like an urn that will never quite be the same. Somehow, with Charlie here, everything has felt, if not great, then at least okay. Survivable. And there's something else too. With Charlie standing next to me, the idea of just being who I am doesn't seem nearly so frightening.

Charlie suggests that we go back to the hotel. It's nearing three o'clock, and the wedding starts at six.

"I know you need a lot of time." He grins at me. "But I have to admit, if an hour and a half is what it takes you to look the way you did last night, I'd wait every night, forever, just to get to see you in that dress again."

Chapter 16

We go to our separate rooms back at the hotel, after we kiss thoroughly just inside my door. And then he scoots me in the direction of my bathroom. "Go get showered," he commands.

I wrinkle my nose. "Do I stink?"

"No, you smell like you. It's driving me crazy." He kisses and nuzzles my throat again, and I lean my head back, indulging in the tingles that make me shiver. "I need you in perfume STAT, or I'm going to haul you to the room on the other side of that wall." He nods at our shared wall.

"Well, in that case…" I move to the door to the hallway, and he gives me a little push back toward the bathroom, laughing.

"Shower. Hot dress. Perfume."

I go laughing, and he sends me a wink as he closes the door behind him.

The dress I chose is a little bit shorter than I remember, and the back a little bit lower. But it's a perfect fit, and the high neckline makes up for the extra leg, I tell myself. Once I have my hair twisted up into a chignon with about a million bobby pins, my gold, dangly earrings in my ears and my ultra-tall heels on my feet, I decide not to wait for Charlie to come get me.

He opens his door with a toothbrush hanging out of his mouth and a mouthful of toothpaste.

His eyes widen and roam over my body shamelessly. "*Mmmfffggg*," he says.

The goosebumps that I thought I'd gotten under control return with a vengeance.

I saunter in, my confidence soaring to unseen heights, and Charlie disappears into the bathroom. After the water runs for a moment and I hear him spit, he's back.

"Sweet Jesus, Daisy," he says with a look of real concern. "You're so gorgeous I'm going to be struggling not to kiss you all night."

My chest squeezes almost painfully.

"Why wouldn't you want to kiss me?" I blink innocently.

He waves a hand up and down my body in a sweeping motion. "I don't want to mess up all your hard work."

He's looking delicious, his skin still slightly damp from the shower. He's put some sort of product in his hair that makes it somehow look both tousled and sexy and tidy at the same time. A pale blue tie hangs around his neck, undone. His shirt is untucked from black slacks and the top three buttons are open, so that a triangle of tanned skin is only just visible. Just enough for me to want to put my lips there, at the hollow between his collar bones. I could spend a week studying each part of him. I would slide my hands over his shoulders and chest and back, kiss my way to his navel, and live there for a while. I want to bury my face in his hair, until I become inured to his scent and am able to function properly again when he's around. Although I'm not sure that will ever be possible.

"You can mess it up," I say. "I don't care."

It's the first time in days I haven't felt stressed about this wedding—about how I'll look or what people might be whispering when they think I don't see. I've almost forgotten that my mom is going to officially become Michael's wife in a matter of minutes now—the wedding is set to begin in exactly thirty.

Charlie holds his tie up from his neck and looks at it. "Hang on," he says and opens his closet doors where a hanger of neatly draped ties displays a multitude of colors. It's exactly what I expected his closet to look like. Rows of pressed shirts and slacks. A few suit jackets. Three pairs of shoes are lined up in neat rows like ducklings.

"How about this one?" He turns and looks at me, holding a slim, blue tie with little white dots stitched into it. "It'll go better with the dress, right?"

I grin at him. It's perfect.

He disappears into the bathroom again, and my feet are already feeling pinched from the shoes, so I sit down. My dress can have creases. I don't care. *It doesn't matter.* If people think I don't look perfect, it's not my problem. Everyone can stare at me and comment on the dress all they want. It doesn't matter.

Charlie emerges after a minute, shirt tucked in, tie neatly done. He goes back to his tidy closet and pulls out a black suit jacket and hitches it up over his shoulders, and buttons the top button.

He turns to face me. "Is this good? Will Mother approve?"

He looks incredible. Tall and handsome. His freshly shaved jaw is cut like marble. "*Everyone* will approve. Especially Peg."

He chuckles as he walks over to where I'm sitting on the edge of his bed.

"There's been something I've been meaning to ask you."

A zing of apprehension runs up the back of my neck. "What's that?"

He takes my hand. "I know these two people who happen to be getting married, and I was wondering if you'll be my date."

My head falls back as I laugh. "Are you asking me out, Beamer? Even though I'm an old lady in a twenty-six-year-old body who likes to knit and drags all her worldly belongings with her everywhere she goes?"

"It's called crochet," he says pointedly, "and yes, that is exactly what I'm doing. I'd like to be your *real* date. No pretend."

I lean in and kiss him on his soft lips. I'll have to reapply lip gloss and he'll need a tissue, but it doesn't matter, because he's Charlie, and I'm quickly discovering that I can't *not* kiss Charlie.

He runs a hand affectionately down my back and toys with the spot where the dress meets my skin. "No pretend," he says.

We get up to go downstairs, and while he wipes his mouth clean, I go to my room to grab a tube of lip gloss—clear this time—and swipe it across my mouth.

"Okay. Let's do this."

"Nervous?" he asks. "Filled with dread?"

I think for a moment. I might be a little bit nervous, but the sense of dread, I realize, has been dissipating since yesterday. Since Charlie and I sat down and went over our story for the rehearsal dinner. I smile. "No. No dread."

His eyebrows rise, and he looks impressed. "Alright. Let's do this, little Mini."

I lift a foot to display my towering shoes. "Not mini. Medium."

The wedding is on the second floor of the hotel, where the ballroom is located, and a sweeping terrace is shaded with an elegant white canopy.

We file in with the rest of the guests, drawn to our seats by ushers, and I make brief eye contact with Walter and Peg. Peg waves enthusiastically, but Walter gives her hand a downward tug and she vanishes into her chair. We take our seats at the front. As predicted, the wedding is enormous. Michael is well respected, and my mother makes friends easily, so I imagine their social circle is substantial. Judging by the guests already present, the guest list must have included well over two hundred names. A stunning array of pink flowers arches over the minister and the spot where they'll say their vows, and white linen curtains are tied back at each corner. Michael's brother, Uncle Jack, stands to the right, with his hands clasped in front of him.

Charlie sits next to me and grips my hand in his lap, stroking my wrist with his fingertips, sending tickles up my arm. Rob and Gabby sit on the other side of the aisle, and she has her hand placed between his shoulder blades. For the first time I feel happy that Rob has someone here, supporting him, too. I think, if it weren't for Charlie by my side, I wouldn't be as calm and self-possessed as I am at this moment.

Music from a string quartet rises and falls, and then a woman with a headset dressed in all black darts over and whispers in the violinist's ear and the music transforms into Pachelbel's "Canon in D." The low hum of the guests' whispers sinks away. A little girl, Michael's grandniece, comes toddling out through the double doors in a white cloud of a dress holding a little wicker basket filled with petals. Her round hands drop clumps of pink on the white carpet and stops at one point to pick one off a man's shoe where it landed.

"I'm sorry," she chirps in her light child's voice, and everyone smiles and *awws* as she finishes tottering up the aisle where her mother takes her by the hand and kisses her proudly before leading her back to their seats.

Then, my mom's matron of honor, Lydia, proceeds down the aisle in pink to match the flowers, and stands opposite Michael and his brother, waiting for the bride. And that's it. The doors to the building close, and all rise. After a beat the doors open again, and my mother emerges, stunning in a narrow white lace dress with fluttery little cap sleeves and a sweetheart neckline. She's radiant, her smile wide and eyes shining. My heart swells at the sight of her. Her happiness is undeniable, and it's beautiful to see. It's the first time since I learned of her affair that I feel truly, genuinely happy that she's in love. Despite everything that's happened—our difficult, tangled relationship, her demands and her needs, and the shame and guilt— in this moment, at least, my heart is full of nothing but love for her.

She glides down the aisle, her eyes fixed on the front where Michael stands, his own gaze locked on her, and the chemistry between them, the affection and love, radiates and sweeps through the onlookers like a gust of wind.

Unexpectedly—unbelievably—my eyes fill with tears.

"Their chakras are aligned," Charlie whispers into my ear, and a little laugh-sob bubbles up and out of my lips. I don't have a tissue. I never anticipated this and came unprepared, so I'm swiping below my eyes with my fingers, and a woman behind me taps me on the shoulder and passes me a hankie. I take it gratefully and dab at my face and my nose. My mother passes her bouquet—peonies and tumbling orchids—to Lydia, and turns to face Michael, who watches her with nothing but tenderness.

Maybe this is what it's all about, after all. I don't know what Michael's marriage to Rob's mother was like, but life is short. It's a fleeting moment. A flash of brightness that vanishes back into creation before the universe even takes note. Maybe, when happiness finds us—when we find our person—we just have to take it and be grateful, and not question it too much as the fates weave into existence whatever future they have in store for us. I don't know what my mom has been looking for all these years, but maybe she's found it in him. Maybe she really did find her home, at last.

The vows are beautiful. They've each written their own, and my mother talks about the moment she knew she was in love with him, and Michael tells her she's everything and promises to spend the rest of his days working to make her happy.

When they walk down the aisle together, her veil slips from her elegant updo, and she grabs it, laughing, and tosses it over her shoulder, more carefree than I think I've ever seen her. The photographer catches the moment in a snapshot that will be worthy of a frame.

I sniffle, and Charlie gives my hand a squeeze to make sure I'm okay, and I give him a squeeze back to let him know that I am. I'm okay. We're going to be okay.

The guests mill about in the ballroom, sipping champagne and cocktails, and nibbling on passed hors d'oeuvres. Peg attempts to track Charlie down, and we flit about the room, dodging her while I giggle at Charlie for getting himself into this mess. He pulls me behind a human-sized arrangement of hydrangeas and presses his lips against mine in a soft glide that makes me giddy, and I slide my arms around his neck. "Thank you," he whispers against my mouth. He presses his forehead to mine. "For letting me be here with you."

I never imagined this. I never imagined being so happy on this day. Being so full, with love for my mother, tenderness and laughter and something else that I don't understand and am afraid to question blooming within me. A fragile, tender sprout emerging from the hard soil, still frostbitten from winter, but softening and warming with the sun.

We emerge from behind the towering floral arrangement, and Rob comes over, looking downtrodden and miserable. He has circles under his eyes like he hasn't slept, and Gabby grips his hand in hers, and she smiles although it doesn't quite reach her eyes. She still looks spectacular, and I tell her so.

"Dad wants us for photos," Rob says to me. "Just us."

I look to Charlie. "Are you going to be okay by yourself?"

He gives me his wicked grin that I know means he's got something up his sleeve. "Peg is right over there, and I think Walter might be bored, so I'm going to be just fine," he says. "Go have this moment."

I walk off with Rob, a distance between us like we're strangers, leaving Charlie and Gabby alone together, and I can't believe I'm not bothered by it. But I'm surprising myself this evening.

Before we reach the terrace, where I see my mother and Michael through the open doors, smiling as Michael dips her, and the photographer's shutter snaps as fast as a typewriter, Rob stops. He turns to look at me. He's wearing a tortured expression.

"What's going on?" I ask. "You look terrible."

"Gee, thanks," he says. "You, on the other hand, look beautiful. You're glowing."

Maybe I am. Maybe I'm finally coming to terms with this. With the bizarre family dynamic that I'm going to have to find a way to live with. I don't want to let go of my mother. And things between us aren't okay, but I want her to be happy. I always have.

"How can you be so happy, Daisy?" Rob says with accusation in his voice. "I watched you tear up during the vows. You looked like you did at Cara's wedding. But this is just so…" He snorts in frustration and breaks eye contact for a moment before returning his gaze to me. "He *left my mom for her.*"

I sigh, rubbing my hands down the sides of my dress. My little clutch dangles from my wrist and bumps against my thigh. "I don't know why I'm okay with this right now, Rob. But I guess I'm just realizing that we have two choices. We can decide to accept what's happened and move on, or we can be bitter and resentful and push them away. Neither choice will change what happened, but going with the first one might just stop the bleeding."

He grips his hair in a fist and turns away in exasperation before looking at me again. "She *destroyed* our relationship, Daisy. Look at her." He frowns in her direction, "It's like she doesn't even realize. Or she doesn't even *care* what she did. And you are just okay with that?"

I shake my head. "Deciding to come to terms with the fact that it happened isn't the same thing as being okay with it. I'll never think what they did was right. Not completely, at least. But I think I might be finished being angry about it."

I don't know if that's entirely true. There's still so much for me to figure out. But I can't keep being filled with the shame and resentment that's been eating away at me like lye. None of this was my fault. Nor was it Rob's. As Charlie has said repeatedly, she is the adult. Michael is the adult. It's not the kids' jobs to figure it out.

He frowns deeply. "You're just enabling her. You always did. You were always afraid of making her unhappy, or trying so hard to make her happy and then hating yourself for bending over backwards for her. Your speech last night, and the way you're smiling and… celebrating…" He closes his eyes, and his lip curls in disgust.

But it's not just her, I think. It's Michael too. And it's *certainly* not me. Whatever my relationship is like with Mom, it didn't cause this. It's a separate thing. If Rob thinks it was just my mom, and her alone, who caused this, and if he thinks I somehow let it happen, he's lying to himself. But maybe that's what he needed to tell himself to bring himself to be here today.

I take a breath. Both frustrated and sympathetic, because while I understand his feelings, they can't be my cross to bear, and I realize I can't allow him to blame me just because it makes him feel better. I have a right to protect myself.

I huff a short breath, and steal myself for a moment before I speak. "Rob, I'm not the reason your dad cheated on your mom. I'm not the reason *our* parents had an affair. Your dad was part of it too. And," I add pointedly, "I am not my mother. You keep seeming to forget that fact. You've *been* forgetting that fact since we found out about this whole thing. It's time for you to get it straight and accept it. This isn't my fault.

"I'm here, just like you, trying to muddle through this thing and come out the other side in one piece, with my relationships intact and my heart still beating. So, I'm sorry if I don't have time for you to question my choices. You made yours already, and when you did that, you lost the right to question mine."

Rob pales slightly and shoves a hand through his blond hair.

"Shit," he mutters under his breath. We stand for a drawn-out moment. I watch him drag the toe of his shoe across the floor. The sound of the photographer's hectic photoshoot has died down, and I imagine we're being missed, but I wait.

"I'm not okay, Daisy," he says finally. "And seeing you with…" He glances back to the ballroom where Gabby still stands waiting for Rob, and Charlie has meandered into the crowd. "Seeing you with him made me realize exactly how much we both lost."

I worry for a moment that he's going to ask to get back together, and I can't believe that the possibility of him doing that has somehow stopped being a pleasant one.

"You know, Rob," I say, "it's okay for you not to be okay. I know how loyal you are to your father, but you're allowed to say no. You don't have to be here. If it's too hard, he's not entitled to your presence."

Somewhere in my mind Cara's voice is cheering and gloating, telling me that these are the things I should have been telling myself all along. Why have I never managed to articulate these things until I just said them to someone else?

"You're right," he says with a heavy sigh. "I know you're right, Daisy. I'm sorry. I shouldn't be laying all of this on you right now… and I'm sorry for walking away. I just… I couldn't."

"I know," I stop him. "You don't need to apologize for ending things, Rob. I'm alright."

"I can tell." His eyes shift back to the ballroom where Charlie is undoubtedly now threatening Walter with an offer to read his aura. "It was just so complicated with us."

I don't need him to go over everything that happened again, but if he needs to, I can listen.

"And who knows if we would have even been able to have a healthy marriage," he says, and I nod in agreement. "I mean… we're stepsiblings now."

We both pause and look at each other, and a hysterical little laugh slips out as the absurdity of it washes over me yet again. Rob chuckles ruefully.

"Well, after this wedding, Christmases are really going to be a hoot, right?" I try to lighten the mood, but Rob doesn't laugh.

"I'm just still so messed up about this," he says, "and I keep trying to leave, but Gabby is asking me to stay, and I'm confused. How could he betray her like that? How can I keep being his son after all of this?"

He's talking about his mom. But he might as well be talking about my relationship with my mother. Because what she did, what *they* did, *was* a betrayal. They put themselves before their children, and they put Rob and me in a nearly impossible situation.

"I don't know," I answer honestly. "People do stupid, selfish things sometimes. And the rest of us are left to clean up the mess. But if you don't want to clean up the mess, Rob, that's okay. You don't have to. If you need to leave, you should go. You should take care of yourself."

As I talk, I begin to really believe the truth of my own words. It's easy to know something on an intellectual level; it's another thing to believe it in your heart.

Chapter 17

When the pictures are finished, and Rob and I have had photos with each of our parents alone, and then together, when we've awkwardly stood and pretended like we're all a big happy family, Rob and I return to the reception. A few minutes later Michael and Mom are announced as Mr. and Mrs. Nielsen, and the ballroom erupts in applause and wolf whistles.

We sit through dinner, and I'm served *another* steak, and Charlie and I laugh when we swap our food around. Gabby rubs Rob's back in what I now recognize as a consoling motion. It's the six of us again—Rob and Gabby, Astrid and Tyler, Charlie and me. Our conversation is fairly easy, even though Rob clearly doesn't feel much like talking. It's an elegant affair. The flowers are costly and beautiful, the food is excellent—at least, the non-meat portion of it is—and each guest is gifted with a little authentic Tiffany ornament, not unlike the one my mother brought to Rob's parents the first time they met. Walter must be over the moon about this. And then the string instruments setting the ambience for dinner wind down as a DJ comes in and the dancing begins.

Charlie sweeps me up from my chair. Naturally, he's a great dancer. And he's my date—my real date, not pretend. We boogie goofily to the Chicken Dance, flapping our arms and strutting about like roosters and we line-dance to the Cha-Cha Slide, both of which I am *extremely* surprised were not on my mother's "do not play" list. I swell with pride to be the girl on his arm when he twirls me around and my skirt flutters dangerously around my thighs.

When the music slows, we stand almost still, and he kisses my brow and pulls me into him, his hand cradling the back of my head, just underneath the twist of my hair. I press my nose into his throat and inhale him, and kiss him there.

I'm lost. I'm getting lost in him. I'm not unaware of the fact that what's happening between Charlie and me is at least partly responsible for my comfort tonight. When you feel like this, it's hard to have room for any other emotions—especially anger. Charlie and my desolation have been competing for space, and Charlie is winning an easy fight.

My mother tosses the bouquet, and Gabby catches it and goes dancing over to a startled-looking Rob. But then he grins and kisses her, and as I rest my head on Charlie's shoulder, I smile to myself. I want Rob to be happy. It took me a long time to get to this point, but I seem to have finally arrived, and it feels good.

After a while, Rob and Gabby vanish. Slowly, the guests thin out—women carrying away flower arrangements tucked in front of them, attempting to be stealthy about it like thieves in the night, but it's hard to be stealthy with three-foot orchid branches bobbing all around you. By the time only the most dedicated dancers remain, Charlie and I are red-faced and sweaty, and my shoes were long ago discarded so I could move without pain or risking serious bodily injury.

My mom is swaying with Michael, hearts in her eyes as she looks at him. They look happy. She looks peaceful. When they cut the cake, he fed her a piece delicately, and then she smashed his slice right into his beard and everyone laughed with delight. He still has little flecks of frosting on his chin.

"Should we go?" Charlie asks softly into my ear. His eyes, and the way he's running his fingertips down the length of my spine, tells me that, yes, it's time to go. I nod at him and go to pick up my shoes and purse, and we leave, making our way through the heavy wooden double doors, and out into the corridor beyond.

We're moving in slow motion, like wading through water. The sounds of the wedding reception drift away as the anticipation in my belly mounts. I can't wait to be alone with him again. It doesn't matter how slowly Charlie wants to take things, I'm here for it. His hand lingers at my bare back, and then slides up so that it's around my shoulders and I'm tucked into him. He leans over and kisses my hair. I hear him inhale my smell. "Perfect smell," he says, and I evaporate.

We're in the elevator, and my body vibrates. I bounce a little on my toes.

"What are *you* all worked up about, Mini?"

"I'm really looking forward to another round with David Attenborough," I say.

He laughs softly as he pulls me into him. "What if I suggested we give David the night off?"

My heart turns over in my chest at the meaning behind his words, and I lose the capacity for speech for a brief moment before replying, "You don't think he'd be offended?"

"If he saw you, he would understand."

His lips land on mine and I try to climb him, wrapping my arms around his shoulders and lifting a leg all at once. He chuckles against my mouth, and then flat-out picks me up so that he's holding me with his hands clasped on my backside and presses me against the wall, eliminating any space between us. We've been like this before, making out like horny teenagers, but this time it's different. The urgency is there, but there's no rush. We have all night with each other.

When the elevator doors open, he sets me on my feet and leads me by the hand down the corridor, towards our twin doors. What was fate thinking when it brought us together in this way? When Charlie was led into my life at the time when I needed him the most?

Charlie slides the key card and opens the door, and I don't even bother getting mine out of my bag. He's leading me in backwards. My eyes never leave his. There's so much tenderness. So much care. So *much*. The door swings closed behind us.

I expect him to want to undress me. To unhook the straps where they meet at the back of my neck and let my dress glide down my body. But instead, he pulls me into him, and we tumble sideways onto the bed. My shoes fly from my hands. My clutch rolls across the carpet. He wraps his arms around me and pulls me into him. I nuzzle him, envelop myself in his smell. Kiss his neck and savor the salty taste of his skin.

"I'm so glad I found you, Daisy," he says into my hair as his body shivers under my mouth. "You don't even know."

I do know, though, because Charlie hasn't just been my savior this weekend. He's awakened something in me. Some newfound belief in myself, and gratitude for the things in my life that matter. That are meaningful.

"I do know, Charlie. I do, because I feel the same way you do," I say as I kiss his throat.

The tip of one of his fingers finds my chin and tilts my head up, and my nose bumps him. His hand slides up to my jaw, and he holds the side of my head as his lips find mine. It's a tender kiss. Gentle and reassuring. I inhale deeply through my nose, and then release it as I open my mouth for him and his tongue slides against mine. My thigh glides up over his, and we lie like that, kissing, tasting each other, inhaling each other, until I feel his breaths develop into pants through his nose.

"Daisy," he murmurs, and I think he's about to put a stop to things, but instead his hand moves to my back, and he pulls me closer. He turns and takes me with him, rolling me so that I'm on top of him and in control. My thighs straddle him as I lean down, and he groans when I grind my hips. Heat is pooling in my core. An urgent need, unmet for days, flaring to life. This whole evening was foreplay. This whole *weekend* with him has been foreplay. Every time he grazed my skin, or ran a finger down the line of my back, or whispered something in my ear that made me laugh, he had me biting my lip. He grips my hips as I move against him, and our breaths are both fast and shallow. "Oh God," I groan as I move on him, sending sparks of pleasure shooting through me.

"Take my shirt off," he says into my mouth with short, staccato breaths. "Is it okay if I take my shirt off?"

I nod and lean back as he sits up. We're face to face, my legs wrapped around him. I work the top buttons around his throat, while he handles the ones at his wrist, and then he peels his shirt up over his head, revealing his tanned, firm chest, dusted with coarse hair, light from a summer spent outdoors. I kiss him across his jaw, down his throat and his hands slide from my hips up my back, splaying across the span of my shoulder blades, and then down again to trace the line of my underwear through the silk of my dress, at the crease between my thigh and hip. He pulls back and looks at me seriously, both the question and answer in his eyes. *Can we? I think we can.* The only thoughts I have now are coming as feelings. My heart filling, my body throbbing, the need to touch him and feel him on me. In me.

I reach for the hook at the back of my neck, holding my dress in place. "Is this okay?" I ask. His eyes are dark. The rings of his irises just a sliver of green around wide pupils.

He nods. "God, yes." He watches me intently as I reach back to unfasten them. He slides his hands up my legs, from my ankles, over my calves, tracing circles around my knees, and then his hands glide up. "I hate this dress, Daisy."

I squirm impatiently as he runs his fingers under the strings of my underwear.

"I mean it," he says. "I was hard all night. Even when I was talking to Walter. It was a nightmare."

I start to laugh, and then stop as he lifts the dress over my head, so that I'm bare before him, utterly exposed. My breastbone is being battered so hard by my heart that it might break.

He tosses the slip of fabric to the side, and then he starts to laugh.

"What is it?" I ask. I run my feminine to-do list through my head at lightning quick speed. Everything shaved, polished, waxed.

"What are those?" Charlie asks, looking at my breasts, and a rush of relief and giggles pour out of me.

"I forgot." I laugh. "I forgot I was wearing them."

He runs a finger along the edge of a nipple cover, and goosebumps spring up all over. "Can they be removed?"

I shake my head seriously. "No, Charlie. I'm afraid they're permanent."

He bites my neck and digs fingers into my ribs, and I squeal with giddy delight.

"What are they?" he asks again, peppering my face with his lips.

"They're nipple covers."

I help him peel one off, and then the other. There's a ring of red flesh on each of my breasts, where the glue was, but I barely have time to feel self-conscious before Charlie has his mouth over one of them and my back is arching at the sensation of his warm, wet tongue sending tingling shivers through my body. "Oh God," I breathe into the air as my head tips back.

He kisses each of my breasts, running his tongue over the sensitized skin, and I shiver. "Perfect breasts."

The rest is easy. He flips me back over so he can shake himself out of his shoes and pants, and I lift my hips for him so he can slide my underwear down and off. He spends time there, listing his favorite parts as I blush and giggle until his tongue touches me, and I lose the capacity for speech altogether, and all I can do is pant and moan and arch with shaking legs until I fall to pieces.

He hovers over me on his elbows, my legs spread around him, my arms sliding up his back as we kiss each other hungrily. My hands wander, exploring him. Learning his body. And then there's a foil packet, and Charlie pressing into me as I gasp at how good it feels. How good *he* feels.

We move together, rising and falling like the waves of the ocean. The world has fallen away again, and all that exists is us. His eyes dark and the cords of his neck visible as he hangs on to his restraint.

"Fuck, Daisy," he moans.

"I know," I breathe back.

He slides his forearm under my backside and lifts me up off the bed, moving his hips into me, first at an easy rhythm, until I start begging for more—faster and harder, until neither of us can hold on a second longer and we come apart together. First me, and then him, falling, falling, down into something deep and thrilling and, for me at least, far more than an orgasm.

I lie with my head on his chest as our breaths calm.

"Perfect sex," he says.

"Perfect sex," I agree.

Chapter 18

We wake to Charlie's alarm clock going off. It startles me, and I sit bolt upright from where I'd been lying with my head on his shoulder.

"Shit. I'm sorry." He scrambles through the sheets and shuts it off.

He leans back over to me. "I have a meeting, but it's in the hotel."

He moves to kiss me, and I turn my head because of the dragon breath and it lands on my cheek.

"Oh no, you don't." He laughs and grips my cheeks in his hands so I can't escape, and kisses me again, firmly on the mouth and I relax into him, unable to resist his touch.

"Why do you have a meeting?" I whine at him. "It's Labor Day. Isn't the point that you're supposed to be *not* laboring?"

He shakes his head ruefully as he stands before me entirely naked. "There's a big deal about to go through. I'm lucky I only have to be there for the first part. This place is going to be swarming with lawyers all day."

"Oh no," I say in horror.

He goes to the bathroom and I hear the shower running, and then he gets dressed with clipped efficiency. "Don't move. I'll be back in two hours. Order breakfast."

"Don't tell me what to do." I pout at him, and he grins before he grabs his wallet and laptop bag, and he's gone.

It isn't until I'm alone that last night comes rushing back to me. There's a post-wedding brunch at eleven o'clock, and I ruminate over the idea of going. It's seven now, so Charlie should be back by then, in theory.

I wrap myself in one of the robes from his bathroom and poke my head out into the hallway, to avoid any awkward encounters with wedding guests, before I sneak over to my own room. The contrast between Charlie's tidy room and the mess I've created is startling. And when I go to the bathroom to go through my morning routine and look in the mirror, I'm met with horror.

This is what Charlie has been looking at since last night?

I didn't bother to wash my face when we got back, and my carefully crafted smoky eye has turned into two inky black runs down either side of my face. The hair that I was too horny and then too exhausted to deal with came unpinned in my sleep and has turned into a squirrely nest of brittle, hairsprayed straw on the top of my head. My skin is strangely blotchy, and when I open my robe, I find my nipples ringed by two angry red circles, like terrifying, bloodshot eyes. I must be allergic to the glue on those pasties, because the flesh is slightly raised with little bumps like hives, but at least they don't hurt.

He's such a liar, I think, with all his talk of perfect breasts and eyes and ears. I look like the girl from *The Ring* if she'd been dolled up and sent out to meet people. All I need to do is crawl through a television screen and the effect would be complete.

I set to work attempting to undo the damage. I'm determined for Charlie to return to his room to find a living human waiting for him. So, I get in the shower and scrub my body clean. I shave everything, yet again. I wash my face once and then stick my head out to check the mirror, and wash it once more. I pull bobby pins from my hair one by one and lay them on the marble ledge meant for soap, and lather in shampoo, rinse, and lather again. It takes a bucket of conditioner to get the tangles out.

I attempt to clean the remaining glue off my breasts with a washcloth and soap, and when I'm out of the shower I tend to them with lotion and make a mental note to stop at a pharmacy to get some cortisone.

When I'm finished, with my hair wrapped up in a towel, I put on a clean pair of fresh underwear and then put Charlie's T-shirt that I slept in back on, because it would be insane for me not to spend as much time inside of his smell as possible. When all of my work is done, and my breath has been restored so that I don't risk an attempted murder charge if I accidentally talk to someone, I go back to Charlie's room.

The whole project took an hour, which means I have an hour to go before I get to see him again. I'm giddy and impatient, and I struggle to pay attention to an episode of *The Office*. You know things are bad when Michael Scott can't distract you into forgetting about the clock. I pick up the phone and order room service and ask them to wait until nine o'clock before they deliver it, so I can eat with Charlie.

Finally, the time passes, and I hear the robot noise of the door's lock sliding open. Charlie's brow is furrowed and he generally looks stressed, but when he sees me, his face relaxes into an easy smile.

"You showered," he says.

"I can't believe you were going to just let me continue to exist like that without saying something!" I accuse him.

He laughs and comes over and draws me in for a kiss. "You looked perfect."

"And now?"

"I can't tell a difference," he says, shaking his head. "Did you do something? Did you change your hair?"

"*Stoppp!*" I protest. "I could have been arrested walking around like that!"

"Don't worry, Mini, I would have bailed you out, and then I would have hosed you off." He sets his bag down and kicks off his sensible airport shoes.

I giggle and scoot over in the bed so he can get in next to me.

"Did you eat?" he asks, glancing around the room for a room service tray.

"Food's on the way," I answer. "I got you the eggs Benedict again. How was the meeting?"

He rubs his forehead with his thumb and forefinger and shakes his head. "Horrible."

"Really? What happened?" I turn so that I'm sitting cross-legged, facing him.

"My firm is representing a business trying to acquire another, and neither side will budge on their demands. And to be honest, our client is being a real prick."

I frown. "I'm sorry."

He's silent for a moment, his elbows resting on raised knees, as he stares at Michael Scott attempting to revive a CPR dummy.

I watch him as he thinks. He's wearing his lawyer face.

"I'm going to quit my job," he says.

"Are you?" I lean back as I study him.

He nods. "I've been thinking about it for a while, but I've been too afraid to take the leap."

"What changed your mind?"

He looks at me, "This weekend. You."

I shake my head vigorously. "Oh no. Don't do that. Don't quit your job just because I think I can save the world. That's a *bad* idea, Charlie."

"I was thinking about it before this weekend too. It's not just because of you. But remember in the taxi when you asked if I work for the bad guys?"

"Yeah." I nod my head slowly, waiting for him to continue.

"Well… I do. I really, really do. And I don't want to anymore. And there's probably some things I should tell you about my work—"

The knock at the door interrupts him, and I grab a robe and go to answer it. It's the same bellman who brought my food in when I forgot to put on pants, and he looks relieved to see me dressed.

I let him wheel the cart in and set the food out, since my body isn't screaming at me to mount Charlie as soon as possible, although I do plan to do so in the not-too-distant future.

I sit down in front of the little in-room dining table and grab a fork. "What did you want to tell me?" I ask, looking back at Charlie where he's still sitting, leaning against the headboard of the bed.

"Nothing." He scoots forward to join me. "It's not a big deal."

We eat in silence, both hungry after all the sex and the morning without food.

"So, what do you want to do with the rest of the day?" he asks.

The fact that we are going to be spending the day together is a given. I don't even need to ask. It's our last day together. His flight leaves tomorrow morning. I'm headed back the day after. We haven't discussed after. Not yet. But I think there will be an after. I hope there will be a lot of after.

I'm enamored with him. The way he touches me in public—not possessive, but protective. So I know he's in my corner. He has my back, both literally and figuratively. I love watching him think. The way he read the information about each animal at the zoo, and the way he nodded when he'd finished and I could see him filing the information away and prepare to shift to the next one. And his attentiveness. The degree of consideration he has for the people around him. The fact that he wouldn't even kiss me when the chemistry between us was already so strong it had become combustible, because he was concerned I was in too vulnerable a position.

I set my fork down with a strawberry speared on the end of it. "There's a post-wedding brunch in an hour. We could go drink awkward mimosas with Diane and company."

"Would *you* like to do that?"

I shrug a shoulder. "Do I want to? Not necessarily. But this whole thing hasn't been as bad as I thought it would be, and I think I should."

So, of course, Charlie agrees to go with me. I love having him here, but I don't need him here. Not anymore. I'm okay, I think. If Charlie got called away on a moment's notice, I would be fine.

The brunch is on the patio where Charlie and I first sat at a bar together, but a banquet has been set out with a buffet overflowing with every food imaginable. A chef is making to-order omelets, and there's a raw bar. Charlie and I beeline it towards the bartender offering Bloody Marys and mimosas and, for some particularly poorly situated attendees, something called a Bartender's Breakfast.

The sight of Tyler, more than a little ashen, standing next to Astrid, makes me decide that I should just ask for a watermelon juice.

Rob and Gabby are sitting at a table in the corner with plates full of eggs and toast, and Charlie and I go over and join them.

I look around the patio, but I don't see Mom or Michael anywhere. Maybe they're having a post-wedding lie-in. I put the kibosh on that train of thought right then and there. Nothing good lies down that road. Gross.

"Good morning." Gabby smiles at us, and even Rob manages to lift the corner of his mouth. "Not eating?" Gabby asks. She's been carrying the conversational baton rather heroically, despite a few speedbumps.

"We ate in the room." I glance over at Charlie who appears proud of the fact that I let it drop that we spent the night together.

"We should have done that," Rob says.

"Oh, but this food is so good!" Gabby says cheerily and gives his shoulder an encouraging squeeze.

Tyler and Astrid sit down with us shortly after we arrive at the table, and we all scoot our chairs together to fit them around the four-top. I take a corner since I'm not eating, and Charlie squishes his chair up next to me so that Astrid can fit in on his other side.

"A little worse for wear?" Rob asks his cousin.

"Dude." Tyler rests his head in his hand. "You have no idea."

"Tyler decided it would be fun to go out to an after-party," Astrid says. "And apparently—this didn't come from Tyler, by the way, because he was too drunk to remember—someone thought it would be a good idea to play a drinking game where they took a shot every time they said 'Jose Cuervo' to a song *called* 'Ten Rounds with Jose Cuervo.'"

This is funny enough that even Rob starts laughing.

Astrid holds her hands out in disbelief. "I mean, who on the planet Earth thinks that that's a good idea?"

Tyler stifles a gag and forces down a sip of his Bartender's Breakfast. "I'm never drinking again," he says miserably.

"Said everyone with a hangover, ever," Gabby adds.

"When do you guys head out?" Astrid asks the table.

"Our flight is this afternoon," Gabby says and leans in like she's sharing a secret. "Michael treated us to business class."

A resentment box gets ticked in my mind, but again, to my continuing surprise, I no longer care.

"Lucky," Astrid says with a note of envy. "We leave tomorrow afternoon. I'm going to Diane's ladies' spa day."

Gabby sulks a little. "I wanted to, but Rob has to get back to work."

"How are you guys spending your last day?" I ask Astrid.

"We were planning on hitting some museums," Astrid says. "But I think that's going to be a solo venture now."

Tyler has given up entirely, and he's now resting his elbows on his knees, hanging his head, taking slow, deep breaths.

"I can't," is all he says.

"You can't what, honey?" Astrid asks, reveling in punishing him for his sins.

"Continue existing," Tyler moans.

A man walks by with a large plate of oysters, and that's when Tyler gets up in a hurry and speed-walks towards the bathrooms.

"Is he going to be okay?" Rob asks, watching him cross the room, dodging a woman holding a plate piled high with shrimp.

"Fine." Astrid waves a hand. "This isn't the first time Jose Cuervo's come calling. But I should probably go make sure, just in case." She smiles apologetically at us and rises to go nurse her ailing husband.

"When do you guys go back?" Rob asks. He seems to have brightened a little bit and I'm encouraged.

"I leave on Wednesday morning so I can do the spa thing and have some time to collect all of my belongings."

Rob and Charlie both chuckle, and Gabby looks between them. "What?"

Charlie throws an arm around me. "Daisy has a pathological

inability to travel without bringing everything she owns along with her."

"It's a pretty serious condition." Rob nods. "Specialists will be required."

"It's okay, Daisy. I overpack too," Gabby says in solidarity.

Rob and Charlie exchange a glance, and their attempts to stifle their laughs fail.

"It's not that bad," I say to defend myself, even though it is.

When we get up to leave after saying goodbye, and Rob actually offers Charlie his hand to shake, Gabby asks me to hang back a second.

We stand behind a topiary of an elephant and donkey shaking hands.

"I just wanted to say, I'm sorry if I was a little awkward at first." She fidgets with a charm bracelet on her wrist, running her fingers over each little ornament before letting it drop.

"Oh, Gabby, you weren't, of course not," I start to dismiss the apology.

"No, I was." She grabs my wrist. "I was really defensive. It was just hard, walking into this really bizarre family dynamic and feeling like the fifth wheel. And you're Rob's ex-fiancée and I know the only reason you two split up was because... well, you know."

"To tell you the truth, I don't think that's the only reason we split up," I tell her sincerely. "It was insane, if I'm being perfectly frank, but if Rob and I had really been on the same page, we could have found a way through it. Rob and I just weren't each other's people." I shrug a shoulder, like it's just that simple.

"You think so?" Gabby asks.

"Yeah, I do," I answer. "And I think Rob is crazy about you. I think he's going through all of this so you can be included in a big family event, and he wants you to be a part of his family."

Gabby's big blue eyes fill with tears. "That means so much, Daisy. And if we're both being honest here, it wasn't until I saw how in love Charlie is with you that I stopped feeling so insecure. But you two are smitten."

"Oh, I don't know about that…"

"I do," she says firmly, "The way he looks at you, when you don't realize it. It's like seeing someone falling in love over and over again."

My expression grows serious as I attempt to maintain my composure, even as an eruption of fireworks in my stomach make me feel faint. A champagne-fizzy feeling overflows up into my chest, right up to my heart, and then I can't help it: a smile breaks out over my face.

"See?" she says and starts to go.

"Wait." I stop her, collecting myself. "I'm sorry too. You weren't the only one feeling defensive and left out, Gabby. I shouldn't have said those things at dinner. And I apologize."

Never in a million years would I have imagined that Gabby and I would leave this wedding as friends.

She smiles softly. "That's alright, Daisy. This hasn't been easy for any of us." And then she gives me a hug with her long slender arms that I hated her for and that don't bother me one bit now. She has beautiful arms.

"I guess I'll see you at Christmas," I say, and she laughs at the realization, that keeps coming over us all again and again, that while this wedding is over everything else is just beginning, and we are going to have to learn, and keep learning, how to be a family.

"I guess so," she says and raises her eyebrows at me, and then goes back to join Rob at their table.

Charlie and I leave brunch and wind through the restaurant out into the lobby.

"So, what do you want to do? It's only noon," Charlie says, "You feel like a museum?"

"Not really," I answer.

"You want to go back to the room?" He raises an eyebrow at me and gives me a filthy look that makes me drag my bottom teeth between my lips.

"How do you read my mind so well?" I ask.

He taps his head with his pointer finger. "It's not a perfect brain. But it's pretty good."

"Daisy!" a voice echoes after us from across the lobby. "Daisy!"

I turn around and see my mother striding towards me with long, intent steps. Her heels echo sharply on the marble floor. My grasp on Charlie's hand loosens at the look on her face as she approaches. A thunderstorm rumbles behind her eyes. Adrenaline shoots through me, clearing the haze of the dream I'd been walking through just moments before.

"What did you say to Walter Peterman?" she demands in an angry, hushed voice.

"Who?" I ask in confusion until realization dawns on me, and if it weren't for the look on her face I would already be laughing.

"Walter. Peterman," Mom says in a clipped tone. "He seems to believe you're dating some… guru or something. And you're moving to a *commune*?"

Next to me, Charlie's shoulders start to shake with laughter, and it's catching. I'm laughing too. Heavy belly laughs that have me bending over and gasping.

My mom stands there, aghast at our display.

"It's not funny." Her eyes are rimmed in red, as though she's been crying. She grips me by the arm in a bruising grasp like I'm six years old again and drags me into the little library side room where Charlie first consoled me.

"Ow! Mom, stop," I protest as I stumble after her.

"What did you say to him?" she demands.

"I didn't say anything," I answer honestly, all laughter gone now. Charlie stands just outside the door looking conflicted. Unwilling to intrude but unwilling to leave me.

"You must have said *something*. He came up to me this morning and said he was *sorry*. He felt *sorry* for me, Daisy! Can you imagine? I'm humiliated, on my wedding weekend!" Her tone is ferocious. Angrier than I remember her being since I told her I was going to work in environmental conservation, like, as she put it, a "hippie." "How could you do this to me?"

Do this? How could I do *this*? To *her*?

"What? Mom," I attempt to calm her. "Who cares what Walter thinks? Just tell him it was a joke."

"A joke?" she says in disbelief, as though the possibility is offensively absurd. "Walter sits on the board of Citibank, Daisy. He's very important in my social circle. You know how much this weekend meant to me. *Everyone* is going to be talking, and I needed you. I *needed* you to be the girl I raised you to be this weekend. Was that really too much to ask?"

The familiar guilt comes pouring back, my mother's insecurity and need for acceptance sluicing cold water over my head and erasing any of the warm feelings I'd managed to nurture into life. I open my mouth, on the cusp of begging her not to be angry with me. About to go offer to apologize to Walter myself.

Charlie has walked into the room, closing the sliding doors behind him, and he places a protective hand on my shoulder. The moment I feel him, it breaks me out of the shame spiral. How could I do this to *her*? How can she not *see* what I've gone through to try to make her happy?

And it hits me all at once, in an unwelcome, hard realization—I will never live up to her expectations of me.

I'll never be the daughter she wishes I was, or the person she hoped I would become, because that girl that she imagines is someone else entirely. I will never get her approval. And every time she does something to hurt me, I will have to be the one who picks herself up. Who dusts herself off and who lets it go. I can wait forever for an apology. It won't be forthcoming. I will forever have to shrug off hurt after hurt after hurt, and my mother will continue to believe that I am the one who is letting *her* down.

"Daisy didn't do anything, Mrs. Nielsen," Charlie says, defending me. "It was me. I was just pulling his leg a bit, and it got a little out of control. I had no idea he would take me so seriously. I'll go tell him myself."

My mother dismisses him with a shake of her head. "This isn't the first time Daisy has disappointed me like this, Charles." It's very like her to use formal names when she's angry.

She turns back to me, her face white, her eyes steely. "You owe me an apology, Daisy. Right now."

Charlie's hand on my shoulder tenses. "Daisy has been *exceedingly* gracious throughout this entire weekend. If you're embarrassed it's my fault, not hers," he says firmly.

"No." I shake his hand off. Not because I don't want him here, but because I need to stand on my own two feet. When I say this, it needs to come from me alone. Not me and Charlie.

"Charlie didn't do anything wrong. And neither did I. We were having a little fun. It was a completely harmless, innocent joke. It's not like someone pulled their pants down at your ceremony. No one died. You're blowing this completely out of proportion."

Her eyes widen at my backtalk.

"If you're embarrassed," I continue, undeterred, "it's *your* fault. Not mine. And certainly not Charlie's."

"You think this is *my* fault?" she gasps, pressing her manicured hand to her chest, missing the point entirely.

I fight the urge to stamp my foot into the ground. To grab her shoulders and shake her.

"Do you have any idea how hard it was for me to come here this weekend, Mom? Do you have any idea what I've been through over the past year? No. You don't," I say, my temper building. The need to say all of the things that I've been holding back, all at once, pushes away any desire to keep this calm. "Because Diane Nielsen, previously Thomas *only* thinks about herself. I'm not your accessory, and I'm not your emotional support animal, and I'm *definitely* not your showpiece. I'm your *daughter*. And you hurt me, Mom. *You* hurt *me*. Not the other way around."

My mother's face darkens.

"When you and Michael—"

"Oh." She waves a dismissive hand. "Don't bring him into this, Daisy."

I throw my arms out. "How can I not? How can I *not* mention the fact that your relationship *ended* my relationship? How can I not mention the fact that while you enjoyed your engagement, I was picking up the pieces of my life, as was Rob, as was Michael's ex-wife? I don't understand you, Mom. I don't understand how you don't see anyone but yourself!"

"You told me," she says, pointing a trembling finger at me, "that you were okay. You told me that you and Rob had been having problems. You told me you weren't even sure you should have been engaged to begin with!"

It's true. I did say all of those things. After Rob and I ended, I questioned the relationship heavily. We could have been happy together. But there were already cracks, and what our parents did deepened those cracks until the whole thing shattered. But that is so, so not the point.

"You're right," I say, "I did tell you all those things. But I shouldn't have. I should never have given you an excuse for what you did. And yes, our relationship wasn't perfect. But it was our relationship to figure out. The position you two, our own parents, put us in was completely unfair. And then you both expected us to just… be okay with it? To celebrate with you? You are so lucky that Rob and I were even here this weekend."

I never should have suggested to my mom that the fact that there were problems—private problems that we *maybe* could have worked through, or maybe we couldn't—made what she did okay. I never should have let her off the hook. But that's what I've *always* done. I apologize for *her* actions. Or I find excuses for them to make myself okay with how she behaves. What Rob said last night was true. I've been enabling her, and it's time for it to stop.

"Mom, I don't *care* that you feel embarrassed right now, because what you did to me is so many times worse that there isn't even a number large enough to describe it. It… it was…" I stutter, flustered and angry, as I search for words to express a quantity large enough, but find that none exists. "It was *infinity* times worse," I spit at her, even as I choke back tears, swallowing a lump the size of a baseball that has lodged itself in my throat. "Infinity!" I say again, for good measure.

As I've ranted, my mother has shrunk. Back into a girl. Back into the version of herself that comes to me when she's feeling lonely and I'm the only one who can save her. The only one who can tell her she isn't alone or abandoned.

Once, when I was in college, she called me in the middle of the night on a Friday in tears, because she believed no one in the world loved her, and even though I had an important exam to study for, I caught a flight back east at six o'clock that morning and spent the weekend consoling her. Reminding her that I would always love her.

That remains true. I do love her. I always will. But I can't live my life for her anymore. I can't continue to bear the weight of her pain or make excuse after excuse on her behalf when she hurts me.

"Daisy," she pleads as I begin to turn away from her. "Oh, Daisy, I'm sorry. Forget the whole thing. Let's just be friends again."

But I can't forget. It's all too real. Too visceral. I want her to be happy, but it can't be at my expense. Not anymore. I look at her as tears course down my cheeks.

"I'm not your friend, Mom. I'm your daughter."

"Daisy, it's my wedding weekend," she implores.

I gesture in the direction of the hotel restaurant. "Go and have your wedding brunch. Enjoy it. But I'm finished. I'm done."

I turn away from her a final time, and walk across the lobby to the elevators, and Charlie follows, at my side as he always is. We don't speak the whole way back to our rooms. In the elevator, I slump against the wall with exhaustion as the adrenaline in my blood ebbs. Charlie says nothing. He doesn't touch me, as if he knows I'm already on sensory overload and it would be too much. When we reach our doors, we stop. "Do you want to come in? Do you want to talk?"

I sniff and wipe a hand across my nose. I want to curl up and sleep for a thousand years. I want my own pillow in my own bed. I want to forget the generous feelings from yesterday, when I was so awash in happy hormones that an earthquake would have felt like a carnival ride.

"I want to come in, but I don't know if I want to talk," I say.

He nods. "Okay."

Charlie moves me about like a marionette. He sets me on the edge of the bed and slips my shoes off my feet. He pulls back the duvet, and I climb in, pressing my face into the cool pillow and pulling my knees up to my chest, just like I did in that same little library room a few nights ago, and he tucks me into the blankets, pulling them up to my chin and pressing the edges in around my feet. I laugh-sob as he does this. A little flicker of light in the darkness.

"I'm glad I can at least make you laugh a little bit, even though you're hurting."

"You can always make me laugh, Charlie."

He removes his own shoes, and slides into the bed behind me, wrapping his arms around my body and holding me against him. His heart thumps against my back in a steady, reassuring rhythm. I'm shaken by what just happened. I shouldn't have let my guard down with her. I should have expected something like this. The warmth that I felt towards her yesterday is draining away, leaving me feeling like a discarded doll, battered and worn, forgotten in the bottom of a child's toy chest.

Charlie's breath skates across the back of my neck, warm and soothing. He rubs a hand up and down the side of my arm, reminding me that he's here. He's got me. He always seems to. He keeps picking me up, and encouraging me, and urging me to believe in myself. To be okay with *being* myself. When he stepped in between my mother and me, there was something so protective about him. Like he couldn't stand to see her go after me. I love him for that right now.

That thought warms me, and with the steady thump of Charlie's heart at my back, his breath gently tickling me as it moves about the hair at my nape, his arm firmly settled around me now, holding me close to his heat, I fall asleep.

Chapter 19

I don't know how long I sleep for, but when I wake, I'm in the same position. And Charlie still has his arm around me, like he's been holding me in place, protecting me from any more battering. He must have gotten up at some point, because the curtains are closed, and the room is dim and cave-like. Like I've retreated from the world, gone into hibernation. I breathe in deeply, not quite a yawn.

"Are you awake?" he says softly, almost a whisper.

I wriggle and turn in the bed in response, so that I'm facing him, and I tuck my head under his chin. He kisses me my hair, and I nuzzle in.

"I'm sorry," I mumble.

"Don't be," he says. "How do you feel?"

"Exhausted," I say as I smell him. "Sad. But otherwise okay."

He kisses my forehead.

"You were magnificent. You're so strong, Daisy. I wish I could be like you."

His hand rubs circles between my shoulder blades. "You're such a beautiful, strong girl. Funny and clever and bright. I don't see how she doesn't see that. But I do. And everyone else does too."

"I just wish she loved me," I say into his chest.

"I think she loves you, in her own way. You wouldn't have so much power to hurt her if she didn't care."

Tears run sideways from my eyes and form a wet spot on the bed, and on Charlie.

"I'm making you all snotty."

"I love being snotty," he answers. "It's my favorite thing. Next to being your fake boyfriend."

His nose is in my hair, and he gives me a nuzzle. "Perfect girl," he whispers.

I lean my head up to him and kiss him, and he seems hesitant at first, like I'm too fragile. But his mouth softens and then his hand slides from my back to my hip.

We undress each other slowly, wordlessly, sitting up in the bed as we take each other in. His T-shirt goes over his head, and then mine. Our lips meeting again and again between each gesture. He unclasps my bra, and winces when he sees the angry skin of my breasts, still red and inflamed.

"Does this hurt?" he asks.

I shake my head. He kisses each breast tenderly, like he might be able to make them all better. Like he can make *me* all better. Like he can heal the wounds in my heart and soften life's blows.

I can't fix this for you, he says with his mouth, *but I wish I could.*

The sex is slow and languid. His forehead barely leaves mine as we gaze at each other. My lungs are filled with him. My body. My heart. Until there isn't any more room for pain. Just Charlie.

When we are finished, I finally look at the clock. I slept for three hours.

We lie facing each other. He strokes my hair back from my forehead, running strands through his fingers and toying with the ends. Our feet are tangled together, my knee tucked between his.

"How are you feeling?" he asks me.

I'm feeling confused. How can pain and pleasure coexist this way? And how is Charlie nudging out the hurt and replacing it so that, while, yes, I'm sad and the wound is there, its impact is not nearly as profound as it would be? He's sharing it with me. He's carrying some of the weight, and it's something that we go through together.

When the blowup happened with the family, it had created a fracture between Rob and me. Like we were standing on two different ships, sailing away from each other. The hurt and angst we both felt so keenly did nothing but push us apart. He withdrew from me, like there was no more room when he was so consumed with darkness. It subsumed him. It stole him away. And eventually, I think I became the thing that he resented. He resented my attempts to keep things whole between us. My insistence that we could love each other enough, that nothing else mattered.

The way Charlie looks at me now makes me float. Makes my insides soft and melty, and I don't understand how I came to feel this way so quickly. It's frightening.

But I don't say any of this to Charlie. I don't want to risk this fragile thing that exists between us. I wrap it up like fine china and tuck it away inside of myself.

"I'm feeling… hungry," I say. "I could eat. How about you?"

Relief passes over his face. "That's a good sign that you have an appetite. Let's go get some food."

We get dressed, our clothes wrinkled from being in bed, but neither of us bothers to even mention it. It doesn't matter. We walk through the hotel looking like vagabonds, and Charlie takes me to the place where I ran into him after I saw Gabby and Rob for the first time, just down the street.

We step into the dark bar, the neon beer signs casting blue and red light across the room. A placard at the front asks us to please seat ourselves. We pick the same booth where we sat last time, and our feet lock under the table, my one foot between his, like not touching each other isn't an option.

A surly college kid who looks like he spent the whole night in the library comes and takes our orders, and we both ask for beers. Charlie orders a burger and shoots me an apologetic look.

"Don't apologize." I laugh at him with our server still standing there looking impatient. The veggie menu isn't exactly robust, so I get a basket of fries and a garden salad. Strange combination, I know, but I'm in need of the comfort food and a salad alone isn't gonna cut it.

"So," Charlie begins when our orders are placed, and we're sipping the foam off our beers, "I was wondering, when we get back to Denver, if I can take you out to dinner?"

A flutter erupts in my stomach, and I'd like to lean across the table to kiss him.

"You mean like a real date?" I say with my best coy face and flutter my lashes at him.

"Just like that."

"I don't know… I thought this was just a fling," I say as I rub the condensation off the outside of my glass of beer with my fingertip.

"Like a vacation friend?" His grin goes lopsided.

"But I guess I'll take you out for a test drive in Denver."

"Please, no more road-rage incidents if you do."

I give him an evil smile. "Buckle up, Beamer, because Mini Cooper is about to be back in action."

My heart is lighter now. The altercation with my mom has faded away into the background. Charlie and I could sit here and do the postmortem, but instead we chat and flirt.

"You never told me what you like to eat, besides ice cream and vegetables."

"I can eat French," I say, "but I love Italian."

"Done," he says. "Endless breadsticks are in your future, Daisy."

"Can we get ice cream after though?"

"For my flavorite? Anything you want."

Our food arrives, and I shovel French fries in like I'm coming off a diet.

"Do you think it'll be weird? When we're back in Denver?" I ask. I'm trying to picture him in a different backdrop, when we both have jobs to attend to and friends that, if all goes well, will need to be introduced.

"There's no way it'll be weird. Not after this. This is weird. Denver will be a cinch."

"I'm not going hiking with you," I blurt out. "At least, not a lot. Maybe on your birthday. If we make it that far."

"We will," Charlie says confidently.

"I hiked with Rob, but I don't like hiking. I like to jog and go bike riding, but I don't want to pretend to be into hiking."

I hiked with Rob for the same reasons I've done so many things—because I'm addicted to pleasing the people around me. And I've decided I'm going to stop doing that.

He leans forward in his seat with a conspiratorial look. "Daisy, you don't have to hike with me—you shouldn't do anything you don't want to do just to make other people happy—but there's something you should know."

I tilt back a little, apprehensive. "What's that?"

He's going to tell me he's about to hike the Pacific Crest Trail and he's going to be gone for four months. I just know it.

"I don't like hiking either," he confesses.

"What?" I break out in another laugh. "Then why did you say you did?"

"I didn't say I *like* hiking," he points out. "I just said that I hike a lot."

I raise an eyebrow at him as I munch on a French fry and pick up another. "Why," I point the fry at him, "would you hike if you don't like it?"

"Do you remember what I told you, about how Sarah and I split up?"

"Of course."

"When that happened, and I essentially became a non-functional human being, I started developing all this restless energy. But I didn't want to have to talk to anyone. I just wanted to be alone, so I started hiking. It always felt like a chore, but it also cleared my head. When I was sweating it out on the trail and hating every minute of it—it truly feels like punishment—"

I nod enthusiastically at this statement.

"It matched my mood, and eventually, after enough time slogging away, it would empty my mind. And I would come home so exhausted that I could sleep at night."

I frown at the thought of Charlie—sensitive, considerate Charlie—feeling so terrible that he had to punish himself just to get through life.

"I'm sorry you had to go through all of that," I say sincerely.

"It's alright." He slides his hand across the table to put it over mine. "In the end, it was good for me. Spending a lot of time alone let me do some soul-searching, and I learned a lot about myself."

"Like what?" I ask.

"Like that I don't like hiking, for one thing. And that I hadn't been happy for a long time before the breakup happened. Ultimately, it turns out, the thing that hurt the most was the way it happened."

I relate completely.

We walk back to the hotel. It's around four o'clock in the afternoon, and despite it being a holiday, the traffic is heavy and people in business attire mingle with vacationers on the sidewalk.

"How about a movie?" Charlie asks as we stroll hand in hand.

"At a theater?"

"I was thinking in our room."

Our room. I smile to myself.

"I think that sounds great."

We walk through the glass doors to the hotel, opened for us with a smile and a nod from a uniformed man, and I remember to thank the gods once again for the invention of air conditioning.

"Charles!" a man's voice calls us, and Charlie pauses.

"Oh, hi, James," he says to the middle-aged ginger man swinging a briefcase in corporate attire. "You just getting out?"

"Yeah, the meetings dragged. So much for the long weekend. But you know." He shrugs. "Billable hours."

Charlie chuckles. "Don't I know it." He looks to me. "Daisy, this is my colleague, James. He works in the DC branch of my department, with Mark. James, meet Daisy."

I give James a wave.

"Nice to meet you, Daisy," James says with a polite smile and a passing glance before turning back to Charlie.

"I've gotta get going. My wife has been texting me non-stop all afternoon. We were supposed to take the kids out on the boat."

Charlie says farewell, and just as James turns to leave, he stops and turns back briefly. "Hey, by the way, man, great job on the Matchless Mountain deal. Alex said you were a real bulldog."

Matchless Mountain.

The words hit me like birdshot, stunning and visceral. Charlie was on the Matchless Mountain deal? The deal my team and I worked so hard to stop. The land we petitioned the governor to try to get the state to purchase and turn into a park. The deal that I spent the last six months pouring my heart and soul into, while I hid myself from my imploding personal life. The project I told him about. He knew I was the lead on the project, that it was my brainchild, that it crushed me when I failed.

James is walking from the lobby, out into the sunshine of a beautiful, carefree afternoon.

I turn to look at Charlie, and I see his face falling in slow motion. I release his hand. My ears buzz. He was on the deal. He knew, this entire time, that I had been on the other side, that I was the one he defeated, and he never said a thing. I rifle through memories as I watch Charlie's hands come up. His lips part and he inhales, ready to try to explain.

My jaw falls open. Everything is happening as though I'm watching from somewhere else.

I see Charlie in the cab, telling me he works for the bad guys. Charlie telling me he wishes he could do something courageous. Charlie telling me he wants to quit his job. Charlie telling me he has something to tell me, and then never actually doing it.

This was it. This was what he wanted to say, and he didn't have the guts. In fact, when Mark tried to talk about their work at the bar, Charlie put a stop to it. He lied to me. He lied by omission and let me fall apart in front of him and pour my soul out about my most personal, deepest secrets, while he knew that he'd been working against me and the things I believe in, all this time.

A horrible, nauseating notion comes over me. What must he have thought of me, knowing I was the one he defeated? Has he been pitying me? Thinking of me as a fool? He claimed to be a man with convictions—he told me he admired me. Maybe he's been lying about more than just what he does for a living. Maybe he's been lying about how he sees me. About the sort of person he wants to be. Maybe I was just an easy target. A silly girl with silly ideas, not someone to be taken seriously, respected, regarded as an equal. Not someone entitled to know the truth of our connection. He slept with me, all while withholding this information from me.

I pinch my eyes closed, shaking my head, wanting to say something but unable to speak.

"Daisy," he says as he reaches for me. "I wanted to tell you."

I take a step back, away from him.

"But you didn't, Charlie. You didn't tell me." I'm shaking my head at him. "You knew how much that meant to me, and you didn't bother to let me know who you really were."

"Daisy." He sounds flustered. "Just give me a minute to explain. Can we just go upstairs and talk? Please?"

The pleading look in his eyes makes me want to go, and then Mom's pleading look comes back to me and I realize I can't. I can't listen to him tell me why this is okay. I can't listen to him explain away an omission of this size. I can't put my own feelings aside when I'm this hurt.

"I didn't know," he's saying as I shake my head and take another step backwards. His voice echoes across the lobby, and a few lingering hotel guests are looking at us. "When you told me you'd been working on that campaign, I didn't know how much you'd mean to me. How important you would be."

"It's okay, Charlie." I force a hollow laugh. "Of course you didn't know. How could you have known?"

He nods slowly, like he might be making some headway. He holds his hands in front of him like he's trying to negotiate with a feral animal.

"But I did mean something, didn't I?" I ask. "I thought I did. You meant something to me at least, Charlie. I told you everything. I let you in, completely." I press my hand to my chest. "You meant something to me, and I thought this was starting to mean something, whatever it was."

"Don't say that. Don't say *was*."

There is fear in his eyes, his brow creased and his lips downturned. I can see his mind working, trying to figure out a solution, trying to find an angle he can use to bargain his way out of this.

"This was just a vacation fling, right? I wasn't important enough for you to be transparent with me. I wasn't important enough for you to take a risk."

"No!" he nearly shouts. "It's the opposite. You were too important to take the risk. I was scared. I was scared you would hate me and refuse to talk to me. And think that I'm some… soulless…I don't know, monster or something. That I don't have a conscience."

The loitering hotel guests have stopped whatever they were doing, and are watching us with curious, intrigued eyes. This will make for good gossip later. I couldn't care less.

"Do you?" I ask. "Do you have a conscience? You pushed the deal through." I sneer, "You were a real bulldog, apparently."

I don't know if I'm being fair. I don't know what kinds of lines to draw around myself. I've been a doormat for other people for so long that I don't know how much to accept. How much give and take and forgiveness I need to offer. I wish Cara were here, to tell me how to draw boundaries in the proper places. I don't know how to do that yet. I've never learned. But there is one boundary I know that I need to establish——that I began to establish with my mother this morning—and it's that I won't apologize for who I am, and I won't accept being used or taken for granted. Not anymore.

He opens his mouth to plead with me again, but I stop him with a hand. "Please, Charlie. Just don't. I can't. I can't think right now. There's too much going on already."

Charlie exhales hard, as his head drops forward and his eyes squeeze shut. The look of hurt on his face nearly breaks me. He looks like a dog that's been kicked.

"I'm just so sorry, Daisy. I'm really, really sorry."

I speed walk to the elevators, forcing myself not to run. I hit the button and look back. Charlie is standing in the same place in the lobby, his bereft hazel eyes following me, but he doesn't move.

Chapter 20

I don't start to cry until I'm in my room. And then, big, wet, choking sobs take over. They wrack my body as I lie in my bed, in the middle of the clothes strewn carelessly about the room. I press my face into a cool feather pillow to muffle the ugly sounds that I'm afraid Charlie will hear from next door if he's in there. Between the fallout with my mom and Charlie's revelation, I feel like I'm drowning. Underwater, too deep even to see the surface, holding air in my lungs for as long as I can before I'm forced to release it and see the last bubbles of oxygen rise into the black, out of reach. Alone, no life raft in sight.

I grasp my purse with trembling hands and call the only person I have left. The person who has picked me up a million times and who I trust like no one else in the world.

She answers on the first ring. "Daisy?" she says with concern. I never call without texting first. We only talk on the phone when there's a story too big to tell with our fingers.

"Cara," I say through gulps of air, "I need to tell you something."

Cara listens patiently on the other end of the line as I unload about the whole weekend.

I tell her about Charlie, about how we met and the spark, and the fake date, and then the real date, and how something was happening between us, and then everything was happening all at once. I tell her about my mom. The prank on Walter and how she flipped out on me, and the way that Charlie was by my side when I finally stood up to her. I tell her about Charlie's omission. What he hid from me and how much it hurt to hear those words from James's lips, and how badly I wanted to just brush it under the rug and tell him that it was fine. But I couldn't. I just couldn't this time.

When I'm finished, Cara is silent. In the background, I hear her mother's voice saying something. I didn't even ask her if now is a good time to talk. I didn't even bother to ask her how her grandmother is doing. But Cara listened anyway. Like she always does.

"Give me a second," she says. The sound of a door opening and then closing comes through the line.

"Okay," she says. "I'm alone. I didn't want to talk about this in front of my family."

"Oh my God, Cara," I gasp over a sniffle, "I'm so sorry. How's your Nana?"

"She was discharged yesterday. She's fine."

I nod. "Okay. I'm glad."

"First," Cara says, "I just want to tell you how proud I am of you for standing up to Diane. I know that wasn't easy for you."

"Thanks," I say in a small voice.

"And it was a long time coming, Daisy. Maybe doing it this weekend didn't feel like the ideal time to you, but it needed to happen."

I nod even though she can't see me.

"So, you met this guy, and you really liked him, and I'm guessing you slept together?" she asks.

I nod into the phone again, and she takes my silence as assent. "And it turns out he was lying to you."

"Yeah. Or… I mean, not lying, exactly. But he didn't tell me this really important thing. And I told him about the Matchless Mountain project. I told him that it was something I personally had worked on. He could have told me a million different times. He kept talking about how he feels shitty about the work he does and how he wants to do something better. He could have just come clean, and I think… I would have been okay with that. If he had just told me."

"As far as I'm concerned, Daisy, him withholding that information is as good as lying. Especially if things got far enough for you to sleep together. If things were that serious and intense, he *definitely* should have told you. So, to me, that's a big red flag."

I sigh into the phone.

"And I think you have enough on your plate as it is. You just went through what might have been the most stressful weekend of your life. And you had this blowup with your mom that you're trying to process. You don't need to give more emotional energy to someone who didn't respect your right to know all the facts before he took you to bed."

From out in the hallway, I hear a door swing shut, and I wonder if Charlie is on the other side of the wall now. Just feet away from me.

"You don't think I overreacted?" I ask.

"It doesn't sound like it to me. You were emotionally fragile already, and then this happens. You don't *owe* him anything, Daisy."

The concept of obligations is a recurring theme this weekend… and, it seems, in my life. The problem I have is that my entire sense of obligation and entitlement is so warped that I don't know how to navigate them on my own. But Cara confirms everything I was feeling. I can't ignore my instincts just because it's easier not to.

When I'm off the phone, I start picking up my room. If I lie down, I'll just cry, and I don't want to cry anymore. I pick up all the T-shirts and fold them and lay them flat in my suitcase. I start collecting underwear and sort them, putting the dirty ones in a little linen bag, and place the clean ones in the side pocket of my suitcase. I sort out my makeup and put it away, because I won't need it again on this trip. There aren't any more events.

As I clean, and my room becomes tidy again, I think everything through, filing each event into its own space in my mind. My relationship with Rob, and now also Gabby, goes on a shelf, like a house plant that was on the verge of wilting but has been tended to and just needs some time. My relationship with my mother is placed on a workbench. It's in disrepair, but I'm not finished with it yet. And Charlie. My heart aches when I think about him, as I fold slacks and blue jeans and zip up garment bags. Charlie, whose face I'd learned to read, who thinks my nose is perfect, and who held me up when I wasn't sure I could stand. I don't know where to put him. He lingers, floating in my head space, taking it all up.

I turn on my television set and turn it way up, afraid of hearing anything from his side of the wall. Even the sound of him watching TV would rip me apart. As *The Real Housewives of Atlanta* fight it out on screen, I pace. My room is clean. My bag is mostly packed. I relive the last six days over and over again. The airport incident that feels like it happened years ago. The first time I noticed the color of his eyes. His hand on my back. His face when he saw me in the red dress. His lips on mine. And the sex. God, the sex. And, more important than anything else—the way he supported me, when he didn't have to do anything at all.

I go to my door and grab the handle a thousand times, ready to cross to the other side of the wall and talk to him. To hear what he has to say, and to forgive him, and to beg him to forgive me for my reaction. I let go of the handle a thousand times more. Cara's voice is in my ear, reminding me that I don't owe him any more of my emotional bandwidth. I sit on my bed with my crochet blanket in front of me, chewing my lip, hoping that Charlie might knock, hoping that he won't.

By nine o'clock I'm exhausted. I'm sitting on my bed in my pajamas working on a green stripe in the baby blanket, and there's a tap on the door.

I spring to my feet, and then freeze. Maybe I won't open it. I stare at the door in frozen silence, and there's another tap. A little bit harder this time. I take a deep breath and steel myself, and walk across the room.

I open the door slowly, and find my mother standing on the other side, looking small and contrite. My heart drops.

"Mom," I say, my voice breaking on the word.

"Daisy?" Her eyebrows tilt up with concern. "What is it?"

Tears fall down my cheeks at the sight of her, and memories of my mom holding me as a child come rushing back. Without asking, she wraps her arms around me and pulls me into her. Her perfume surrounds us in a cloud.

She pulls back. "I came to talk things out," she says.

"We need to do that," I agree. "But right now, can you just be my mom?"

I'm exhausted. I'm too overwhelmed to have this conversation with her right now, and if I'm really being honest with myself, I want her here, despite everything.

"Oh, Buttercup. Of course I can."

She sits down on the bed, and I rest my head in her lap while she strokes my hair. "Did something happen with Charlie?" she asks.

I nod my head. "I don't really want to talk about it." I brace myself for some sort of reprimand. Some suggestion that I did something wrong, but it doesn't come.

"Okay."

Eventually, we move so that she's sitting next to me, leaning against the mountain of pillows. I let my head fall sideways on her shoulder, and we watch bad reality television, of which she does not approve, until finally I pick up the remote and switch it off.

She turns and looks at me. "You're ready?"

"Yeah," I say. "Let's talk."

She scoots up so that she's sitting straight up, against the headboard of my bed, and I turn to face her, laying the remote on the side table next to me.

This is a conversation I've had with my mother countless times. And it usually goes like this:

My mom apologizes that I'm upset. It's a classic *sorry not sorry*. And then we go over the events that brought us to that moment, and my mother explains to me why whatever it was wasn't her fault, and she often suggests that some of it is, in fact, my responsibility. And then I end up apologizing to her. Or we agree to forget the whole thing. And finally, when that's done, we move on, like nothing ever happened.

But that's not how it's going to go this time. I won't let it, so I brace myself.

My mom looks at me. Maybe it's because it's obvious that I've spent the evening in tears, but her face isn't as hard as I was expecting. "I'm very hurt, Daisy. Maybe I overreacted, but I think, given the circumstances, that it wasn't too unreasonable for me to simply ask for an apology from you."

She waits for me to answer. Waits for me to tell her that I was the one who was wrong. I hold myself still, gripping a pillow in my lap.

My mouth itches with the urge to placate her. I grit my teeth against the words fighting to come out.

"Well…" she says after a moment, "you're not going to say anything?"

I blink a few times. "I know you're upset," I say carefully, "And I'm sorry that you're upset. I'm also sorry for how I said things. But the truth is, I didn't say anything that I don't, in fact, feel."

Something comes over her face now. A shadow passes behind her eyes, and then vanishes. She tips her head to one side. "All of it?" she asks.

I nod.

She takes a deep breath, looking down into her lap, as she thinks back to this morning. "You said you feel I treat you as an accessory and… an emotional support animal?"

"That's right," I say.

She sighs heavily. "I don't think you're a showpiece, Daisy, and I wasn't precisely sure what an emotional support animal is, but I did google it, and I would venture to say that I don't think of you as one of those either."

In other circumstances, the thought of my mom googling emotional support animals would be rather funny. But not right now. I chew my lip. I don't want this to turn into an argument. I want to actually talk with her. I want to get to the bottom of our relationship so that we can start repairing it.

"You might not be aware that you treat me like those things, but you do. You've told me you don't like the choices I've made regarding my career. You're always worried about the impression I'll leave on your social circle. You don't like my clothes or my job or even the place where I live, Mom. You never take responsibility when you do something that hurts me, but you always expect me to be there for you when you're the one who's feeling bad."

I see her face start to close when I say these things, and I get worried about where this is heading. Soon accusations will be levied, and she will storm off.

"You've never told me any of this before today," she says in a small voice.

I swallow and twist my hands into the fabric of the pillow. "I guess I was just afraid to."

"You felt afraid to talk to me?" She appears taken aback by this.

"I didn't want you to be upset that I was angry. When I was growing up, you always said that it was just me and you, and I, I don't know… I felt like I had to make sure you weren't upset. You're my mom, but I'm your best friend. It's what we do for each other."

At this, her face crumples. "Oh, Daisy," she says in a voice I'm not sure I've ever heard before. She sighs heavily. "I didn't realize it was this bad between us."

"Mom—"

"Wait." She cuts me off, and then sighs deeply, as though giving in to something. "I think there are some things about my life that I need to tell you."

I frown while she takes a deep breath, her hands clasped together in front of her, like she's steadying her nerves, or praying, and she starts from the very beginning.

"When I was a little girl, my family was very poor."

I nod. I know this already.

"I don't mean, *we buy our clothes at Goodwill* poor. I mean, real, hard, rural poverty. We didn't have running water. The electricity was on and off. My mom didn't know how to read because her parents didn't send her to school."

This I did not know. My grandparents are both dead. I never met them, and my mother has no relationship with any of her living relatives.

"We lived in a holler in West Virginia that I've never taken you to, because going back feels…" She thinks, pursing her lips. "Impossible. I wouldn't be able to do it."

I've never once in my life heard my mother use the word "holler" in a sentence. But when she says it, it doesn't sound alien on her tongue.

"One winter, it got so cold that my brother got hypothermia and my parents resorted to building a fire in the middle of our living room. But my dad was… he wasn't a good father, let's just say. Or husband. And my mom couldn't leave, because she had nowhere to go."

"Mom, why didn't you ever tell me any of this?" I say, astonished.

"I'm not telling you this because I'm looking for sympathy. But I think it will help you to understand some things about me."

I nod, waiting for her to go on.

"Unlike your grandmother, I was sent to school as a child. I walked." She smiles a little at me. "And I know what you're going to say. *'Was it uphill both ways?'* And the answer is, of course not. But it might as well have been, because education wasn't taken seriously in our household. I often had to argue my way into going. My dad was a very suspicious man, and he didn't think book learning served much purpose in life.

"But I took it seriously, because I knew it was the only way I was ever going to get out of there, and I was terrified that I would end up like my mother—desperate and exhausted and hopeless, and completely trapped. Sometimes, I would steal a copy of *Vogue* from the corner store when my dad sent me to pick up cigarettes. I would slide it up my shirt and stick it into the waistband of my blue jeans.

I suspect Mr. Byrd knew what I was doing, but he felt sorry for me. Everyone in town knew I was one of the Thomas kids. We had holes in the bottoms of our shoes, and our dad spent five out of seven nights stumbling drunk."

She gives her head a shake, as though to slough off the memories.

"Anyway, I looked at all these pages of glamorous women, living glamorous lives that were so different from mine, they might as well have been living in an entirely different country. But it was enough to know that there was something else out there, and that maybe I could have it.

"When I got to New York I decided that I wasn't going to go back. Not ever. And then I decided that if I was going to have a completely different life, I was going to be like one of those women from the magazines. I had already gotten myself so far. I was at a good university on scholarship, far away from the mountains. I had a job at the university bookstore, and it was enough to keep me in shoes that didn't have holes in the bottoms. That alone was a big deal. Transforming myself one more time didn't seem like that much further to go. I had done the hard part, I thought, so why not reach for the brass ring?

"I decided to study art history because I thought that was what society girls studied, and I worked on my accent until it was all but gone. And then I met your father, and he was just like the man I always imagined I'd like to marry. His family was wealthy, and he wore the best clothes and drove a gorgeous car that he had a parking spot for, right in the middle of Manhattan. His family vacationed in the Hamptons, and he never had to worry about money at all. He spent money like money didn't even exist for him. Like everything in the world was free for the taking. It was so different from anything I had ever known, and I wanted to be a part of that world. Part of a world that just seemed completely free from struggle, and fear."

I'm listening with rapt attention. I've never asked detailed questions about my father. I've only ever dismissed him as the man who rejected us.

"I fell in love with him so fast, and he said he loved me too. He liked the fact that I still had a little bit of my dialect. He said it was cute. We couldn't get enough of each other. But, your dad was also a little bit of an alcoholic, I think. And he was spontaneous, and one night, after he'd been doing cocaine at a party—it was a different era—" she says with a sideways glance, "he asked me to marry him and of course I said yes. The alcohol and drugs didn't seem like a problem. Not compared to what I had seen in my life, at least. I hadn't even met his family."

She sighs. "So, we had a quickie marriage and I moved into his apartment, and then I found out I was pregnant with you. I'd only just finished my degree. At that point, it became necessary for Erik to introduce me to his parents, and when his mother met me and heard the way I spoke and noticed all the little things that gave me away as not being from *their set*, she was horrified. And in the end, your father chose them."

I grit my teeth against the force of the anger that hits me when she says this. I knew we had been unwanted, but hearing her say it, and seeing the look on her face as she does, is truly a gut punch. The pain is still raw for her.

"My saving grace was the marriage, and the fact that he had already come into his inheritance. I was about to be alone with a baby and a degree that, unless you're well-connected, isn't very helpful for getting a job. Despite all my experience with poverty, I was very naïve, and I had no real sense of who I was. All I knew was who I *wasn't*. I wasn't a hillbilly from the holler anymore, and I wasn't good enough to be in your father's club of people. So, who was I?"

She looks at me now with tears sparkling in her eyes, like she's really asking me. But then she says again, "I was your mother. That's who I was. I was your mother, Daisy. You were my little savior."

I swallow hard. "But I can't save you, Mom. I was just your kid."

She nods. "I did know that. But I suppose what I'm trying to say is that *you* were my only sense of identity. I couldn't seem to find another."

"Is that why we moved around so much?" I ask.

"Maybe. For whatever reason—and believe me, I've asked myself why more times than I can count—I couldn't settle down. Every time I started to put roots down, I got antsy and nervous, and so I moved us again."

"Why do you think you got antsy?" I ask. I've completely forgotten about the argument we had earlier. My mother has never bared her soul to me like this before.

She sniffs and pulls a tissue from the box next to the lamp. "I've spent my life asking myself that question. All I know is that for years I couldn't forget the way your dad rejected me… and you. The way he just… threw us away. Nothing ever felt right after that, and I never felt right. I felt… like I was just never going to be good enough. That anyone who really got to know me would reject me."

For the first time in my life, I think I'm starting to understand my mother. Her restlessness, her obsession with what other people might think of her, her incredible need for me to be there for her, no matter what. Even when she's the one who fucks up. She needs the love from me to be beyond unconditional. She cannot tolerate criticism.

"Mom," I say, and though I should be too dehydrated at this point to form more tears, it seems I'm not, because I'm hugging her and, yet again, I'm crying.

"I'm so sorry, Daisy," she says as she wipes her nose. "I don't know why I didn't tell you any of this, but I think, on some level, I thought I was protecting you from it."

"Mom, you *should* have told me," I say. "I never understood what was happening when I was a kid, and why we had to keep picking up and leaving every time some place started to feel like home."

"You were just a little girl, Daisy. You couldn't have understood. And I didn't even understand myself, not then. It's taken so much therapy for me to realize it."

"You see a therapist?" I say in shock.

"I do," she says, nodding and laughing a little bit at my astonished expression. "Her name is Jeanine. I started seeing her after the affair with Michael came out. He convinced me to do it."

I'm stunned.

"Jeanine thinks that I have a hard time taking responsibility for things. And that I don't have enough self-worth and I try to get it from other people." My mom looks at me with large, vulnerable eyes. "And it seems she's right."

I feel my resolve begin to crumble. Seeing her vulnerable like this is overwhelmingly difficult. I begin to reach for her but she stops me.

"I don't see you as an accessory, Daisy. And I don't expect you to make me happy all the time. I understand that you believe that about me. But I want you to know it's not true."

I think for a moment that she's reverting to denying my feelings, but she continues, "Daisy, all I want for you is happiness, and for you and me to be okay. And if my issues from my past have gotten in the way of that, then I am truly, from the very bottom of my heart, sorry. And, perhaps most importantly, I want you to know how sorry I am for what happened with Michael. But I can tell you one thing—it was never about you. I wasn't trying to steal something from you, or wreck your life, or wreak havoc."

The pain in my heart at everything my mom has just shared with me is so acute it feels like it's been pierced.

"I never really thought you did anything to intentionally hurt me, Mom," I say. "What burned so badly was the fact that you seemed not to care. You just… dismissed it."

She's shaking her head, wiping tears away from her eyes. Her makeup is a mess. "I think I understand that now. I'm so sorry, Buttercup. I love you. I promise you I only want the best for you. The thing about your career… it wasn't about appearances. Not really. It was just about wanting you to make a decent living. I don't want you to struggle. You refuse to accept any of the money from your father. And excuse my language, but your salary is crap."

I laugh through the crying. "It is, Mom. It is crap."

We wrap our arms around one another. She pulls me in to her, holding me against her chest, kissing my hair. "You're my baby girl. I never thought you were supposed to be taking care of me. I'm sorry if I treated you like that was your job."

Forgiveness. Real, honest, sorrowful forgiveness washes over me. Everything she's said—my new understanding of her, her heartfelt, meaningful apology, all of it—makes it possible for me to finally, tell my mom that it's okay, and for once, to actually mean it.

"I love you, Mom," I say. "I should have explained all of this to you a long time ago. I shouldn't have spent so much time resenting you." We cling to each other and cry together, so that we are both snotting on each other's shoulders.

"I'm so sorry I didn't let you be who you want to be, Buttercup. I'm so sorry I let my shame and insecurity get in the way of being your mother. And I'm so sorry you feel like you have to parent me. I know you're not the parent. And I promise I'm going to try to be better, okay?

I'm nodding, wiping my nose.

"Okay, Mom."

We take turns apologizing to each other—me, for never being honest with her about how I felt, her for being obtuse enough not to see it when I was hurting. Layers of misunderstanding are peeled away. Mom isn't a bad person. She's not even a bad mother. She's just a human.

Somehow, we end up lying down next to each other, and I tell her my favorite thing about each city we ever lived in. She tells me she didn't want me to go to school in Colorado because she hates the mountains and has done ever since she moved away from them.

As we talk, I can feel the exhaustion of the weekend settling over me, and my eyes start to drift closed.

My mom kisses my cheek, and her tennis bracelet grazes my skin, just like when I was a child. Her perfume lingers in the sheets around me.

"Goodnight, sweetheart," she says. "I love you. So much."

"I love you too, Mom."

She switches off the lamp, and goes out through the door, and I fall asleep.

Chapter 21

I sleep, and sleep, and sleep. I wake up at dawn to pee and go back to bed. It's like my body and brain have decided that they've had enough, and they've gone on strike.

When I finally wake, it's with a start. It's eleven o'clock in the morning. I've slept for twelve hours straight, and I'm still groggy, but I have a strange sensation that there's something I've forgotten. Something that's missing. A puzzle piece that's out of place.

I relive my conversation with my mother. The revelations and the years of hurt that those revelations began the process of washing away. And my realization. All I ever wanted to hear from her was that she was sorry. Those words. Among the most important in the dictionary.

I'm sorry.

Charlie had said he was sorry. He'd said it again and again. And I wouldn't listen. I wouldn't hear a word he had to say, because I was so angry and so hurt that I couldn't see past his mistake. But maybe that's all it was—it was a mistake. Maybe he never meant to hurt me. Maybe he really was scared. And if there's anything I've learned this weekend, it's that everyone is carrying something around with them. Struggle, and vulnerability, and fear are all inevitable parts of the human condition. We're all damaged goods, walking around in the world, pretending that everything is okay. But I didn't even give Charlie the chance. I'm not the only one between the two of us who has been through a lot. Not even close. And I realize now, I fucked up. I should have listened. That doesn't mean I had to forgive him. But I should have at least heard him out.

It's eleven o'clock. His flight was scheduled for this morning. On a thread of hope as slender as spider's silk I run into the hallway and bang on his door, but there's no answer. My head falls forward against the wood, and I thump it twice.

Stupid. Stupid.

I'll go to the restaurant next to check for him there. Maybe his flight was delayed? Or maybe I heard him wrong? I already know I'm lying to myself.

"Miss?" A housekeeper pushing a cleaning cart approaches me in the hallway. "Are you okay?"

I stare at her blankly. "I'm sorry. I'm fine."

She looks awkward, her hand on the handle of the cart, and her eyes darting between me and the door number beside me. I glance around and down at myself. Maybe I forgot to put pants on again. But I'm wearing my sleep shorts.

"I'm here to turn this room over," she tells me. "Are you at the wrong door? Can I help you find your way?"

My shoulders drop as I shake my head. He's definitely gone.

I return to my room and pick up my phone, about to send him a text message begging for the chance to talk to him, and it hits me: I don't even have his number. It was never a necessity. Charlie was just always available—in the room right next to mine. He called me on the hotel phone, and I still didn't think to ask for his information.

I've been so wrapped up in my own world that I didn't even get the contact information of the man who I've been falling in love with. Because that's what was happening, wasn't it? I was falling in love with him.

Chapter 22

I go downstairs and eat breakfast at the hotel restaurant in a state of total misery. The worst thing about meeting someone at a hotel? Everything reminds you of them. Every single place in this entire building holds potent memories of Charlie. While I'm eating, I stare at the table where we had dinner that first night. The couple currently sitting there keep glancing over their shoulders at me like I'm with the FBI.

The prearranged ladies' spa day is at one, and I don't feel at all like treating myself. I've got a pit in my stomach the size of a jet liner. I can't believe how stupid I've been. I looked at Charlie's work profile again, and considered dialing his office number and then dismissed it outright. I wonder if he's going to be in the office today. I miss him. It's been less than twenty-four hours, and I miss him so much it feels like I've been flayed.

I stare at my phone, willing it to ring, like Charlie might somehow develop sudden psychic powers and know my number, and that he should pick up the phone and call me.

But what if he doesn't *want* to call me? What if he watched me shut him down and decided that I've got more issues than he can deal with, and that it's just not worth it?

I open my Instagram app and make my account public, and I turn off the privacy settings on my long-abandoned Facebook page.

Please find me, I will him. *Please just message me, and I'll come to you.*

I linger at the table for far too long. The lunch rush is starting in earnest, and the annoyance of the exceptionally polite wait staff starts to break through, and their smiles begin to look a little bit crazed. It's twelve-fifteen and I have absolutely nothing to do with my day, so I finally admit defeat and accept the fact that I'm going to the spa.

***

The space is beautiful, and because this seems to be the one place in this hotel that I haven't been with Charlie, I don't have the urge to daydream or weep when I walk in. Calming Zen music plays over concealed speakers, and the walls are covered in white, textured stones set at irregular depths so that they bounce light and cast shadows in every direction.

"Hello," says a woman with a name tag that reads Adelaide when I approach reception, "welcome to Lotus Spa." She speaks in a hushed, soft voice. An ultra-calm monotone as if any auditory variation might launch her delicate clients, who have come to be de-stressed, past their tether's breaking point.

"Hi," I say. "I'm, um, here for the ladies' spa day? My mom is Diane Thomas, or, um, Diane Nielsen?" Everything is coming out like a question.

"Ah, yes, the Nielsen party," she says and taps lightly on her keyboard. "May I please have your name, Miss?"

"Daisy? Thomas?" I say as though I'm not sure.

"Our attendant will bring you back, Miss Thomas," she says.

A small dark-haired woman in all black appears by my side from nowhere, and I actually jump a little when she says, "Right this way."

I'm ushered to a locker room, where I change out of my street clothes and wrap myself in a robe that's waiting for me. I slide my feet into terry cloth slippers and am then led to a private room where I find my mother and her friends lounging in reclining seats. My mother's face lights up when she sees me, and I'm all at once glad that I came. My despair over the Charlie situation has been so profound that I've barely reflected on the conversation Mom and I had last night. But it was an enormous milestone. I don't feel any judgement radiating from her now, and I'm not sure if she's different or if I'm different, or if it's just that now I understand her in a way that I didn't before.

Ultimately, it doesn't matter. What matters is that we are genuinely happy to see each other. She's surrounded by friends, so I squeeze in just quickly enough to give her a kiss and tell her how happy I am to see her, and then wander off to find myself a spot.

Astrid is sipping a glass of champagne and motions for me to join her in the empty lounger by her side.

"How's Tyler doing?" I ask when I sit down. Another woman dressed in all black steps out from behind a curtain and proffers a tray of petit fours and a glass of champagne, and again, I startle a little.

"Oh, he's almost back to himself. I made him do yoga with me this morning, down by the water! The hotel set it up for us."

"Oh, that sounds nice," I say, though my mind wanders back to Charlie telling Walter that he's a yogi. Nowhere, it seems, is truly safe.

"Tyler tried to refuse to go, but I told him I would take the kids and leave him if he didn't."

I stare at her with a carefully controlled, blank expression.

She breaks into a smile. "I'm just kidding, Daisy! I told him he owed me one for me wiping his forehead with a damp washcloth while he puked."

"Oh," I say, relaxing into a laugh. We should have spent more time with Astrid at the wedding. Charlie would love her.

The spa treatments are a dream of hot oil and lavender fragrance and hands all over every tender spot on my body, rubbing out knots and lulling me into a trance. I'd like to say I enjoyed it. I feel guilty for *not* enjoying it, when I know Michael and my mother must have spent an absolutely nauseating sum to make this happen.

My mind wanders as my body is pampered and rubbed. I think about money, and what it means to people, and what it does, or doesn't do, for people. A big part of who Mom is hinges on her impoverished beginnings. It's not something I've ever had to experience because of decisions my mom made long before I was born—when she was a child with an iron will and the determination to make a better future for herself, against tremendous odds—and because of the twists and turns in her life, tragedy and heartbreak, my life has been a comfortable one.

It's very easy for me to say that money isn't important, but that's coming from a person who has never had to think about money. Even when I'm laying out my monthly budget, there's always the knowledge that, should I fall, there's a safety net to catch me. And that knowledge has always been unconditional—not just because of the trust fund—but because I always knew that, despite everything, my mom would be there. I have no idea what it's like not to have security. Not even close. Charlie doesn't do what he worries is bad for the world because he's a bad guy. He does it because his childhood taught him that money *is* important. At least in our society it is. Money buys more than nice things. It buys a trip to the doctor's office, and to the dentist. It buys cancer treatment. It buys security. It buys safety.

There is an element of indignity in poverty, not because being poor is undignified, but because desperation is an insult to a person's dignity. It hurts. And that damage is so visible in my mother, I can't believe I didn't see this clearly until right now.

The decision that Charlie made to become an attorney was born of the same essential driving factors that have led my mom through such a strange and rootless life. The fear of poverty lies within them both. It's an essential ingredient to what makes Charlie who he is. And maybe the work he does isn't noble, but it protects him. It's his armor, just like my fancy dresses and makeup were armor for me this weekend. Just like Charlie himself was my armor. He did that for me. And, moreover, the experience of poverty might be why Charlie is one of the most thoughtful, empathetic people that I have ever met.

The memory comes back to me of Charlie slipping a bill under the boot of a man sleeping on the street, and even though I'm lying on a massage table being pampered in one of the finest spas on the East Coast, I groan at my own stupidity. My brain is hysterical with glee at the fact that it can show me *this* many ways in which I've fucked up. It's a record-breaker. The massage therapist takes my sounds of agony for pleasure, and the pressure increases. I wince, but I don't say anything, deciding that wearing a hair shirt might be precisely what I deserve.

My own invisible privilege has completely blinded me, and I'm only fully comprehending it now. I'll need to explain my revelations to Cara and enlist her help. Maybe we know someone who knows someone who knows Charlie Bond. And if that fails, I'll call his office. I dread crossing that line. I don't want to bring his personal life into his professional life, and I need to respect his boundaries. But I don't just owe him the time to explain himself for failing to tell me the whole truth. I owe *him* an apology as well.

Chapter 23

My mother invites me to dinner that evening, just her and me, and I accept gratefully. She takes me to the restaurant she mentioned, the one with the Michelin star, and I enjoy a seventy-dollar plate of sea scallops and drink a thirty-dollar glass of wine and remember to thank my mother for treating us when she picks up the check.

Mom tiptoes around the Charlie subject, and I'm grateful to not have to discuss it. But when she asks me about work, I can't tell her about it without bringing up the Matchless defeat, and when I do that, I crack. My mom listens like I don't remember her listening to me since I was just a little girl. I tell her everything—that Charlie was never my boyfriend. That he was just some guy I met on the airplane on the way over, and he offered to stand in as my date, and we hit it off, and then something more began to grow. Something beautiful and unbelievable. And then in a fit of hurt and anger, I ruined it.

"Well," Mom says as I finish, "I have to say, that until the end there, that is one of the most romantic stories I've ever heard. He's either out of his mind, or he's absolutely crazy about you."

I sniffle back a tear attempting to escape.

"Oh, honey." Mom lays her hand over mine. "Can't you just call him?"

"That's the worst part," I moan. "I don't even have his contact information. I forgot to get it, because his room was right next to mine."

She's shaking her head. "He's going to reach out to you, Daisy," she says with complete certainty. "This sort of thing doesn't just happen. There is absolutely no way that he isn't, right now, thinking of a way to get in touch with you. Just be patient, darling. It'll work out."

I want to ask her to promise. The way I did when I was a child and I had a cold.

You'll feel better in the morning, Buttercup.

Do you promise?

But she can't promise. All she can do is hope on my behalf. And she does. Her compassion and love for me radiates, and now that I know it's always been there, I'm able to really bask in it. It's like the storm cloud that she and I passed through together has lifted away all the haze we'd been living in, and we see each other clearly for the first time in years.

That night, I barely sleep. Every time I wake up, I open Instagram, just in case he's messaged me. It's empty. My Facebook also shows no signs of life. I have my bags packed and ready to go.

At the airport, I open and close my social media apps compulsively. When the airplane boards, I hang back at the gate until the very last minute so I can keep an eye out for a message. I'll be in the air for three and a half hours, during which time I'll be out of touch with the world.

I'm squished between a middle-aged man named Bob, who has the aisle seat, and who can't seem to stop himself from talking about his upcoming fishing trip, and a stressed-out father who keeps getting up to reprimand his two children who are sitting with their mother in the row in front of us.

"Have you ever tried fly fishing? It's fantastic. The way you lure the fish up to the surface. You should try it," Bob says to me.

"Abbie, your mother said cut it out," says the man on my other side.

Bob didn't get the memo that someone with their nose in a book isn't up for conversation.

"The first time I went fly fishing was with my uncle," Bob says dreamily, directly into my ear.

I smile and nod at him and turn back to the page I'm staring at and not reading.

"Owen, stop trying to take Abbie's pretzels," the father says.

"I love that moment when you get a bite." Bob sighs.

"Mm-hmm," I say.

"Owen, you have to sit in your seat. No, you can't go in the aisle. It's not allowed. Honey, grab his arm. I know, but I can't buckle the belt if you don't get him to hold still." The dad leans over the seat in front of him so that he's curled over the headrest and his butt is in the air.

"Sir, you need to return to your seat please," a flight attendant scolds him.

This continues for the duration of the trip. The outbound flight was like being on a cruise compared to this.

By the time we land I know the makeup of Bob's entire family tree and how his wife prepares their Thanksgiving turkey.

When we touch down, I turn into one of the passengers I loathe, and I catapult myself from my seat, standing awkwardly as I wait for the door of the plane to be opened.

I switch my phone out of airplane mode and open Instagram again and close my eyes as the disappointment washes over me.

Once I'm in my car I call Cara over Bluetooth on the drive back to my apartment, and when I arrive, she's used her spare key to let herself in. She wraps her arms around me in a crushing hug and squeezes the air out of me. I bury my face in her mass of curls.

"So, there's more to the story, huh?"

We sit down on my tufted blue sofa and wrap ourselves in quilts like we always do when we settle in for a chat, or a movie marathon, or really anything. We both prefer to live as human burritos.

I explain my revelations to her, and she listens as attentively as she always does. She's delighted when I tell her about my mother's apology, and surprised when I tell her about my mother's background. When I get to the part with the realizations I had afterwards, falling like dominoes, one pushing on the other, until the entire, carefully constructed picture changed into something else, she smiles.

"That's a lot of learning in a short span of time, Daisy."

I nod. "I know."

When I first encountered Charlie—on the road when we were both stressed out and pissed off—I'd mentally decided that he was suffering from affluenza. I think, maybe, that I've been the one suffering from it all along. That I've just taken so much for granted.

Cara and I set to work on our laptops, scrolling through friends' Facebook pages, looking for some connection. I google and search the white pages, to no avail. I search for University of Colorado alumni listings with no luck. I didn't get Mark's last name when we were at the bar, so I can't try to look him up, either.

Finally, I look at Cara, and say, "I could call his office?"

My hands are clammy with nerves. I really don't want to do this. Charlie clearly doesn't want to be found, and there have been no overtures on his end. If he really wanted to reach me, he could have by now. I think I've already blown it. But I *have* to try. I won't ever sleep again if I don't try. I'll always be wondering, *what if?*

I get my phone and open the web page again and look at his bio. The only email that's listed is the generic one to his office at large. I click the link to the number at the top of the screen.

The phone rings, once, twice, and then a woman answers, "Bikram, Jones, and Cummings."

"Hi," I say hesitantly, "I'm calling to speak with Charles Bond?"

"I'm afraid he's out of the office today. Can I direct you to his voicemail?" the woman asks politely.

"Oh…" I think about it long enough that the receptionist thinks the line has gone dead.

"Ma'am?" she asks. "Are you still there?"

"I'm sorry, I'm here. No, I don't need his voicemail. Thank you."

Cara looks at me with pain in her brown eyes. She loves me, and my angst is making her hurt.

"It's okay." I give her a feeble smile. "I'll figure it out."

Days pass, and I go back to work. I bury myself in work, using it as a tool not to think about anything else. My own social media remains inactive. The silence is deafening.

Donna compliments me on a brief I write about the endangered red wolves of the Southeastern United States. I sit through conference calls and staff meetings. My colleagues crack jokes, and I laugh. And through it all, I'm hollow. I've now spent as much time without Charlie as I spent with him, and yet I ache. I return to the home-work-gym routine that got me through the first months after my break with Rob. Cara and I eat lunch, and she chooses not to raise the subject.

The following Wednesday—officially one week since I left DC—I decide to try his office again. I'm desperate.

When I call, the same voice greets me, but when I ask for Charlie, she says only, "I'm afraid he's no longer with this firm."

I hang up, utterly defeated. I should have left a voicemail last time. I missed my last chance to reach him.

Charlie is gone.

Chapter 24

I decide that I ought to see a therapist. If my mom can do it, I certainly can too. I book an appointment with a woman I find on a website with local listings.

Her name is Jennifer, and she has a kind face and a disarming air that makes me feel like I can tell her anything. Her office is decorated in earth tones and shelves full of framed images with inspirational quotes from famous thinkers. We discuss the rootlessness of my childhood, the strained relationship with my mother, my breakup with Rob. She's shocked when I tell her what our parents did. I talk about Charlie and the weekend I spent falling for him, and the end of it all. We talk about what moving on looks like.

It takes a month for me to start to feel like myself again, for me to return to venturing out with friends, and going back to cooking real meals and not just boiling pasta every night. My mom and I start having regular phone calls. She had a wonderful trip to the Maldives, and she and Michael are house hunting in Northwest DC, ready to move out of the apartment they've been sharing. She talks about getting a dog, which is something that she's never been interested in before because it wasn't conducive to her transient lifestyle.

She tells me more about all the work she's doing with Jeanine and tells me that Peg has gotten Walter to start doing yoga with her, and that he actually *thanked* her for opening that door for him. Apparently, he's lost weight, and all the stretching has been good for his back swing and his golf game is the best it's ever been. I wish I could share this with Charlie. He would find it absolutely hilarious.

At work, Donna announces our next push, and we all buckle down. I'm grateful for the added pressure at work. It means my mind will be extra occupied, and maybe the constant, dull ache in my heart won't be the first thing I think about every morning.

Another month passes, and I've begun to let go. I've begun to accept that Charlie was like a comet—a flash of brightness across a dark expanse, lighting everything up in an astonishing display—but fleeting and mysterious. Donna tells us all that she's going to be out for the next two days. She sits on the board of a nonprofit dedicated to protecting watersheds, and she's on their hiring committee.

While she's out, things relax a little bit, as they are wont to do when the boss is out of the office. In the middle of the afternoon, Casey, our intern—a role I once filled, before I was hired—flicks a folded-up paper triangle at me, and we end up abandoning our work for a game of table football that the whole office gets into.

At the end of the week, Donna is back, with her wife in tow, and announces an impromptu office party. The bottle of bourbon emerges from her bottom desk drawer, and we fill paper Dixie cups and ask what we're celebrating.

"Blue Water found their candidate, and he accepted the position today. He starts in a week," she says with delight. Ordinarily, hiring someone for another agency isn't cause for celebration, and I suspect that Donna is just in the mood. The new hire will be focused on reducing the use of harmful chemicals in industrial farming.

Cara runs out to buy chips and salsa, and we gather in the

conference room to play trivia. A few people call their partners, and our Friday afternoon turns into a party. At six o'clock, the group decides to move things to a local bar. When we are about to go, Cara pulls me aside.

"You look tired, Daisy. And I don't really want to go to a bar and watch everyone get sloppy." She pats her pronounced baby bump. She's five months along. "Do you want to have a snuggle party at your place? I'll bring cake."

The offer of cake and movies with Cara is far more tempting than a night out at a bar, and I smile gratefully. "That sounds good."

Cara follows me to my apartment complex in her Honda, and I park in my spot while she drives around the corner to the visitor spaces. It's a three-story building with open-air corridors, and each apartment's door opens to the outside. I sling my purse over my shoulder and grab an armful of papers that I plan to look at over the weekend. I haul myself up the stairs to the second floor, and then down the stretch of balcony, with my head down, looking at my phone. I tap Instagram open, as I still do at least twice a day, just in case Charlie has had a change of heart.

"I promise I'm not stalking you."

I startle so hard my feet almost leave the ground and my papers fall from my arms, and I have my keys out in front of me before I even look up, ready to jab my attacker in the eyeball.

Charlie is standing outside of my door in an untucked polo shirt and khakis, and I swear, even though I knew he was beautiful, my mind had somehow tempered it, like it was trying to protect me, and I'm overwhelmed by the sight of him. His hair is rumpled, and he looks tired, but his hazel eyes are the same as they always were, kind and full of tenderness, his lips just as full, his jaw just as strong. The surge of love that sweeps over me nearly knocks me over.

"Charlie," I breathe.

"Daisy, I'm sorry to turn up at your apartment like this." He holds his hands out in apology. "It's totally inappropriate and boundary-crossing, but I need to talk to you in person, and I wasn't completely sure if you'd read anything I write to you."

I want to fling myself at him and beg his forgiveness. Tell him how stupid and short-sighted I was. Tell him that I fell in love with him over the course of five days, and I don't understand how it happened, because I didn't believe that things like that *could* happen, but that I haven't felt like myself since I left Washington. I haven't felt whole since the last time he held my hand.

Instead, I say, "How do you know where I live?"

He gives me a small, uncertain smile. "I found Cara through your Instagram page, and she said I should just come here. She said she thought… you might be willing to listen?"

I look behind me for Cara to come up the stairs, but she's not there. She lured me here with the promise of cake, and instead she brought me this. The best thing I could have possibly hoped for. It's so, so much better than cake. She might be the best person I know.

"I've been looking for you high and low, Charlie. Yes, I want to listen. And there's so much I want to say."

His eyes carry hope and apprehension, and he runs one hand up and down the strap of his ever-present laptop bag.

"Do you want to come inside?" I ask, and he nods.

"That would be good, I think."

I unlock the door with trembling hands, struggling even to get the key in the lock, and lead the way inside, grateful that I vacuumed and picked up yesterday so that Charlie doesn't think I live my everyday life the way I live in a hotel room.

He steps inside, and his eyes sweep the room, taking in the tufted navy-blue couch with yellow blankets and embroidered red pillows. The potted plants that sit in the windows, reaching for the sun. The posters of every city I've lived in hanging on the walls. The shelf with the silver spoons.

"It's so… tidy," he says with surprise, and I can't help but laugh in spite of all the tension that vibrates between us like a violin string that's been plucked.

"It turns out I'm not a hoarder in real life."

"I wouldn't care if you were," he says, "I might try to get you help, but I wouldn't care."

He takes a step towards me, and then hesitates. "Should I take my shoes off?" He looks down at the carpet that still has tracks from the vacuum on it.

I shake my head.

We sit down on the sofa, facing each other.

Charlie takes a deep breath, about to begin, but I stop him.

"Charlie, before you start, there are some things I need to say to you."

He looks abashed, like he thinks I'm about to give him a firm scolding. I don't blame him. The last time he saw me I was irate.

I take a breath, collecting myself. I wasn't prepared to give this speech today. The words end up coming out in a rush.

"I'm so sorry about the way I reacted. I should never have yelled at you like that. And I should never have refused to listen to what you had to say. I've been trying to reach you to apologize, and I couldn't find you, and…" Tears prick, threatening to fall, and I swallow hard. Charlie's eyes are so soft. Full of nothing but understanding and concern.

"You have nothing to apologize for, Daisy. You had been through so much already, and I should have been forthright with you from the very beginning. But, when you told me what you did for a living, I didn't know... I could never have anticipated what was about to happen. How much you would mean to me. And when I did realize what was happening, I was so scared to tell you. I was so scared you would hate me for it and refuse to see me again, and I just couldn't bring myself to risk it."

The hard truth is, I might have hated him. Before I got to really know him, I might have written him off as a lost cause. I didn't understand yet. I didn't understand all the things I *needed* to understand in order to properly love Charlie, and give him the grace he deserves. That knowledge makes the tears come harder, my lip trembling and my nose beginning to run. I swipe the back of my hand across my face impatiently. I need to really listen to him, attentively, the way Cara always listens to me. I need to give him the chance to say all the things he needs to say.

"So then, I thought, I would wait to tell you the truth. I would wait until I had fixed things."

"Fixed things?" I ask.

"After the rehearsal dinner, the night of David Attenborough," he explains, and I smile at the memory, "I started looking at job postings. And I knew I was going to leave the firm I was at. Getting to know you... it woke me up. It woke me up to the person I want to be, and I've been too afraid to be, my whole life."

A slow realization dawns on me.

"I didn't want to tell you what I did, because I thought, if I told you *after* I had left my job, that the blow wouldn't land as hard. And you would be able to forgive me."

"Charlie." I reach for his hand, and he takes it gratefully, gripping it hard in his. Both of our palms are coated in sweat. "You should have told me about the Matchless thing, but you never owed me an explanation for your work. It's not my choice to make for you. I have no right to judge you for wanting to earn a decent living."

Now Charlie's eyes well with tears, glistening against the gold and green. Seeing Charlie cry cracks my heart into pieces. I don't want him to ever feel sad, about anything. I want to cover him with my body and shelter him from anything bad that might come his way.

"You could have reached out to me. I made all my social media profiles public, and I was checking every day, and I was so scared I had ruined everything."

He swallows, and I watch him work to prevent the tears from falling. Our fingers are lacing with each other now, one finger after the other, like we are being stitched back together.

"I know," he says. "I looked at every picture you've ever posted. I didn't reach out to you because I hadn't found a new position yet, and I was afraid I would have to go back to corporate law, but then I got called for an interview, and I accepted it today."

I already know the answer, but I ask anyway. "What job did you take, Charlie?"

He smiles. "I got a job with Blue Water. It's not a legal position, but they think my background working on real estate contracts will be helpful. And to be honest," he says, laughing through all the emotion, "I think I was so earnest that I might have guilted them into offering it to me."

I'm so full of love that my body can no longer contain it and I gulp through a sob that forces its way out. "I'm so sorry I ever made you feel badly. I can't believe you did that. You didn't need to do that for me, in order for me to…" *love you.* I don't say the words. I can't. I can't scare him again.

"I wanted to do it, Daisy," he says. "I didn't do it for you, so much as I did it *because* of you." He rubs his thumb across my hand, sending fire through me. My chest is burning, and my stomach is twisted into a knot. "I've been wanting to do it for a long time. It wasn't until I met you, and I saw how courageous you are, and how you stand up for your beliefs, and how… *true* you are to yourself, that I finally got the guts to do it."

"Charlie…" I choke. "I missed you. I missed you so much you have no idea."

"Yes, I do," he says. "I haven't slept in weeks, Daisy. I've been stalking you online like a maniac. I got an Instagram account just so I could see your face every day."

I'm crying helplessly now, and the tears run freely. I probably look just like I did the morning after the wedding, but I don't care. Not at all.

"Charlie." I sniffle. "I'd really like to kiss you right now."

His lips turn up into a smile as light fills his eyes, and he pulls me into him, back into that space that I fit into so neatly. The place that feels like safety and warmth, and as joyous as Christmas morning. But Charlie is more than a gift. He's my heart, and it's bursting.

His arms wrap around me, and his lips meet mine. Gentle and then urgent, as though we need to make up for all the kissing we haven't done, that we could have been doing, if we both hadn't been so short-sighted. So afraid of getting hurt.

"Daisy," he says my name over and over again, as he peppers my face with his lips, and then returns them to mine. "Daisy, you're so special."

"So are you," I answer into his mouth, grasping him, trying to climb onto him.

"Wait," he says, and I pause as renewed uncertainty springs to life in my belly.

"There's something else I need to tell you, and it might be bad. I don't know." His eyes shift between mine as he studies me.

I give my head a little shake. "What?"

"I just need to say it, because I don't think I can go a second longer without saying it."

I wait, my arms still around his neck. Our faces are so close together that all I can see are his eyes. His warm, beautiful eyes.

"I'm in love with you, Daisy. I fell in love with you two months ago, and I haven't stopped. And I know it's insane that I'm saying this. You don't have to say anything back…"

The rest of his words are lost when I crush my mouth to his. I'm smoke, vanishing into him. I kiss him like I'm suffocating and he's air. I climb onto his lap, and he has his arms around me as I bury my nose in his hair, taking in his perfect smell. The smell that comes from him, and no other place.

"I love you too," I say. "I love you so much."

Charlie picks me up, holding on to me with strong hands. "Where's the bedroom?" he demands, like it's not a question.

I stop nibbling his jaw just long enough to gasp, "Through the kitchen."

Charlie carries me back, through the apartment, to my little bedroom, where, yes, there is a pile of clothes on the floor. And a basket of clean laundry that I probably won't get around to folding.

We fall onto the bed without letting go of one another. His hands shake as he undresses me, pulling my crisp blouse out of my skirt, and pulling my shoes off my feet with impatience. We're both in a hurry, unwrapping each other as our hearts unspool and tangle together.

"I love you," he murmurs the entire time. When he brushes my skin with his fingers, when he kisses my body and worships me with his mouth, and then he's inside of me.

"Perfect earlobe," he says when his teeth brush against it. "Perfect hips," he says when he grips them.

When I'm on top of him, hovering over him, and we move in synchronicity, his eyes are somehow dark and tender at the same time, until they blank, and he's lost, and I'm lost, but I don't feel like I'm falling this time, because I already fell. And I already landed, right into him.

We lie together after, and the windows grow black with the night, but we don't let go of each other. He holds me and I nuzzle him until, finally, hunger forces us to relent, and Charlie goes to my kitchen and scrambles eggs for us, and we sit at my table and eat with our feet locked together. I tell him about the revelations from my mother, and when I share the fact that she's in therapy he's as astonished as I was.

The next morning is Saturday, and we go to the park, and then Charlie makes good on his promise to take me to dinner. First, we eat heaping mountains of pasta, and then later we lick ice cream cones and make ridiculous puns at each other while we watch children playing, sticky with sugar.

"I love you," he says.

"I love you more."

We're cheesy and silly, and we look at each other with stupid expressions that say everything.

The weeks that follow are a dreamy, gooey haze. Charlie starts his new job, and he loves it. I meet his father and lean down to hug him in his recliner like I already know him. I introduce Charlie to Cara, and she apologizes for ever thinking there could have been a red flag.

We go out to dinner with Rob and Gabby, and the conversation is easy and fun. We end up going to a bar where we play foosball—girls versus guys, and Gabby and I kick their asses and high-five each other. The boys demand a rematch, and we do it again.

And Charlie and I settle into a routine. The sort of thing that happens when someone becomes ingrained in your life. We meet at his apartment after work, because it's halfway between our offices. It's as neat as I expected it would be. His style is minimalist and clean. His furniture is Scandinavian. He moves his things out of a drawer to make room for me. And then another drawer, and another, until half the bedroom becomes mine.

Cara gives birth in the hospital, nine days past her due date, and after her sisters, I'm first in line to hold her baby boy. He's wrapped in the green and yellow blanket I made for him. His face is all squished, and his little hand grasps Charlie's finger with an impressively strong grip. Billy looks so proud I think he might take out an ad in the newspaper.

"His name is Stuart," Cara says from her spot in the hospital bed. "After Billy's grandfather."

"He's so perfect," I say in wonderment. Such a tiny, perfect human, with his whole life ahead of him. He's going to be ensconced in love. He's the first grandchild in Cara's family, and her parents have already set up a nursery in their home so Cara and Billy can get a break when they need one.

After a few weeks, Cara is ready to re-enter the world. She's sleep-deprived and exhausted, but no less radiant. Billy looks like he's been run over and laid in the street for a few days before anyone bothered to collect him. Stuart sits in his baby carriage, gurgling and marveling over his newly discovered feet, while the four of us eat brunch. Cara drinks a mimosa and is immediately tipsy.

"God, that's good," she says, stretching her arms up over her head, and we laugh.

Charlie's foot brushes against mine under the table, and he grips my hand in my lap. I smile over at him, wondering if maybe there will be a little one in our future. I don't know what will happen, but I'm happy. I'm happier than I think I've ever been, at any time in my life.

And then, eventually, Charlie asks me to move in with him, and our styles meld into a tasteful, eclectic mix. My posters line the hall between our living room and our kitchen. His sofa now has a basket full of my blankets next to it so that Cara and I can cocoon ourselves. Charlie likes romantic comedies, so he often joins us when we have girls' night, but sometimes he goes out with his friends so Cara and I can have time together.

But at the end of every night, no matter what we're doing, it's just Charlie and me again. And I think it always will be. I think that this is it for me. The long, strange road I've been on has led me here. To him. To home. Where I belong.

Acknowledgements

Daisy and Charlie's story came to me all at once, and I wrote the first draft over the period of just a few weeks, during which time my husband was abandoned to deal with our entire household singlehandedly. He also served as my first editor without complaint. For better or for worse, if it weren't for him this book would not have come into existence, and I owe him my undying gratitude.

I also would not have seen this process through if it weren't for the support of my mom, who has been my biggest cheerleader throughout every part of my life.

Additionally, I must thank my wonderful editor, Sarah, who provided the perfect blend of encouragement and critique to keep me going.

Hristina, Melissa, and Justin: thank you for listening to my ideas, reading chapters, and generally supporting me even when I thought I was going to quit. You are, quite simply, the most amazing friends.

About the Author

Anna Harbom lives in Maryland with her husband, son, and dogs. When she isn't writing she usually has her nose in a book or is outside in the garden. She loves to travel, eat good food, drink good wine, and spend time in the company of good friends.